D0477314

Glenn Hoddle

Glenn Hoddle

The Man and the Manager

Brian Woolnough

First published in Great Britain in 1997 by
Virgin Books
an imprint of Virgin Publishing Ltd
332 Ladbroke Grove
London W10 5AH

Copyright © Brian Woolnough 1997

The right of Brian Woolnough to be identified as the author of this work has been asserted
by him in accordance with the Copyright Designs and Patents Act 1988.

This book is sold subject to the condition that it shall not, by way of trade or otherwise, be
lent, resold, hired out or otherwise circulated without the publisher's prior written consent
in any form of binding or cover other than that in which it is published and without a
similar condition including this condition being imposed upon the subsequent purchaser.

A catalogue record for this book is available from the British Library.

ISBN 185227 628 2

Typeset by TW Typesetting, Plymouth, Devon

Printed and bound by
Mackays of Chatham, Lordswood, Chatham, Kent

Contents

Acknowledgements

You would think writing a book about Glenn Hoddle would be easy. The story is there in place – one of the most gifted players this country has produced who shone for Spurs and Monaco, then managed Swindon and Chelsea before taking over England, the job of his dreams. In fact, it is far more complex than that. Glenn Hoddle has always been more than just a footballer and a manager. He is a private, almost shy person; sometimes a reluctant superstar. He's a caring, deep-thinking man with strong religious beliefs. There were times when – certainly as a player – he wrestled with his own confidence. This is the first book that has tried to get behind the man and the manager, the player and the person.

It's a fascinating story that I enjoyed writing because I have always had the utmost respect for Hoddle, first as a player, then as a manager and friend. I would like to thank all those managers, coaches, team mates, friends and family for helping me paint the picture. Their contribution was invaluable. They helped me open the door to a book about the real Glenn Hoddle.

Preface

Derek Hoddle knew exactly what to expect when he cycled the two miles home every day from his work as a fitter. His five-year-old son would be sitting on the doorstep of their house in Harlow, Essex, a football trapped between his little feet.

Derek often used to do overtime, but his son would still wait. Even if Dad did not come home for two hours, he waited. And when Derek finally arrived and nipped into the kitchen for a cup of tea and a sandwich, he was continually pestered to hurry up. Time was precious for this little chap. He wanted to go to the park and play football.

Football, you see, meant everything to Glenn Hoddle, even at five years old. The first ball his parents ever gave him was a red rubber one that bounced about the floor. Derek and Terry thought he would throw it. Glenn didn't. He kicked it. And then there was his favourite ball, which he would take everywhere with him. If his parents wanted him to do something or go anywhere, they would often use this ball as a bribe. 'Get in the car, Glenn, we're going out,' they would say. 'And we've got your ball.'

Derek, who played a good standard of amateur football with Harlow, Ware and Edgware, realised straight away that his son had been born with a rare gift, which is why he didn't mind rushing off every night to play at Harlow's Town Park, situated just behind the family home. Glenn was so skilful, even at a tender age, that some of Derek's work colleagues would stop at the park on their way home, lean their bikes up against the fence, and watch Hoddle Junior perform his skills. 'The tricks he could do were fantastic,' recalls Derek proudly. 'It was as if the ball was tied to his feet by string.'

He particularly remembers a family day out at Bognor. No

sooner had they arrived than he and Glenn were off down the beach, passing the ball to each other. They skipped around a couple half asleep on the sand. The man was wearing a handkerchief with knots tied in the corners on his head, and as young Hoddle flicked the ball up and trapped it in front of him, he sat up, rubbed his eyes, and said, 'How old is he then?' 'Five,' came the reply. 'Blimey,' said the man, 'he'll play for England one day.' Derek says he will never forget that moment for as long as he lives.

Derek's wife Terry didn't approve of her husband playing so much football with Glenn. But Derek loved the game as much as his son. The grass under a tree in the back garden of their Harlow home is still worn today, where Glenn, his brother Carl, and Derek played. When the weather was bad, or the nights closed in during the winter, Glenn substituted a ball of wool for a football, which he kept off the floor for hours and then shot through the legs of an armchair.

Of course, all football-loving dads played with their sons. My own father did the same as Derek, returning home to find a whole gang of us waiting to play football or cricket. The local park is where dreams start.

My favourite club as a boy was Arsenal, and when I was old enough to go to my first football match it had to be Highbury. To this day, I can still sense the excitement of coming out from the underground into the open and hearing the banter of the programme sellers and the man with a loudspeaker ushering you towards your turnstile. The first game I saw was Arsenal against Preston in the late 50s. Tom Finney played for Preston, Tommy Docherty broke his leg and Arsenal won 2-0. The sight of the pitch took my breath away when I got to the top of the terrace and looked down at Highbury for the first time. Like Glenn Hoddle, I wanted to be a professional footballer when I grew up. I wanted to be Vic Groves.

The difference was that Glenn Hoddle, from the moment he could kick a football, was special. He was destined to be great, and Derek Hoddle knew it: 'When Glenn got older and played in practice matches I used to look closely at the other boys to see if they were just as good. They never were.'

Glenn, like his father, was a Spurs fan. Derek's favourite player was Jimmy Greaves, while Glenn loved Martin Chivers. If he wasn't playing, Derek took Glenn to White Hart Lane, and even if they couldn't get a ticket Glenn would insist on standing outside the gates to collect autographs of his heroes. It was the signatures of Chivers and Alan Gilzean that he treasured most. Ironically, it was Chivers, the former England centre forward, who spotted Hoddle for Spurs while presenting the prizes at a football finals day at Harlow Town Sports Centre.

It was always Derek's ambition to play in the same side as his son, and he was nearing 40 when it finally happened. Glenn, then in his teens, joined his dad in a Sunday morning side, and they won the league by fifteen points. In the matches Derek won the ball and gave it to his son, marvelling as Glenn made and scored goals, and generally bemused the opposition. 'He was the best player by a mile,' says Derek. 'I retired proud and happy.'

Hoddle was so talented that when as just a young boy he went to watch his father play senior amateur football on Saturday afternoons, the club asked him to go on to the pitch at half time and entertain the crowd with his tricks and skill. He kept the ball up in the air for the fifteen-minute interval. It was easy. The boy, Derek told everyone, had been born with the skill, balance and grace of a footballer. He knew he had been blessed. However, Hoddle Senior never pushed his son into the professional game. While other fathers screamed at their sons from the touchline, Derek stayed in the background – because he knew that one day it would happen.

Glen Hoddle's story started in the park with his dad, just like millions of other football-crazy boys. Derek recalls with amusement how when it got to nine o'clock in the park and dusk was settling, Glenn refused to go home. 'He would have stayed out there all night playing football if he could.'

He would sit on the ball, his head in his hands and tears in his eyes, shouting, 'Dad, I want to stay and play some more. Don't you know I'm going to play for England?'

And he did.

When he was twelve years old Glenn told friends that one day he would manage England too.

And he did.

1 Game One, Game Won

Moldova 0 England 3,
Goalscorers: Barmby, Gascoigne, Shearer

The twelve-year-old boy's dream became reality for Glenn Hoddle on Friday 30 August 1996. Here he was, the England coach, flying to Moldova for his first match. The boy, as they say, had done good.

He had selected his squad, faced the press and met the players for the first time at England's attractive Bisham training head-quarters, on the river near Maidenhead. And now this was it; this was for real. He sat on the chartered Britannia Airways aircraft with his players in front of him, his new bosses around him and the media behind him at the back of the plane. I wondered what was going through his mind. It's not always easy to tell what's going on in Glenn Hoddle's head.

One would reasonably presume that he was thinking about his career – a career that took him from his beloved Spurs to the South of France with Monaco and then to Swindon and Chelsea as player-coach. It had been a smooth ride to the biggest job of all. Indeed, some would say he was lucky to get it. What had he actually achieved to be given such a glittering prize at the tender age of 38?

He was without doubt a player of immense talent, and yet he never convinced English coaches that he was the finished all-round article. He won promotion with Swindon but got no higher than eleventh in the Premiership with Chelsea. There was an FA Cup Final against Manchester United, but Chelsea lost 4-0.

So why was he sitting here on this plane heading off to Moldova? He was certainly not the Football Association's first choice to replace Terry Venables. The difference was that he wanted it, while others said no. Hoddle will tell you he was destined to become England coach.

His CV probably needs only two words – Glenn Hoddle. It is a name that is right up there with the men who are respected from different generations of English football, like Bobby Charlton, Billy Wright, Kevin Keegan, Gary Lineker, Peter Shilton and Bobby Moore. It is half the reason he got the job. The FA liked his name, his image, the fact that he had respect and the way he played. And he was a young, modern-day thinker who would keep our game at the level left behind by Venables' controversial and arguably unnecessary departure.

So what was really going through Hoddle's mind as we took off? 'Pride,' he admits. 'And the job in hand. To win a World Cup tie on the road to France 1998. My mind was focused.' Certainly not to get rolled over in Moldova. If the media were behind him on the flight going out, they would have been on top of him on the return journey if the result was not the one required.

It was certainly very difficult to tell whether Hoddle was nervous. He rarely shows outward signs. He doesn't swear in public – well, not much anyway. His expression doesn't alter much, although it does light up when he laughs. He is not a table-top thumper, a shouter, a screamer or a finger pointer. He is a cool, calm character.

There were no give-away signs when he met the media for the first time as England coach, the day after Venables had lost that dramatic European Championship semi-final against Germany at Wembley, or when he announced his first England squad or gave press conferences before and after England's opening match on the road to the World Cup. He was as cool as you like.

That has been the hallmark of his whole career. Unflappable under pressure. He was the player with the ability to control the situation while being closely marked or kicked. If in trouble give the ball to Glenn, the Tottenham players used to say. And the FA did just that.

He got his squad right, more or less sticking to the players who had got so close in the European Finals, and even persuading Stuart Pearce to come out of international retirement. There was, as expected, an England lifeline for Matthew Le Tissier, the inconsistent Southampton star dumped by Venables. Hoddle identified with the skilful forward because he himself had been misunderstood as a player. He could see the same thing happening to Le Tissier.

There was also a first appearance for David Beckham, the Manchester United youngster tipped by so many to be one of the great stars of the next ten years. Beckham had already made his mark on the season, scoring a wonder goal from the halfway line against Wimbledon. They could close the goal of the season competitions on day one, Beckham's effort was so superb. David Batty was also recalled by Hoddle, while he axed Blackburn goalkeeper Tim Flowers and brought in Liverpool's David James.

It was the selection of Le Tissier that was the most significant, though, and the most telling of the Hoddle era. 'When I was playing,' he explained, 'I always felt we had the talent in this country, some of it not used. Since being given the job I have been playing fantasy football. Now this is real and I am happy with these players.

'The season is early and of course there will be changes along the way. Le Tissier and I need to have a chat. I need to find out his positives and negatives. I need to work with him and, yes, I see a little of myself there. He has a future to look forward to and the door is open. It is up to him and others whether he goes through it.

'Matt has got immense talent. At international level you need highly technical players. I need to work with him and find out what is going through his mind.'

The chat Hoddle referred to was not restricted to Le Tissier. Hoddle took it upon himself to sit down with all of his players on a one-to-one basis during his first months in control. It was a good piece of man-management and allowed him to get closer to the squad.

Le Tissier returned from Moldova happier and more relaxed about his England future. 'It is up to me now,' he said. 'I feel that here is someone at last who wants me to play for England. There is no better feeling than to be wanted.'

Hoddle would have liked a training get-together before meeting up for the Moldova trip, but it was impossible. As every football fan knows, the English programme is so congested that the England manager's wishes often come last. It has been a complaint from all the England managers before Hoddle. So when he met his players, some of them for the first time, he had to use his time well. He only had a couple of days to get to know them and prepare them as well as he could before the flight on that Friday before the Sunday game. It was not ideal, but there was no alternative but to get on with it. 'I have never been a complainer,' says Hoddle. 'There is absolutely no point in dealing with negatives.'

Hoddle was to use all his time well. Over the first three matches, he had a series of meetings with players. The meetings were valuable to him because if you want to be in Hoddle's gang you need to be the right make-up. And if Hoddle likes you, he is extremely loyal. He not only had to make up his mind about his men as players, but as people too. It was an important period for him in his England managerial career. In Le Tissier he clearly saw something he liked.

Le Tissier's selection was not lost on Venables, who had been portrayed as a villain for continually overlooking him. 'I did not pick him because I did not think he could operate in the system I wanted to play,' said Venables. 'And I was not going to change that system for Le Tissier or anyone else. Of course I appreciated his skill but he was not for me – not in my England team and how I always intended them to play.'

Beckham's selection was exciting for everyone. Here was a superb fresh young midfield talent. Alex Ferguson, however, was not so sure if he was ready for international recognition, and he voiced feelings, some of them in private, that England had come too soon for Beckham. He and Hoddle spoke on the telephone about shielding the youngster from the media, even from the team, but it was surely an overreaction from Ferguson. At 22, Beckham was not a teenager, and it was clear that he had a head on his shoulders that could cope with the pressures. Most other countries in the world would have picked a talent like Beckham long before his early twenties.

Beckham did face the media at Bisham before the squad flew to Moldova. He was sandwiched between Hoddle and the FA's press executive David Davies at a little table, and made all the right noises and said the right things. There has never been a great interview obtained with the player sitting alongside his manager. How is a player supposed to voice his true feelings when worried about saying the right things? But the FA did Fergie proud. Hoddle even interrupted the interview to request that the questions should not be just concerned with playing for England. It could be argued that press days with England are becoming too organised in favour of the FA, and it is unlikely to become more relaxed with Hoddle because dealing with the media has never been his favourite pastime.

David Batty's selection brought this response from Hoddle: 'A vastly underrated player. He passes the ball much cleaner and better than most people give him credit for. I have always been a Batty fan.' Batty clearly could look forward to a long England career under the new coach. Hoddle lost Darren Anderton, Teddy Sheringham, Robbie Fowler, Steve McManaman and Steve Howey through injury and surprisingly only called up two replacements – Aston Villa's Mark Draper and Andy Hinchcliffe from Everton. 'I have got enough players and quality to do the job,' he announced confidently.

There was no Tony Adams, because of the injury he suffered in the European Finals. Adams should never have played in Euro 96. He had a dodgy knee that needed rest, treatment and perhaps an operation, but the Arsenal captain desperately wanted to play, because he wanted to win something for his country. He needed seven painkilling injections during England's run to the semi-final, and at one stage he was held down on the dressing-room treatment table, screaming in agony, to have the injection that enabled him to go out for a second half. By the end of the competition, Adams emerged with his reputation higher than ever but his knee in a mess. He missed the start of the 1996–97 season because of the operation he needed.

Venables always liked Adams. He was his kind of captain – a players' player who anyone would want on their side in a crisis. Adams, however, had been to prison for a drink-driving offence, and Venables, who took the job under a cloud of controversy, did not want to upset the FA. Instead he chose David Platt, who like Gary Lineker is a safe bet. Come the European Finals, however, it was Adams who led the team out. Platt was not even a first choice in the team, and even when they both started a game Venables gave the armband to Adams.

The fact that Adams was an alcoholic, which became public knowledge at the start of the 1996/97 season, gave Hoddle a big problem to solve. He had yet to talk with the hero skipper of Euro

96, who was out of the Moldova match because of injury. This meant that he had to name a new captain, but would it be long term or short term, and would he wait for Adams?

Hoddle, like Venables at the start, went safety first and gave the job to Alan Shearer, top scorer in the European Finals. He announced the decision just as the squad were about to board the plane for Moldova, saying that Shearer was not just going to be a one-off and would certainly be his captain on the road to the World Cup. This view, however, seemed to strangely change after Hoddle's third match, the impressive win in Georgia. Shearer was missing this time, with a groin injury, and Adams returned as captain. Hoddle then said that Shearer had been aware from the start that the captaincy issue would be reviewed after he had led the team for three matches.

The difference between Adams and Shearer as captain is obvious. Adams is the street fighter; sleeves rolled up, tackling like a runaway truck, screaming at his players and the first man over the top of the trenches. He can also play a bit too, as Arsene Wenger realised when he took over at Highbury at the end of 1996. He encouraged Adams to play more football and go forward with the ball to join his attack. 'He has more technical ability than I thought,' said Wenger. Adams now led by example from the back and the front.

Shearer sets his example through goals. He is Mr Cool, the man with ice for nerves. 'Nothing makes me nervous,' says Shearer. 'Not off the pitch or on it. I take it as it comes.' Hoddle went for that approach in his captain and significantly said, 'He has a great reputation around the world, with all players and especially with referees.' So he had the right image. The FA, no doubt, could not believe their luck. After the controversy of Venables they now had Hoddle and Shearer, a whiter-than-white combination, although many people would argue that a captain should play behind the strikers. Just look at Bobby Moore, the greatest of them all, and Dave Mackay, Frank McLintock, Steve Bruce, Tony Adams, Graeme Souness ... And Shearer could never be called a dream captain in a journalist's eyes. He's a superb player and professional, of course, but his first comment as England captain was: 'There are eleven captains out there ...'

All the preamble and endless press conferences were almost an irritation for Hoddle. He has never looked comfortable with the press, and there was often an annoyance in his voice, especially at Chelsea. But the media has never been bigger than now and he must come to terms with that. The plane to Moldova carried more press men than ever before on an England trip. It was the first game for a new manager, Euro 96 meant that interest in football was at an all-time high, and everyone wanted a piece of the Hoddle action. He was public property now. Hoddle, however, just wanted to get on with the football.

His approach to training had an immediate effect on the players. Hoddle's experience of playing abroad meant a slight change in emphasis from the Venables era. Paul Ince, formerly with Manchester United and now Inter Milan, explained: 'The training is different. It is a bit like training as we do in Italy. You spend a lot of time warming up – twenty-five minutes maybe – and another twenty minutes on skills – keeping the ball up and so on – before going into a game. With Terry it would be five to ten minutes warming up, then a game, then practising crosses and all that.

'It's all geared to the same thing really, but the boss has played abroad and seen how they train and maybe he's trying to follow in their footsteps. We started to play in a new formation under Terry, a more continental style, and now under Glenn Hoddle we are training like that as well.'

Hoddle's warm-up man is John Gorman, his assistant at Swindon who almost followed him to Chelsea. A Scot, Gorman waited for the sarcastic comments from the players – and got them. That was inevitable. But he has always been a players' man and swapped jokes and jibes with the England players to break the ice on day one. He is Hoddle's buffer and has always been happiest in that role. 'I'm a Scot but proud to be with England,' says Gorman. 'England winning matches and getting to the World Cup is all that matters to me now.'

Gorman is a friendly man who is liked throughout the game. Tactically he isn't on the same wavelength as Hoddle, and he doesn't have that kind of respect in the game, but he is immensely popular with players and they respect his honesty. Significantly, he has never let Hoddle down.

Hoddle also introduced Ray Clemence, his former Spurs team

mate, as goalkeeper coach, and Peter Taylor, another Tottenham old boy, as full-time manager of the Under 21 squad. Hoddle met Gorman for the first time when they played for Spurs, so it was a trip down memory lane when England joined up at Bisham.

Taylor's role with England is significant. Hoddle wants all his England side to play the same way and Taylor, who works well and is an inspirational figure for young boys, is keen to build up the Under 21 side.

'In the past too many players have dropped out. You got the impression from the outside that it was not taken seriously enough. I intend to go out to the clubs, meet the managers and players, and change the attitude.'

Hoddle added: 'I want to create the club atmosphere and system where the players all down the line are gearing themselves for the first team, playing the same way, so they are ready when and if called upon. I see it as a long-term progression. It makes sense. For so long the English player has had a closed mind. Now, with the influx of foreign players and the arrival of younger coaches, players' minds are being opened. Ten years ago, if someone had said that we are going to play with a flat-back three, the players would have been up in arms and you would have had trouble convincing them. But times are changing and so is football – and that can only be healthy.

'I know how I want my England side to play, eventually, but I'm not going to change things in five days. That would be drastic and wrong. It's going to be gradual. There will be subtle changes. It's going to be a slow evolution, certainly not a revolution. My thinking is long term. But I have to get results. If I don't win matches then there's no long term for Glenn Hoddle. It's my head on the chopping block.'

One former Spurs man who was not kept on was physio Dave Butler. He had been a member of Venables' staff at White Hart Lane and for the two-and-a-half years of Venables' England reign. Hoddle, however, brought in Gary Lewin from Arsenal and Butler discovered he was out from his friend and another England physio, Alan Smith at Sheffield Wednesday. Not surprisingly, Smith was acutely embarrassed after talking to Butler and then realising that he did not know he'd been replaced. It was disappointing handling by Hoddle; a poor piece of man-management.

By the time Hoddle got on the plane he knew his team. He had picked it a million times in his mind, long before he came down on his final selection. David Beckham was always going to play. He is definitely a player Hoddle wants around him all the way to France: 'He selects his passes in a mature way, way beyond his years,' explained Hoddle. 'Beckham is a player who sees the furthest pass first. There are enough around in football who see no further than the nearest ball. If you see the furthest, most penetrative one first, then your options are so much more creative. Beckham has got that ability. He has also got an eye for goal which is a bonus.' Hoddle's reputation as a player was not just about skill – his passing was devastating. His long passing, if you ask anyone who played with him, was the best they have experienced. Hoddle could land the ball in a bucket from 40 yards – and often did in training. He could spot similarities in Beckham.

His first side was: David Seaman; Gareth Southgate, Gary Pallister, Stuart Pearce; Gary Neville, David Beckham, Paul Ince, Paul Gascoigne, Andy Hinchcliffe; Alan Shearer and Nick Barmby. In the second half David Batty replaced Gascoigne and Matthew Le Tissier came on for Barmby. Three players were selected who had not been in Venables' European Championship squad: Beckham, Pallister and Hinchcliffe. Hoddle was confident and in an extremely relaxed mood once the team was announced. 'I would not have taken this job had I not been confident of reaching the World Cup. I am certainly confident of winning this one,' he said. 'I have got the best players at my disposal and my job is to put the jigsaw together. Moulding the team will take time, the one thing I have not got, but it has to be done.'

Surely we could not go three days in a foreign country without Gazza causing some sort of controversy? His moment arrived at the Under 21 game, played, to Hoddle's dismay, on the same pitch 24 hours before the senior game. During the match it began to rain, and the England players who had been sitting in the stand – if you can call it that – scrambled for cover and the safety of a long press box. Paul Ince and Les Ferdinand clambered over a small wall and as Ince drew himself up, Paul Gascoigne could not resist the temptation. Down came his tracksuit bottoms and shorts. One eagle-eyed snapper, ironically working for an agency recognised as an official provider of photographs for the Football

Association, got the picture of Ince's bare backside. It was plastered over most tabloid back pages the next morning under such headlines as 'Gascoigne's New Shame'.

Hoddle was not particularly concerned. He treated it as a joke and certainly did not discipline Gascoigne. It probably got more headlines and bigger coverage because, on that particular Saturday, stories were few and far between. Hoddle had introduced a new rule that no players would be interviewed the day before a match. 'I want their minds totally focused on the job in hand,' he had said. So, Gazza came to the rescue and Hoddle played the incident just right. But Gascoigne was soon to provide Hoddle with a much bigger dilemma; a controversy that was to divide a nation and question the England coach's God-loving standards. But that's another story . . .

Moldova lies between Romania and Ukraine, down near the Black Sea. It was a journey into the unknown and what greeted the England party was a basic hotel, but not the horror story that had been painted back home. The place was cheerless but the weather was warm, the food certainly edible and, for journalists, the phones worked. The pitch was Hoddle's biggest concern. It was bumpy, the grass was too long and uneven and there were pot holes. It was the kind of surface Hoddle hated playing on, and it didn't promise the beautiful game he had hoped for.

The expectancy level, though, was higher than ever. Four months earlier, on warm June evenings, England had wowed the nation in the European Championships. Who will ever forget those days and nights at Wembley? Football did come home and England almost won. It was so close. In 1990 it was the semi-final of the World Cup. In 1996 the semi-final of the European Championships. Germany both times frustrated us. Hoddle's job was to take it a step further in 1998.

Suddenly we found ourselves in Kishinev, Moldova, at the start of a tough-looking World Cup campaign. No friendlies for Hoddle, as Venables enjoyed for two-and-a-half years – every game was pressure, make or break. He couldn't afford to lose one of them, certainly not in Moldova. Waiting along the way were Poland, Georgia and then Italy. Only one from group two would qualify automatically. 'It is the toughest group to finish top of,' admitted Hoddle.

There could be no slip up because the fans would not tolerate it – not after Euro 96. Arsenal goalkeeper David Seaman, a national hero after his penalty saves – 'I walked into the centre court at Wimbledon and all this applause broke out. I turned to see which celebrity had come in. There was no one, then I suddenly realised they were applauding me. It was embarrassing' – admitted: 'The country expects. Because of what happened in the summer it is doubly important we get to France. It is no good us not qualifying, not now. The trouble in football is that it takes hard work to get right up there, and it is even harder to stay there. But we must.'

There was no need for concern. England won easily. It was not convincing or wonderful football, but it was never going to be, not on a poor surface. There were a few early scares as the nerves gripped the players; hesitancy at the back which a better team might have pounced on. Indeed, at times in those opening minutes, Gareth Southgate, Gary Pallister and Stuart Pearce didn't look as though they had ever played before. But once Nick Barmby put England ahead, the result was a forgone conclusion – it was just a question of how many against a very poor international side.

Gascoigne, who played in the game despite an ankle injury, got the second with a header and Alan Shearer lobbed the third, his first goal for his country on foreign soil. Moldova missed a penalty and Le Tissier was given the chance to have a feel of international football again. It was a job done.

David Beckham's debut was impressive, in so far as he coped well with the pressure of the occasion and the poor conditions. Andy Hinchcliffe's arrival for the first time was also smooth, without being edge-of-the-seat stuff. A free kick and corner specialist, and a player with a huge reputation for getting in crosses, he did not deliver a stream of centres or get forward that much, but it was workmanlike.

The after-match press conference was carried out with Hoddle sitting in the dug-out on the side of the pitch, surrounded by flashing cameras and press men. If you weren't at the front you couldn't hear him. His first victory speech was predictable. 'I am glad to have won, of course. I was concerned about the surface and the players handled it well. It was not a classic but three points are in the bag. I could not have asked any more from them. I only met some of them a few days ago and they have done the job I wanted.'

On the surface Hoddle didn't look relieved or excited, but he hadn't looked worried or concerned going into the game either. The only certainty was that Hoddle had big plans for England and this was just the start.

One man who was relieved was his dad Derek, watching the game in his Harlow home. He felt nervous for his son when he turned on the TV, because there's nothing worse than losing your first game as England coach, especially in the World Cup. He only began to relax when the second goal went in and England took control.

He was not surprised England won because nothing surprises him any more about his son Glenn. Since those nights playing in the park he has achieved so much. He and his wife have often said to each other that it has all been a dream come true.

For Glenn Hoddle it has to be.

2 'Who's That Tall Kid?'

Martin Chivers was always being asked to open fêtes or supermarkets and make personal appearances. After all, he was the Spurs and England centre forward. On this occasion it was presenting prizes at the Harlow Sports Centre. It was close to his home and he was happy to do it. The boys were fourteen and fifteen and Chivers, after signing autographs, settled down to watch some football. It wasn't actually a scouting mission for his Tottenham club, but you never know.

One boy caught his eye straight away – a tall lad with long legs and not much muscle about him. 'Who's that tall kid, then?' Chivers asked someone sitting alongside him.

'Which one? Oh, that's Derek Hoddle's boy. Skilful, isn't he?'

Skilful! Chivers couldn't keep his eyes off him. The boy was more than skilful. For someone so young he had amazing balance, awareness and passing range. Chivers' mind raced. I must tell Tottenham about him, he thought to himself. He contemplated dashing off there and then to make a phone call, but he didn't think it would be polite, and anyway, he might miss the prize-giving. So he settled back in his chair to watch some more of this lanky lad Hoddle, amazed that a scout from another club hadn't snapped him up already.

The next day he gave the name of Glenn Hoddle to Tottenham's then chief scout, Dickie Walker. Liking what he saw when he spied on Hoddle, manager Bill Nicholson was informed and the rest is history . . . a star was born.

Chivers recalls: 'I was in my hey-day. I went along to present the prizes at Harlow and Glenn stood out straight away. He was a cut above the rest. His skills were amazing and I could tell after about five minutes that he was a player for the future. Glenn's balance on the ball, even at that age, was uncanny. He stuck out head and shoulders above the rest. He used both feet as if they were natural. I enjoyed watching him then, and have done ever since.'

Hoddle's impact on Tottenham was immediate. He was so much better than all the other boys of his age, and it wasn't long before he was better than the senior players as well. Paul Miller joined Spurs at around the same time. Two years Hoddle's junior at thirteen, Miller, an uncompromising central defender, quickly became a member of the Hoddle fan club. They also became close friends, playing in the same side through to the first team, sharing rooms on away trips and socialising together.

Miller recalls: 'I was big for my age and trained with the older boys. I first saw Glenn playing in the gym. He was tall and gangly but had a great touch. Because of his skill he always stood out. You could tell in those early days that he was exceptional.

'Those matches in the gym were fierce. Very competitive. The club used to encourage them to be physical because they saw it as part of the toughening-up process for boys. It was a masculine thing. Ambitious boys pushing to be the best – showing off, if you like. You had to look after yourself. If you didn't have a good touch you got smashed against the wall. If you couldn't get the ball under control, or release it quickly, in came the next challenge, from any angle. We all tried to get Glenn but none succeeded. He just released the ball or skipped out of the way. He was so skilful.'

Miller believes that the boys from that era were lucky to have caught the end of the Bill Nicholson era. The manager who led the club to the FA Cup and League double, was strong on standards and old-fashioned morals. 'Get your hands out of your pockets, get your hair cut, polish your shoes, remember who you are, who you represent – you know the kind of thing,' Miller recalls.

'It stood us in good stead and I will never forget him. I suspect that pride and those standards are something that Glenn will want in the England squad. People like Bill Nicholson have to rub off on you. He was a larger-than-life legend, one of the game's great managers, and we were young boys at the start of our careers.'

It was only a matter of time before Hoddle made his Tottenham debut. He would have liked it to have been under Nicholson, but Bill resigned before Hoddle was ready. The club's first choice to replace Nicholson was Danny Blanchflower, their former Double-winning skipper and favourite of Nicholson, working with former Leeds star Johnny Giles. It would have been an exciting forward-thinking combination and put Tottenham years ahead of the rest, but the ambitious plan never came off. The job instead went to Terry Neill, the former Arsenal and Northern Ireland centre half. 'The wrong man for the wrong job,' said Miller.

It was Neill, however, who gave Hoddle his first-team introduction. Glenn went on as substitute for Cyril Knowles at home to Norwich on 30 August 1975 and six months later he made his debut, away at Stoke on 21 February 1976. For the records the Tottenham team that day was: Pat Jennings, Mickey Stead, Don McAllister, John Pratt, Willie Young, Keith Osgood, Hoddle, Steve Perryman, John Duncan, Martin Chivers and Jimmy Neighbour. Chris Jones went on as substitute for Duncan in the second half.

Hoddle's first kick in League football came after just twenty minutes of that home game with Norwich. The first thing Hoddle remembers was the size of the crowd. He had never played in front of such a big gathering before and he felt that the sides of the pitch were being squeezed in. 'The pitch definitely seemed smaller,' he admits. The game ended 2-2, and eighteen-year-old Hoddle actually came close to scoring on his debut. He went home that night happy and contented, wondering what the future held for him. His mind raced with the memories of the game; the passes he made, that shot that almost went in. He could never have guessed the future. How could he have known at that stage that he had just taken the first step of one of the great careers of English football.

Chivers couldn't even remember playing in the same side as the man he discovered. He says: 'I chatted with Glenn at the end of the 1995–96 season. Chelsea had drawn at Spurs and I think it was just before Glenn took the England job. Inevitably, we chatted about the past and he complimented me about how I played and my form in those days. I said it was a pity that we never played in the same side together. He was hurt, and looking at me sideways, said: "Don't be silly. You were in the team when I made my debut as a sub and when I started for the first time. Of course we played together."

'I had completely forgotten because I chose to forget the Terry Neill era at Spurs. There was a big exodus after Billy Nick stood down. All my old compatriots started to go and I left for Switzerland with Servette in June 1976. I must have played one or two games with Glenn but it was the end of my Spurs career and not my happiest memories.

'You've only got to look at that Spurs side at Stoke when Glenn made his full debut to realise what a transitional period the club was going through. Donkey Willie Young; John Duncan, who never passed to anyone in his life, certainly not me. He was a dreadful, selfish player. Also people like Don McAllister who should never have been near the Spurs side I had grown to know and love.

'My favourite team was in the early seventies. I can still reel it off. Pat Jennings, Joe Kinnear, Cyril Knowles, Alan Mullery, Mike England, Phil Beal, Steve Perryman, Martin Peters, me, Alan Gilzean and Ralph Coates. What a side. It was a pleasure to play with them. We had a lot of success – four finals in four seasons – and on our day we could beat anyone. The era went too quickly for me. I still can't understand how we didn't do it in the League because the quality we produced was superb. We were always a Cup side though – a threat to anyone.

'How Glenn would have enjoyed playing in that side. Of course he would have got in. Players like him only come around once in a blue moon. Which other Spurs players since 1970 would have got in that team? Only one. Paul Gascoigne.

'Glenn certainly remembers more about playing with me than I do him, and that's a nice compliment. When we chatted after that game between Spurs and Chelsea he said he recalled getting the ball accurately to his feet from my headers as he moved up from midfield. He said that when he came into the side he was not used to such service. He couldn't believe how I, under pressure from big defenders, could deliver the ball into his path so well. It was good to recall the old days and I just wish we had been at our best together.'

Hoddle scored on that Stoke debut, a 25-yard drive past Peter

Shilton. Spurs won 2-1 and the Hoddle adventure had really started. Of course, it was a double thrill to score your first goal against the great Shilton. Hoddle also recalls that during and after the game he was very impressed by the attitude of Alan Hudson, the former Chelsea player who went to Stoke and throughout his career was said to be heading for great things. Hudson became one of the players English football never appreciated, and that is not lost on Hoddle.

During the game Hudson complimented Hoddle on his goal and afterwards told him: 'Keep playing like that and keep your feet on the ground and you'll go a long way.' Hoddle still has his feet on the ground today, even as England coach. He has never let the adulation get to him.

That full debut and goal against Shilton triggered a journey of headlines, glory and frustration. Hoddle came into English football as a boy genius and eventually left Spurs for the continent as a player our game did not completely understand or appreciate. Just before that Stoke game, Hudson had been brilliant for England against West Germany, going off to a standing ovation, and the critics raved about a new genius. He only played two more times for his country! It's now said that Hoddle's years at Spurs fell into the wrong era of our game, but that's a cop out for English football and all the coaches who didn't realise the talent they had at their disposal.

Paul Miller recalls: 'Glenn was the star of the youth team with us and then nipped off to play in the first team. Everyone was on about how good he was going to become. Tottenham are a club with a great tradition of skilful, attacking football and a youth policy which has discovered some great talent. Glenn was one of the first and best off the conveyor belt. Others followed him like Steve Walford, Noel Brotherstone, Chris Jones and Martin Robinson, and they were exciting days.

'We could sense, as youth team players together, that the future was bright. If we stayed together we could enjoy some great years. We knew we, as a group, were the makings of a superb Tottenham era.

'I recall one junior Cup Final against Ipswich when they had Russell Osman, Terry Butcher, John Wark, Alan Brazil, George Burley and Eric Gates – all internationals – and we were bombing along. It was a superb occasion. Glenn even missed a penalty, which was a real rare occurrence. Great memories from a marvellous era.'

The club's first concern with Hoddle was that he was too thin. 'Thin?' says Miller. 'There was more fat on Lester Piggott's whip. The amazing thing was, however, that he may have been skinny but no one could knock him about on the pitch because he was always too skilful for opponents, especially at youth level. They used to see this skinny bloke and target him. You could sense the instruction from the team's hardman: "Leave the tall git to me." But they could never get anywhere near him. Glenn was a one-off. A boy wonder.'

All the time Hoddle was listening to his managers and coaches, talking to his team mates and forming a picture in his own mind. He knew he had talent. He knew he was special, and he wondered how far it would take him. He loved Spurs – he had done from a tender age – and he often asked himself what he could achieve for his favourite club.

He knew he would play for England one day, and others began to think along the same lines. Joe Mercer, the late great manager of Manchester City who did a caretaking job for England when the late Don Revie negotiated a deal with the Arabs in the middle of his international reign, was once asked on television who he would sign. 'Oh, the boy at Spurs,' he said quickly. 'I would take Hoddle tomorrow.' Glenn was only eighteen at the time.

But as his career progressed, question marks began to emerge. Too lazy, too lightweight to dominate matches, not enough work rate, can't tackle. In the end, they drove Hoddle crazy and forced him to quit our game. Why don't managers push the strengths of a player? Why do so many coaches want to find fault? They did in the Hoddle era and it didn't make any sense at all. They eventually lost a great talent.

The same thing happened at Arsenal in 1996. Ian Wright and the then manager Bruce Rioch did not get on for the simple reason that Rioch used his sergeant-major approach to try to turn Wright into something he wasn't. Wright rebelled, lost interest and asked for a transfer. It was a decision that helped persuade the Highbury board to sack Rioch. New coach Arsene Wenger arrived, with his continental approach, and recognised a unique scoring talent in

Wright and so encouraged him. Wright responded by scoring goals again, enjoying himself and getting back into the England squad. 'I am only interested in his strengths,' Wenger said. 'He is a one-off; I have never met anyone like him before.' Great man-management. It was the very same man-management that got the best out of Hoddle in Monaco.

Throughout his playing career, all Hoddle's managers and coaches knew they had a special talent. But only one of them, Wenger, got the best out of him, and that's an amazing indictment of what happened to our game in the 1970s and 1980s. Defenders were told to 'Get Hoddle' and if he couldn't cope in certain games, his own bosses blamed him. He would have enjoyed himself more playing in the Premiership today, with the tackle from behind banned, the influx of foreign players and coaches, and more positive thinking from everyone.

Chivers was one player from that period who certainly appreciated Hoddle: 'When Alan Shearer was sold for fifteen million I was asked by someone if there had been any player from my day worth that amount of money. I fell about laughing. How many would you like, I said? Ten, twenty? I listed off just a few. Dave Mackay, Jimmy Greaves, Bobby Charlton, George Best, Dennis Law – the list went on and on. I would put Glenn Hoddle in there too, and Paul Gascoigne. What short memories people have.

'There were also some great characters in that time – the kind of characters that our game is missing today. Hoddle's skill made him a character. He was special. Glenn was able to pass the ball with the outside of both feet. Look at the records and see the centre forwards who played in front of him during his career. They all got a lot of goals. And some of those strikers were not particularly top class. How many did they miss? It would have been a pleasure to have been a centre forward, playing at his peak, with Hoddle behind you delivering those lovely long balls.'

Chivers is right. All the strikers down the years who enjoyed a full season playing with Hoddle scored more than twenty goals. John Duncan, Colin Lee, Mark Falco, Garth Crooks, Steve Archibald, Clive Allen, Mark Hateley. Chivers adds: 'I wonder how many I would have scored? I was just lucky to play a couple of matches with him at the end of my career and the start of his. Since then I have watched with admiration. If only, if only . . .'

One of Spurs' greatest fans is Maurice Keston, a good friend of former England manager Bobby Robson. He first started going to Tottenham in the 1940s and has seen and appreciated all the greats at White Hart Lane. He recalls: 'There have been some great teams and great players. The Eddie Bailey push-and-run team in the fifties, the Double team in 1961 with Danny Blanchflower and Dave Mackay, and the seventies team of Chivers and Gilzean. I know that Glenn Hoddle played in two teams that had success – the late seventies and early eighties one with Ossie Ardiles and Ricky Villa and the David Pleat team that almost won the lot.

'I don't think, however, that either of those matched up to the three at the top of my list – the push-and-run side, the double-winning team and the seventies side. I do believe that football in this country has deteriorated. Yes, it is quicker and the players are more like athletes, but the skill is not so great. Spurs once had a player called Tommy Harmer, who was the most talented player I have ever seen. I went to reserve games just to watch him. Ron Burgess was my favourite Spurs player of all time and winger Cliff Jones was a sensation.

'If I had to pick my top Spurs players of all time they would have to be Ron Burgess, Danny Blanchflower, Tommy Harmer, Dave Mackay, Jimmy Greaves, Ossie Ardiles and Glen Hoddle.' No John White? 'No, I thought he was overrated,' says Keston.

But could Keston persuade Robson about Hoddle? 'Not a chance,' says Keston. 'I often used to give Bobby a lift back to Liverpool Street after a dinner together and the conversation, always about football, often got on to Hoddle. I told Bobby that here was one of the greatest players of all time. He would not have it. He kept on about Glenn not running backward and forward enough.

'Keith Burkinshaw was the same when he was in charge of Spurs and Hoddle was flying. One season Glenn got more than twenty goals. The next Keith made him defend more and he got three goals, and Keith was happier. To the fans it just didn't make sense.

'Glenn once went on England Under 21 duty when Terry Venables was the manager. He came back and said that in two days under Venables he had learnt more than in two years at

Tottenham. Had Venables been England coach when Glenn was playing there is no doubt in my mind that he would have won more than a hundred caps.

'I believe you have to watch these kinds of players week in and week out to really appreciate them. It's no good popping in for the odd game, seeing a bad performance, and dismissing the player. Over a period you are convinced. I have some wonderful memories of Spurs, and Hoddle figures in a lot of them. The day he went in goal at Manchester United, because of injury, and we won one-nil. His volley against Nottingham Forest, the chip at Watford and his last goal for the club, when he ran from the halfway line and beat the goalkeeper by dummying around him and not touching the ball.

'The Spurs crowd has always loved a big name, a player with magic. We've been lucky down the years. Fantasy football, if you like, because supporters like to dream, to be entertained, to get on their feet and cheer and clap. Hoddle entertained me and won games on his own. The last magical player we had was Jurgen Klinsmann. He was superb. He came to Tottenham with everything against him. The media, the Jewish fans because he was German, and he won them over in one magical season. He took knocks on and off the pitch but never showed them. A really great character.'

Keston also has fond off-field memories of Hoddle. After Glenn had returned from France and became player-manager at Swindon, Keston organised a testimonial game at White Hart Lane for Cyril Knowles. 'I tried to get as many old players together as I could and I contacted Glenn and asked if there was any chance of him turning out. He had been injured for nine months and was only just coming back into playing. I said to Glenn to give the crowd five minutes. They would love it and it would light up the night, I told him. He played the entire game. That is the kind of bloke he is.'

The more games Hoddle played for the Spurs first team, the bigger his reputation grew. The boy wonder, the greatest talent to come into English football for years, an England cert, a magnificent prospect, the magic man, the king of White Hart Lane . . . the tributes poured in.

But it was not to last.

3 The First Breakthrough

I f any of us look back on our lives, we inevitably remember landmarks. Things that happened, places we visited, situations that made us sit up and take notice, people we found fascinating, an unexpected chemistry. Turning points. Glenn Hoddle is no different. He will point to situations and – more significantly – people who changed his life. Arsene Wenger at Monaco certainly; the mother of a former girlfriend, a faith healer, definitely.

Another was Ossie Ardiles – a little Argentinian international who had just played for his country in the 1978 World Cup. He arrived in England soon after that World Cup and it proved to be the biggest transformation Spurs has known.

Ardiles, and his Argentinian team mate Ricky Villa, made a huge impact on English football. They changed the face of the game and were the first foreign imports to be a success, and the repercussions are still developing today. Ardiles and Villa opened people's minds to a new concept of football, particularly the young man who at that stage was the star of the Spurs side. Glenn Hoddle.

Hoddle was ready to learn. He knew he had immense talent. He was in the Spurs first team with his whole career in front of him, and the arrival of Ardiles opened up new doors. Paul Miller explains: 'It was the biggest transformation of our lives. Yes, it changed our lives.

'In came Ossie and Ricky with new wage demands, more money than any of us were on. They wanted – and got – houses, cars and new bonuses. We thought, What is going on here? Because suddenly things were moving at the club. Our salaries went up and football at Tottenham took on a whole new buzz. You had this lovely mixture of home-grown talent, players who had come through the ranks together, plus a bit of experience, plus Ossie and Ricky. They were exciting, great times. We became the most popular club side in England. Everyone wanted to play against Spurs. Apart from kicking Glenn, they now wanted to pit their own skills against Ossie and Ricky.

'Glenn loved it. You could see that. For a start he and Ossie were on the same wavelength. Glenn was the long game, his the short. Glenn all balance and majestic passes, Ossie, quick, nippy, a great reader. They were the odd couple who talked the same language. It was a football language that made them the most devastating pair of midfield players in the country.'

It was Keith Burkinshaw who brought the Argentinians to English football. Burkinshaw, who had been brought to the club in 1975, had worked as first-team coach under Terry Neill before being made manager. A tall, often dour man, he arrived from Newcastle with a straight, honest reputation. Players like that. If they do not respect you, understand or appreciate what you are telling them, or if you try and con them or double talk them, you are finished. When Neill was sacked the board took that honesty into consideration.

Even when Burkinshaw took the club down in his first season, the board supported him. The then chairman Sidney Wale said: 'We appointed you a year ago because we thought you were the right man and we have not changed our opinion now.' Burkinshaw says: 'It was in the 1976–77 season when I took over. Glenn was nineteen then and destined to become the star of the side. He wasn't there yet but everyone at Tottenham and in football knew that he would soon be the main man.'

Burkinshaw watched the 1978 World Cup with interest, without dreaming that soon he would sign two of the stars of the host and winning nation. He had been considering how to strengthen the Spurs side and how to get the best out of Hoddle. He knew that Tottenham, traditionally big spenders and a club that loved star names, would back him if he went to them with a name of a top British player.

It was a phone call out of the blue from a friend of his, former Sheffield United manager, the late Harry Haslem, that was to transform Spurs and the whole direction of English football. Burkinshaw recalls: 'Harry rang me up and in the conversation asked if I fancied the little Argentinian who had played so well. "You know, Ossie Ardiles, that super little midfield player," Harry explained. Apparently, Harry had friends in Argentina who had told him that Ossie was available and wanted to play in English football.' Burkinshaw put the phone down, suddenly excited about the prospect of such a signing. He knew the fans would be elated. Something told him to go ahead.

'It was a very simple transaction,' he says. 'After getting the support of the club we flew over to Argentina and the deal was done very quickly. No snags or hitches. Heaven knows how long it would take today, with so many agents to go through, and the such like. It was not until I got to Argentina that I realised Ricky Villa was also available. In our conversation with Ossie he told me that Villa would also like to come. I went to South America not sure if I would sign Ardiles, and returned with two world stars.'

Burkinshaw could not have known the impact they would make or the effect they would have on Hoddle and his Tottenham side. 'I didn't buy the two Argentinians to mould around Glenn; it just worked its way into that situation,' Burkinshaw said. 'The whole thing just clicked and the next few seasons turned into the greatest experience of my career.

'What a side that was. We were not the best defensive team but, going forward, by Christ, we were wonderful. I lived with the defensive problems. A lot of clubs may not have been able to but I could not sacrifice what I had in the other half of the field. It was the Spurs way. I tell you what, during that period, I would have paid to watch us play. Yes, even as manager I would have gone through a turnstile with my money. We were that good, that entertaining. It was a very satisfying period for me to manage.'

The double signing cost Spurs just £750,000. Hoddle admits that Ardiles and Villa were complete strangers to him when the Spurs players met the new arrivals for the first time at a pre-season photo call. It was Peter Taylor, now Hoddle's England Under 21 manager, who broke the ice. Taylor had brought a dummy thumb with him and when he held out his hand for Villa to shake, the big Argentinian pulled the thumb off, to roars of laughter. It was the start of a great relationship between the Argentinians and English football.

Hoddle calls the signings 'sensational', saying they were quite definitely a turning point of his career. 'I learnt so much from them. They came at a great time for the English game and my own development.'

Ardiles had never been to London and never heard of Tottenham Hotspur Football Club or Glenn Hoddle when he was told there was a possibility of a transfer to an English club. 'There were many rumours about transfers after we had won the World Cup,' Ardiles recalls. 'Personally I wanted to go to Europe because of a new challenge but I thought more of Italy, France or Spain. England hadn't crossed my mind. In those days there was no access in Argentina to film of English football. We relied on word of mouth or the odd magazine. I had heard of Kevin Keegan. He was the England captain and top player in that era.'

Burkinshaw, however, was persistent. He arrived in Argentina and convinced Ardiles that his future was in England. It was a journey into the unknown for the little midfield genius but a decision that he has never regretted. He played for Spurs for ten years, apart from a short spell away when the Falklands War was raging and feeling high against Argentina in this country, and has made his home in Hertfordshire. 'In the end the deal was done quickly,' added Ardiles. 'Before we knew what was happening Ricky and I were on our way to Spurs. There were rumours about other clubs but we never spoke to anyone else.'

Ardiles noticed Hoddle straight away when he reported for training. 'He was easy to notice,' says Ardiles. 'He was the most skilful player at the club by a mile. He was very young then and had a great career ahead of him. I would say the chemistry between us started almost immediately. We were on the same wavelength. Football is no different to any other profession; one man admires another person's skill. You want to work with them.'

Hoddle and Ardiles became good friends, on and off the pitch. 'Right from the start he asked a lot of questions. He wanted to know about world football,' said Ardiles. 'He was keen to extend his knowledge.' Ardiles, however, soon noticed a change in Hoddle when he went away on England duty. The player Ardiles believed to be destined to be one of the greats often returned from international duty with a different attitude to how he felt when he was first called up. 'He often returned from England demoralised. It was amazing, and sad, to see someone like him not appreciated. He clearly didn't like what was happening to him, at the club and especially with England.

'It always seemed to be difficult for him. He was the one who was blamed when things went wrong. You have this funny attitude in England. It is always, or was, the skilful player who was the culprit. It happened with Glenn, and certainly happened to Paul Gascoigne. I have no idea why you turn on them. Perhaps they are the easy target.

'I played with Glenn for a long time and to criticise him was absolute rubbish. Why he wasn't appreciated more I will never know. They said that he couldn't tackle or defend; it was rubbish. A lot of people wanted him to run all over the place just for the sake of it. What nonsense they talked. I told Glenn on so many occasions, "Do what you are good at." For me he was always in the right place at the right time. He was always free to receive the ball and create. Those were his strengths.

'The trouble is that people suspect there is something wrong with you if you have so much skill. They look and can't except that you are different because you are better than them. They wanted to find a problem with him, especially, I think, at international level.'

Ardiles has only affection for the Spurs team he played in with his friend Villa. 'The highlight I suppose had to be the 1981 FA Cup Final replay. It was one of those great games you cannot explain why and how it happens. It was a great Spurs team. We were so good, we even made players like Garth Crooks look outstanding. Seriously, I think the team the next season after that Wembley match was even better. We played better football. At one stage we were going for everything until the time ran out.

'I have only happy memories of Spurs. I played for them and managed them and have affection for the club in my heart. I made some good friends, including Glenn. We keep in touch today. I didn't know what I was letting myself in for when I came to England all those years ago. I am happy I made the decision to come.'

The other masterstroke by Burkinshaw was signing Ray Clemence, the England goalkeeper, from Liverpool. He was the final piece of the jigsaw. His experience helped the young Spurs players in front of him. Hoddle calls this side the first of his two favourite Tottenham teams: Ray Clemence, Steve Perryman, Paul Miller, Graham Roberts, Chris Hughton, Ossie Ardiles, Glenn Hoddle, Ricky Villa, Tony Galvin, Steve Archibald, Garth Crooks.

Hoddle has only affection for that team: 'It was a side capable of winning any game.

'I suppose that was the glory because you never really knew what to expect. On our day we were magnificent. Some of the football we played was mindboggling. It just clicked. There was an array of talent that came together. It was a superb period for me and one that I will always remember with a great deal of fondness.'

Ardiles and Villa arrived in the July of 1978, and made their eagerly awaited debuts against Nottingham Forest at White Hart Lane on 19 August 1978, Villa scoring in a 1-1 draw. A Glenn Hoddle penalty in the next game was only a consolation in a 4-1 thrashing at Aston Villa.

That was the trouble with the Argentinians' first season in English football – there was no consistency. Hoddle's great team had yet to take shape and the side only finished eleventh in the First Division, scoring 48 goals. Ardiles got three, Villa two and Hoddle seven, two of them penalties. But once again Spurs proved a better Cup side, getting to the sixth round before going out to Manchester United in a replay at Old Trafford.

Hoddle's finishing was never really appreciated but in the next season, 1979–80, he got nineteen League goals, including seven penalties. Spurs however were again disappointing, finishing four-teenth. They lost in the second round of the League Cup to Manchester United but beat them in the third round of the FA Cup and again went to the sixth round before losing to Liverpool at home.

By the 1980–81 season, Burkinshaw's strongest team was almost in place. Garth Crooks and Steve Archibald were now in tandem up front, and between them they got 47 goals as Spurs finished tenth in the First Division. Tottenham also reached the fifth round of the League Cup and went on to Wembley to win a magnificent FA Cup replay against Manchester City. The replay was one of the great finals in the history of the competition, with

Ricky Villa scoring a fantastic solo winner for Tottenham. Once again they had proved an outstanding Cup team. Could they ever do it in the League? Or more to the point, why couldn't they?

That 1981 final, the 100th FA Cup Final, will always be remembered for Ricky's game. He had been disappointing in the first game, which was drawn 1-1, Hoddle scoring with a shot that deflected off City's Tommy Hutchinson. The replay on the Thursday was a magnificent exhibition of what Cup Finals should be about – excitement, marvellous goals and Villa's winner. The final score was 3-2 and it was the game that really allowed Villa a place in Spurs fans' hearts. Villa said afterwards: 'I had been so disappointed with my performance after the first game. I walked off Wembley miserable and unhappy.

'The replay has only wonderful memories for me. I can still see the goal now; I think about it a lot. It was the pinnacle of my career at Spurs. I can't really describe such pleasure when I saw the ball go in. I just turned away and raced off down the pitch, lost in my own happiness. I think it was Glenn Hoddle who tried to get to me first but I just wanted to run and run.

'I have only happy memories of England and Spurs. Ossie and I didn't know what to expect when we first came. We found a warm club and a team that eventually played some marvellous football. It was what we wanted. I have no regrets about playing in England. There are so many foreign players in England now. Ossie and I are happy that perhaps we set a standard. We made it possible.'

Hoddle's future was questioned after the City victory. For many seasons people were never quite sure whether he would stay or go, and in his own mind there was always doubt. Clubs became interested and he often wondered if now was the time. But he stayed and the 1981–82 season was a massive one for Spurs. At one stage they were going for the lot: the Championship, the FA Cup, the European Cup Winners' Cup and the League Cup.

It was a huge strain on Burkinshaw's multi-talented team and they almost did it. However, a terrible ice-bound Christmas period meant that Spurs only played two matches in December, so the games caught up with them at the end of the season when so much was at stake. At one stage they had to squash seventeen matches into a crazy late five-week period, and it was too much.

In the League they finally finished fourth, when Burkinshaw knew and believed they were the best side in the country. In the Cups they were superb again. They got to the final of the League Cup, losing to Liverpool 3-1, and went back to Wembley for the FA Cup Final, winning a replay again – this time against London rivals Queen's Park Rangers, managed by Terry Venables – with a Glenn Hoddle penalty.

In Europe, in the Cup Winners' Cup, Spurs came into their own, with Hoddle, Ardiles and Villa enjoying themselves in a superb run to the semi-final before going out to Spanish giants Barcelona. They drew 1-1 at White Hart Lane in an ugly, bad-tempered clash, and lost 1-0 to Dane Alan Simonsen's goal in Barcelona.

A highlight of the campaign was a first-round eclipse of Dutch masters Ajax, with Hoddle breathtaking in the first leg away from home. Glenn also scored the crucial away goal in the quarter-final second leg against Fintracht Frankfurt. It was a truly great season, as Miller recalls: 'We were good enough to win the lot but the matches simply caught up with us. In the end it was impossible; too mentally and physically demanding.

'We played sixty-seven games, so many of them squashed towards the end of the season. The crucial games were piling up on us. We did so well to reach two finals and one semi and finish fourth in the League. Glenn was magnificent that season, easily the best midfield player in the country. I had never seen him play better.'

In 1982–83 they again went for the League, once more finishing fourth. Their best run in the Cups was to the fifth round of the League Cup, now called the Milk Cup. It was the next season, 1983–84, that Tottenham produced a magnificent Cup perform-ance to win the UEFA Cup on an emotion-packed night at White Hart Lane. Tottenham drew in Anderlecht with Paul Miller's goal, then drew at home with Graham Roberts this time scoring, and won a penalty shoot-out with reserve goalkeeper Tony Parks diving to his left to bring the house down with the vital save.

What a night that was. It goes down as one of the best in Spurs' famous European history of glory, glory nights. But proved to be the last game for manager Burkinshaw, who announced that he was quitting and bringing to an end a superb era at White Hart

Lane – an era of skill, attacking football and wonderful Cup journeys. He would have loved to have won the League with the side he built, but it proved just too much for him and his attack-minded side.

Burkinshaw looks back on those years with a great deal of affection. At the time, though, he did not realise how lucky he was to have control over such a superb team, including Hoddle. He now says: 'It is easy to be wise in hindsight. But the years have allowed me to think back and reflect on what I had under my control.

'When I joined Spurs, Glenn was seventeen. Whoever I spoke to raved about this fella. When I watched him for the first time he took my breath away. In practice he could do anything. Anything. The ball was a complete friend to him.

'There is no question that he is the most skilful player I have ever seen in English football bar none.

'When I was Spurs manager and wanted to put something across to the other players in training, I would simply ask Glenn to demonstrate. If it was a special free kick, a ball I wanted played on to someone's chest, a situation when the ball had to be brought down, then Glenn just did it. All you did was ask him and it was done. Amazing. He was brilliant.

'It was an instinct thing with him. I believe it goes back to all the work he put in as a boy with his father. I am told that he worked like hell as a kid. No, work is the wrong word. He played and it came easily. There was a net in his back garden at home and he just wanted to work with the ball. It helped him enormously by the time he arrived at Tottenham. We knew straight away that here was something special. A talent like this only comes round once in a blue moon.

'He was tall and slim but because of his skill no one could knock him off the ball. And how they tried. So many times he would have an opponent close to him, or even be on his backside, and still be screaming for the ball. He would shout, "Don't worry about it being tight; give me the ball." It was a supreme confidence; a confidence way beyond his years. I was impressed with him when he made his debut at Stoke. He just came in and fitted into the plan of things.

'He had this tremendous awareness. I can still see him now,

hitting Tony Galvin with those lovely fifty-yard crossfield passes. To a certain extent he was born with a gift. Both feet were strong and effective. He also had this amazing ability to put swerve on the ball with either foot. And even when he was young he had this aura about him. Yes, other players were in awe of him, definitely.

'That period was a hell of a time for me. Who was I? Keith Burkinshaw from the north-east. Down I came and before long took over one of the biggest clubs in the world. We were relegated in our first season and dug deep for resolve. I was not a big name and wondered how the directors would react to me going down at my first try. They were superb and told me that they still believed in me. Today, any manager being relegated in his first season would be dismissed. I was given time and allowed to build a team. What a team it was.

'I take with me some wonderful memories. I recall going to Nottingham Forest, the European Cup holders. We destroyed them. It was magnificent football. We won three-nil and it was possibly the best ninety minutes of football I have had the pleasure of enjoying in my entire career. You know, when everything clicks. It just feels right from the moment you leave the dressing room to the end of the match.

'Then there was the time we went to play at Feyenoord in Europe. The great Johann Cruyff was critical of Glenn before the game. He said that he didn't know what all the fuss was about this player from England. He said that he and Feyenoord would show Hoddle what football was all about. I saw Glenn bristle and I could see the determination in his eyes. In the dressing room before the game he didn't say much because he was obviously preparing himself for what he clearly felt was a great challenge, for more reasons than just winning the game. He had something to prove.

'At half time we were four-nil ahead and Glenn had destroyed them. It was football that gave you so much pleasure. Those wonderful passes from Glenn out to Tony Galvin. How can you beat those forty-five minutes? I sat there contented. Here was my team destroying one of the best in Europe. I have had some wonderful memories, you know. Wonderful.'

Burkinshaw was forced to leave Spurs by chairman Irving

Scholar, who had wrestled control away from the Wale regime. Wale had been the old school. He was the figurehead and let the manager manage. Scholar was a new kid on the block – a fan with a lot of money. He wanted to run the team as well as the finances and be hands on in every way.

There was an immediate clash between manager and chairman and Burkinshaw knew quickly that he would not be able to continue. He adds: 'When I went into that last game, the UEFA Cup Final, I knew it was my last. It was because of Scholar that things broke up.

'The players had known for three or four weeks that it had become an impossible situation. Scholar wanted to run the club and the team and if I was there he couldn't do it. I'm not that kind of bloke. If I am the manager, I manage. It was him or me and as he was the chairman and held the purse, it was me.

'I had to go. I will always be grateful to those wonderful players for pulling out all the stops for me in that Cup Final. We had some great times together. We could so easily have gone on together. Had I been allowed to keep the team together, had I been allowed to manage, we could have won the Championship.

'But because of Scholar, Spurs and I had to go our separate ways. Sad, but that's football. We won three cups and created a fantastic team. I was very sad to leave – I certainly didn't want to. I felt that there were so many good years in front of the team. There were some good reserve players coming through, like Ian Crook and Mark Bowen. But the whole thing was allowed to collapse. Crazy really.'

Burkinshaw knows that he had a gem in his hand in Hoddle. At the time, however, he treated Glenn too much like a rough diamond, and for some reason would never allow Hoddle to go and do his own thing. There were many dressing-room rows and heated exchanges between the star and the manager, even while the match was in progress. Burkinshaw admits now that he asked Hoddle to do a job that was foreign to him. It was always 'tackle back or do more defending,' and Burkinshaw has taken twelve years to admit that he was wrong.

He now says: 'If I had him again I might treat him differently.' Burkinshaw could have stopped Hoddle going abroad, if only he had appreciated him more. Had Burkinshaw used him differently, and had Hoddle felt wanted, he may not have needed to go abroad. But then he would not have met Arsene Wenger and may not have become a manager.

Burkinshaw adds ruefully: 'I tried to form a midfield around him, you know. I did, I really did. I wanted to give him a midfield and a team where he didn't have to worry about defending.'

But that is the whole point of Hoddle's playing career. Burkinshaw never really did. Hoddle was no good at defending. He didn't want to do it and should never have been asked to. He had a talent, like nothing we have seen in this country for generations, and in all truth, Burkinshaw wasted it.

'The players and I are still good pals,' says Burkinshaw. 'That indicates how much we enjoyed it. I still have a great affection for the club. It is a club with a great history and will come again.'

So what was it like to play in that team with Hoddle, Ardiles and Villa? Team mate Garth Crooks delivers this interesting insight into Hoddle the player and person. 'I came down to London from Stoke, where I had played with Jimmy Greenhoff and Peter Shilton. They were the old school. It was a culture shock to play for Spurs. London for a start made an impact. It was a different way of life. The players too were different. It wasn't something I had experienced before.

'My first memory of Glenn is how humble he was. He was down to earth and that image will stay with me to this day.

'It always amazed me, the transformation that took place when he went on to a football pitch. He became the king, the image that everyone thought he was. On the pitch he became larger than life – flamboyant, single minded, determined and exciting. It was only on the pitch when those qualities came out as one. It was an interesting situation that I saw happening before my eyes.

'There is no question in my mind that Glenn's character changed on the pitch. He was loud, for a start, and Glenn was never loud off the pitch. He was tactically aware and became a genius with a football. I would say in that side only Ossie Ardiles was better tactically than Glenn. They could both see the problem and Ossie could always do something about it instantly. It took Glenn a little longer.

'Glenn loves the game, you know. Wait, that's silly, we all love the game. But Glenn drinks, sleeps and eats football, and not all of us do that. He is deep thinking about it; he always was. As a kid, playing with a ball was never hard work for him. Most of us battled with our ability. To him, it came easy. When Glenn was a child he used to play with and master a tennis ball. I never did that. Glenn can – certainly could – do things with a tennis ball that most of us can't handle with a football. With a football he did remarkable things. Like backspin.

'Glenn used to hit a forty-yard pass and the ball would land, bite and spin backwards into your path. I have never known another player do that, never. He could also find space uncannily. When I was playing I always looked for space and if I was in the best position the ball came to me, from all angles, regardless. He could see it.

'We are talking about a genius here. That side we are talking about was a joy to play in. I have never played in a side, before or since, that has given me such satisfaction. Those years at Spurs captured, for me, all the things I ever wanted from football. I couldn't wait for the next game to come. And when I was out there in the middle I often thought to myself, This is wonderful.

'It was a team that couldn't have been strangled by the philosophies of that age. Spurs played a particular brand of football and I was lucky to be involved. You couldn't help but improve. This space thing I talk about was incredible. If I made a yard on my marker the ball would land at my feet. You got to the stage when you just knew it would happen.

'Ah, the memories? Millions of them. I remember receiving one particular pass from him. That sounds funny now but it made such an impact on me. I was out on the left and he was wide on the right, and the ball came at me exactly true. It didn't spin or rotate, it just arrived at my feet as it had left his. He had struck it so cleanly. I will never forget it.

'I'm not often asked about those days, and I get very animated because they were so enjoyable. I felt lucky when the games were going on and I feel lucky now to be able to talk about it with such affection.

'Another memory was an FA Cup semi-final against Wolves at Hillsborough. We got a free kick on the edge of the area and because Glenn was such a free-kick specialist, Archie and I began to laugh. We knew straight away that it was a goal.

'A free kick in that position was like a penalty to us. The tension was incredible but we knew that Glenn would score because we had seen it so many times, in training and matches. We knew our positions when the kick was taken, on either side of the defensive wall. We were only there to follow up if Glenn was slightly off target and hit the woodwork and the ball rebounded. Glenn put the ball down and, as usual, he tapped the ground behind him with the toe of his right foot. It was a nervous thing he always did when taking free kicks. Incredibly, this time he sent the goalkeeper the wrong way with his free kick. He feinted to shoot one way, dummied the other and sent the ball over the wall and into the top corner. We couldn't believe it. In that hotbed, he actually sent the keeper the wrong way from behind a wall of players.

'I have lost count of the times I stood in the middle of a pitch and thanked someone somewhere for allowing me to play in such a team, especially in front of three world class players like Hoddle, Ardiles and Villa. I will always remember them with a great deal of affection.'

He may have been a close team mate and shared many wonderful intimate football memories, but Crooks today is not particularly close to Hoddle. He might try, but it's impossible with a man who does not lower the drawbridge. 'It will take half an hour before he treats me like an old team mate,' says Crooks. 'He's now in a profession that has made him cautious.'

Do the England players know the real Hoddle? Is the draw-bridge ever let down with them? It's doubtful. There are two Hoddles: the public figure and the private man. I know the one somewhere in between. He doesn't like anyone getting to know the real Hoddle, unless you are family.

Paul Miller got to know him better than most, especially in those Tottenham glory days. 'The attacking players loved it in front of him, and us defenders loved it behind him. Graham Roberts and I won the ball and gave it to either Glenn or Ossie. It was easy. The opposition loved to kick lumps out of them and Graham and I often acted as their minders.

'In a lot of games we often used to miss them out for an hour, the ball pinging over their heads in midfield. Against certain teams we had to have a battle before Glenn and Ossie could do their stuff. Many times at half time they came in screaming and shouting because they had not received enough of the ball. We argued back that there was a war going on and that had to be won first. They still wanted the ball but we knew the opposition were just waiting for them to get it and kick them.

'I taught Glenn how to tackle . . . well, of sorts. He could never tackle; still can't. He used to have a go but it was ungainly, awkward and hopeless. I told him to get his studs up. There were times when he almost got it right and went right through a fella and topped him. He got away with it because it was Hoddle and the referees thought it must be a mistake.

'Anyway, we didn't need him to tackle. The bloke had a set of golf clubs on both feet. He could do anything. He had a driver, he had top spin, fade, cut, chip, the lot. In one game at Villa his right foot was quite badly injured. Most clubs would have left him out. We strapped up the right foot and let Glenn switch positions to the left side of midfield. He played everything with his left, pinging passes around, long and short, and playing superbly. As we left the pitch at the end of the game one of the Villa players said to me: "Your mate isn't bad but he's a bit one footed!"'

Miller's own insight into Hoddle the person, rather than the footballer, comes in a story about an invitation to a bar mitzvah. He recalls: 'A friend of mine asked me if I could possibly ask Glenn to attend, as his son was a big Spurs fan. The man said that he would pay Glenn because it would mean so much to his son. Glenn said yes but only if I would go with him. The thought of walking into a room with eight hundred strangers was too much for him. He could play in the biggest stadiums in the world without a second thought but mixing with strangers on a personal basis was almost too much for him.

'He's a shy man. He always liked his Thursday nights out with the lads and married the girl from around the corner. Glenn used to love his pint of bitter but doesn't drink as much as he used to now. I often think he's too serious. His parents have said to me, "Paul, cheer him up, liven him up a bit."

'You sense that he never puts the business of football away. If there is such a thing, he is a football academic. I suppose it's easy to be serious when you are desperate to succeed. Glenn is desperate to become as successful at management as he was as a player. He's got to reach some heights to do that, hasn't he?'

So the picture is forming. Hoddle, brilliant young footballer, adored by fans, appreciated by team mates, but often frustrated by coaches. All the way down the line he was recognised as someone with a huge future in the game. But what as? At this stage he was still fiercely ambitious to win things. He desperately wanted to win the Championship with Spurs and lift a prize with England. He was to have one more crack at that title with a new Spurs side.

4 One Last Try at Tottenham

This book is not about turmoils at Tottenham, the quitting of Keith Burkinshaw, the interfering of former chairman Irving Scholar or the sacking of David Pleat. It is about how Glenn Hoddle lived through those times. It is about the making of Glenn Hoddle, the man and the manager.

By the time Peter Shreeves, Burkinshaw's assistant, had taken control and then lost his job, Hoddle had made up his mind that he had had enough of English football. He felt a deep frustration that he was not appreciated enough by coaches with club and country. So many people had told him that had he played abroad he would have been a superstar – so he decided to find out if they were right.

It was the first bombshell to greet David Pleat when he arrived from Luton as Spurs' new manager. 'I had a massive problem with him,' Pleat recalls. 'Soon after I took over, Glenn came to see me and told me that Irving Scholar had promised him that he could go abroad. And he wanted to.'

Scholar of course had not told Pleat anything about his arrangement with Hoddle. It's extraordinary how many problems Scholar left behind. He bought the club as a fan but sometimes it's hard to believe that he really cared for Tottenham at all. When Scholar eventually sold out to Terry Venables and Alan Sugar, Sugar revealed the complete shambles the club was in as a business. Sugar then had to drag the club through the illegal payments scandal when he knew, and the authorities knew, who was to blame. 'And it was not the bloody present regime,' says Sugar.

Pleat had to persuade Hoddle to unlock his gentlemen's agreement with Scholar and stay. 'I told Glenn that I needed him to give the club one more season. I knew I needed the star of the side to help start things off for me,' he said. 'Thankfully, he eventually agreed. He kept saying that he could go if he wanted to but we came to a compromise. He stayed and I told Glenn that I would make sure that I helped him get a foreign club at the end of my first season.'

Pleat found another left over problem when he started laying plans for his team at the start of his Tottenham career. 'Soon after I got there I told Irving that Ossie [Ardiles] would have to go. He had been there long enough and I felt it was time to end the era. Scholar turned on me and said that I needn't do anything with Ossie. He told me that I was not to get rid of him and that there would always be a place for him at the club. He said that Ossie had been great for Tottenham. So he stayed. I had no idea what Ossie's financial arrangement was with Spurs or Irving. If there were private deals I had no idea what they were.'

So it wasn't the ideal start for Pleat. In the space of a few weeks, Pleat had been forced to persuade Hoddle to play for the club again and been told that a player he didn't want in his side had to stay. There were more problems to follow halfway through the season, when Graham Roberts let it be known that he wanted to go.

Pleat knew that he had been tapped up by Glasgow Rangers. 'In October we went to Liverpool and won one-nil and were magnificent. I recall Chris Waddle destroying Jim Beglin. Our midfeld that day was Roberts, Hoddle and Tony Galvin. But soon after that victory Roberts started to get agitated. He had been approached by a journalist working for Graeme Souness at Rangers and everything got out of control behind my back. When you have a player as strong minded as Roberts who wants to go, and a club he knows wants to sign him, there is only one outcome.' Pleat also knew that Richard Gough, a man he called 'My winner', might need to eventually go back to Scotland because of family reasons.

So it was all the more incredible that Spurs almost did the treble. Just like that superb season for Hoddle's other favourite team with Ardiles and Villa, Pleat's side went for everything. A Clive Allen hat trick on the opening day at Aston Villa set them on their way but for Pleat the side was too inconsistent. He knew he had immense talent on his books and thought long and hard about the best way for them to be moulded into a successful unit. It came to him suddenly, before a match at Oxford in November 1986. Pleat, a man always ready to experiment and one of the most respected men in football for his knowledge and the time he spends on the game, decided to give the English game a first look at a four-five-one formation. It was a gamble – but one he believed would be just right for Hoddle and company.

Clive Allen, a key player in its success, said: 'The manager called a team meeting and said we were going to change things and play like this. He said that if it went wrong and there was adverse publicity he would take the criticism. He told us not to worry. There were a few sceptics, particularly Ray Clemence. He didn't believe it would work and said so. He talked of his successful days at Liverpool and didn't believe a system with only one recognised striker could be successful in the English game.'

Chris Waddle, another deep-thinking man with a high perception of tactics, said: 'The system started at Oxford and just seemed to evolve. As I recall, the players liked it. It saw Clive up front with Glenn in between him and the midfield. Glenn had a licence to do what he wanted. There was an imaginary line drawn between him and Clive and that was his territory. He was a midfield player-cum-striker. He certainly didn't have to go too deep. In that team he didn't have to defend.'

There is the key. Hoddle did not have to defend. For the first time a manager had realised that Hoddle was a wasted genius if asked to back pedal and tackle back.

Waddle adds: 'The system was more like a diamond. Ossie nestled in in front of the back four, I was on the right of midfield, Steve Hodge on the left and Glenn pushed ahead of us with Clive up front. It was very flexible. When we finished attacking we went back to where we started. Glenn picked up tactics very quickly. Even when he was injured he would be waiting in the dressing room at half time with advice about what he had seen from the stand.'

At one stage at Oxford, in the game that changed a season, Spurs were 2-0 down. Clemence was thinking, I told you so, and the system looked decidedly wonky. Then Clive Allen scored, Waddle got a couple, Clive got another and Tottenham ran out 4-2 winners. The atmosphere in the dressing room after the game was a mixture of excitement, relief and expectancy.

Pleat can only be congratulated in bringing new tactics and new ideas to those players. Hoddle often talks about players minds being opened, and those Spurs stars had their horizons changed from Oxford onward. Pleat says: 'I knew I had to do something with Glenn Hoddle. Here he was, the most talented player in the game, and I felt I was not getting the best out of him. I didn't believe that he could do the work when the other team had the ball. Also, Clive Allen was not a worker, a grafter. He was just a great finisher. I didn't want Clive to make runs to the corner flags like, say, Frank Stapleton was doing at Manchester United. We wanted Clive to play across the width of the eighteen-yard box.

'All these things went through my mind until I came down on the plan that started at Oxford. I brought Steve Hodge in to work the left side and Glenn's instructions were to stay loose, Michel Platini style, off the front player. When we lost the ball we defended with eight outfield players with Glenn and Clive the only two not ordered to backtrack. Glenn's job was to link it together and bring other people into the game.'

Once the system had bedded down, Spurs went off on a run that took them to within sight of the domestic treble. From 13 December they played 24 League games, losing only seven of them (three of those were in May when the pressure of time and matches got too much) and conceded only 21 goals. They also reached the semi-final of the Milk Cup, before losing a three-game thriller to arch-rivals Arsenal, and got to Wembley against Coventry in the FA Cup Final. 'It was wonderful,' says Pleat. 'We just kept winning and at one stage went a month without conceding a goal.

'At one time we were going for everything and it looked as though we might do it. The fixtures however built up around us. I had to make a decision and concede the League with about three games to go. It was just impossible. We went to Everton and I played a weakened team to give the Cup Final side a rest. I played Philip Gray, Neil Ruddock, Vinny Samways, Paul Moran and other unknowns and got fined £10,000 which was reduced to £5,000 on appeal. Everton (the eventual Champions) had complained because they believed we had deceived the fans. They won one-nil yet still complained.'

So Pleat's dream team won nothing. They finished third in the

League, were runners up in the Milk Cup, and lost the FA Cup Final to Coventry, 3-2, after a superb match that will go down as one of the best finals. It was Glenn Hoddle's last game for Spurs and he was disappointing in the final. He wanted to say goodbye in style but it just didn't happen for him. The memories live on, however, especially for Pleat.

'Hoddle was one of only two players I have worked with who can play off the front foot. That means they don't have to take the pace off the ball when they receive it or before they deliver it. They can play it away with right or left foot. Bill Nicholson had a wonderful phrase. If Bill went to watch a player and did not fancy him he would come back and say: "He's a waste of time because he doesn't prepare himself right for the ball."

'Hoddle had the knack. The only other player I had was Raddy Antic at Luton. He too was a truly wonderful player and a great technician.

'Hoddle was amazing for a long-legged boy. He looked too leggy and gangly at times but, boy, could he play. He certainly worried me in the first few games. We looked at him and asked ourselves, Can you play in a four-four-two formation? I decided that I had to drop the second striker deep to supplement him or get an extra body in midfield for him. The opposition could play around him because he didn't have the legs or the physical strength to retrieve the ball.

'The position we played him in was an absolute dream. He didn't have to ferret – the ferrets were Steve Hodge and Paul Allen. Chris Waddle on the right held the ball wide, tricked people and gave us that option. It was a marvellous midfield. Waddle was a genius at times, and Paul Allen was a real worker and had a lot more pace than people gave him credit for.

'Then there was Hoddle, the one who could afford to be lazy. We also had Ossie Ardiles sitting in front of the back four. People still recall that side as the Spurs team when the ball was passed from the back through the middle to the top. That is what Spurs fans like. They don't like the ball hit long. Our build up was clever. We created patterns; we had dribblers, passers, scorers, long and short passes, and I always thought that Steve Hodge was the most underrated of the five across the middle.'

It was a system created for Hoddle. We hear of England sides being built around Paul Gascoigne. In 1987 Pleat built a fantasy football team around Glenn Hoddle. Pleat, it appears, was years ahead of his time. Hoddle certainly was.

Pleat adds: 'As a player did Glenn Hoddle fulfil what he was born with? Tough question. Had he been a boy playing abroad then his ideal role would probably have been recognised earlier. Too many people, me included at the start, wanted him to do all the English characteristics of fetching and carrying. That was not him. He was not that man. He knew it all the time. I decided that he needed allies in the team and we employed troops to work around him.

'That team was the best I have handled, with Hoddle superb. We had the best range of passes from him – left, right, high, low – and in an instant the trajectory was changed. He could ping them in all directions and receive the ball as if it was a cushion. That crossfield pass that I saw so many times from him has gone out of the game now. People say it's too safe in English football these days – we're scared of making mistakes because there is too much at stake. Too much money, too much to lose.'

Clive Allen got 49 goals that season and he remembers every one of them. 'It was the best season of my career and I can only describe it as total joy. I knew that however I was playing I would get chances. My confidence about scoring has always been high and so it was pleasure all the way. It was normal for me to get six or seven chances a game and that is a high ratio. It was Glenn who was the main provider for all my goals.

'He was not like any player I have played with. He could find me even if I wasn't looking at him. The ball just dropped over my shoulder. He was the best passer of a ball I've experienced. He wasn't the greatest athlete but give him a ball and he quickly turned into the greatest player.

'What also made him so good was his vision. He could deliver off both sides. He amazed so many people with his balance off both feet. Tactically, he was aware of what he wanted, and the way he wanted to play. The team system benefited him and we benefited from Glenn.

'David Pleat must take a lot of the credit for what happened in 1987. He got the best out of a team of individuals by finding a system that suited us all. I remember the day he told Glenn to be a free spirit and not to be shackled by defensive responsibilities. Others before had asked Glenn to do things he was not particularly good at. He needed the group around him to be effective and within that group Pleat got it right.

'I have many memories. My forty-ninth goal in the Cup Final. I broke Jimmy Greaves club scoring record and that came in the FA Cup semi-final victory over Watford, I broke the Coca-Cola League Cup record of eleven goals (then held by Rodney Marsh) and as far as I know that total of twelve still stands. My abiding memory, however, is not one of my goals, but one Glenn got in his last appearance at White Hart Lane against Oxford. It was an incredible goal and highlighted everything that Glenn was about. He started his run from the halfway line and got through to accelerate towards their goalkeeper Peter Hucker. He dummied Peter without touching the ball. He literally stepped over the ball and sent Hucker sprawling one way while Glenn and the ball went the other, on its way into the net. Superb.'

Chris Waddle called the side The Entertainers and puts Hoddle in his list of favourite players of all time. 'When I was working in a sausage factory in Newcastle, I used to watch Glenn on *Match of the Day*, doing his tricks and scoring those special goals. He was my favourite player then, when I was playing for Tow Law and he was in the First Division. Five years later we were in the same England and Spurs side.

'Everyone knew about Glenn's great skills but it was also his goals that were memories for me. Not many people talk about his goals. He had scored some great ones before I arrived. The one against Forest when the Spurs goalkeeper cleared it and the ball didn't hit the ground, nor did a Forest player touch it, before Glenn volleyed it in. His chip against Watford. When we played together against Wimbledon once I remember a free kick late in the game, when we were winning. It was a Cup tie and I said to Glenn to give it to me and I would waste time down by the corner flag. He just put the ball down and curved it into the top corner. Then that magnificent goal against Oxford in his farewell to the fans at White Hart Lane.

'If Glenn had the space, and the ball, he was like a quarter back in American football. He just delivered the pass. The further away from you he was the better the chance you had of receiving it. He never really liked the simple option. If he was on the right and I was going down the left channel, I just ran. The ball arrived, sure enough, just in front of me. Sometimes he didn't see the short pass; he loved it long. He used to say to me, "Just run and I'll hit you." It's advice I have passed on to players I have been with ever since. I say to them, "Don't watch what I'm doing. Don't wait. Let the other player react." Too many players just stand and admire a pass they have made and wonder what the next player is going to do. They sometimes forget they are playing with you. In that Spurs side a great benefit to Glenn were the runners around him.'

By the end of his Spurs career, Hoddle was established as the most skilful player in football. Too many times for his own good, however, he failed to deliver when it mattered, like in the Cup Final against Coventry, his farewell appearance. In that 1987 final Hoddle was man marked and upstaged by an almost unknown, in Coventry's Lloyd McGrath.

Glenn had so desperately wanted to go out on a high but it was not to be.

Spurs were left to troop away at the end of another Spurs era. They were left with the controversy of a sponsorship scandal. They had played without the right shirts and some of them hadn't even carried the sponsors' logo, creating bigger headlines than Spurs' performance. It was a bitterly disappointing way to go out for Hoddle.

The trouble with great players is that the expectancy level is so high. They set a standard and people are disappointed when that level is not reached. Hoddle also blamed coaches. He appreciated what Pleat did for him but at international level he felt deep frustration. To most people the tall player who always wore his shirt outside his shorts was a marvel. To a lot of people inside football he remained an enigma, and remains one today.

One player who didn't admire the Pleat era at Spurs was Paul Miller, Hoddle's friend who had been replaced at the heart of the defence. 'I thought Pleat was a fish out of water,' says Miller. 'He had come from the corner shop at Luton and struggled to run one of the biggest supermarkets in England. He was out of his depth and I don't believe he could handle the star system.

'There were rows. In his first week David and Glenn had a row about skill. Pleat said to Glenn something like, "The amount we pay you, you're entitled to turn it on like that every game." Glenn told Pleat that what he earned was nothing to do with him, and that it was between him and the chairman.

'Pleat demolished a good side when he arrived. Peter Shreeves took over from Keith and inherited a team that Keith admits should have stayed together. Pleat chose to change it. When he took over he inherited fourteen international players. But he meddled in what was good. He sold me, Graham Roberts and Mark Falco and dropped Tony Galvin. Most of the young players who had grown up at White Hart Lane no longer wanted to play for them. I think Pleat and Irving Scholar were the worst thing to happen to Tottenham.

'They ruined the old traditions. No one questions Scholar's loyalty to Spurs but, like Pleat, he was right out of his depth. Scholar got rid of Burkinshaw, sacked Shreeves, got rid of people like physio Mike Varney, the training ground was sold, good players were let go and not replaced. It may have looked great on the outside but underneath things were going wrong. It wasn't the same club any more.

'While Scholar was there, there were always allegations of dodgy deals and whispers in the background, which wasn't what we, the young players who loved the club, had been brought up on.

'But when Pleat went and was replaced by Terry Venables, it wasn't much better. Terry brought all his cronies in. I called it Tottenham Spivspur then. The class has gone out of the club. The style and grace that was once Tottenham was no longer, and still isn't. This season [1996–97] Spurs don't play in the traditional style. We just hit it long like Arsenal and Wimbledon used to. It's a wealthy club again but without a class team.

'Tottenham are part of my life and I still care about the club, but it hasn't been the same since Pleat broke up the old side when he arrived.'

Strong stuff from Miller. Pleat is hurt by any criticism surrounding Spurs because he feels he was successful. The record shows that in his only full season they almost did the domestic treble. He was sacked soon into the next season after being caught kerb-crawling and was very unhappy when a newspaper claimed that Venables, who had come from Barcelona, had found the club a shambles when he took over. Pleat says: 'I was hurt because our record that season was better than any of Terry's subsequent seasons.'

In the summer of 1987 the Spurs era that had seen Hoddle dance through two great teams and more than a decade of skills and thrills, came to an end. Hoddle left for the South of France, Ardiles finally passed his sell-by date, Richard Gough returned to Scotland and others came and went. Soon into that season Pleat was sacked and Terry Venables arrived from Barcelona.

The Spurs fans were resigned to Hoddle going by the time the Cup Final came and went. Pleat had kept it a secret for as long as he could and the players, especially those close to him, had known for a long time that his frustration with the English game would send him away to find comfort, satisfaction and, most important of all, appreciation.

One of those players was Chris Waddle. He and Glenn became friends while playing for club and country. 'The first time I met him was when I was called up for my first England cap, against Northern Ireland in Belfast,' Waddle recalls. 'We had chatted in training and over dinner and then when we were both named as subs we sat together on the bench.

'I suppose as the newcomer I was the centre of attention. There had been rumours going around about me joining Glenn at Tottenham and the photographers closed in on us as we sat down to wait for the game to start. They kept shouting, "Look this way, Chris" – you know the sort of thing. Glenn asked me if I minded the attention and when I said I would prefer if they left me alone with the match so close, he walked over to the cameramen and made them retreat.

'We became closer after that England game. A year before the 1986 World Cup in Mexico, England went to Mexico to prepare and that, I suppose, is when the friendship really formed. When we got back I signed for Tottenham from Newcastle. I suppose you could say that Glenn had done a good job selling Spurs to me. It was an illegal approach, if you like, but had been done without breaking any rules. I enjoyed the two years we had together before he left for France, and that season in 1987 when we went for everything was superb. I called us "The Entertainers" because some of the football was superb. I recall getting fourteen goals, second only to Clive Allen's forty-nine. If you play in a side with Hoddle you know that chances will be created and for a spell everything clicked. We certainly deserved to win something.'

The friendship blossomed so much that Hoddle and Waddle even made a hit record together. Waddle remembers how it started purely as a joke. 'We had been invited to a sponsors' awards ceremony at Coventry and at the end of the evening – and, significantly, after a few Dutch-courage drinks – Glenn and I got up on the stage and sang. A good friend of ours, Pat Nelson, said we were good enough to make a record. We just laughed and said, "OK Pat, you fix it, we'll sing it." '

Needless to say, the boys were surprised when a few days later Nelson called and said they were to be auditioned, and could they meet at a house in Barnet. A guy called Bob, who had written songs for the Nolans, was there, and after listening to them sing, announced that they 'could easily make a record'. He produced a few songs for them to look at and practise and Hoddle and Waddle eventually chose one called 'Diamond Lights'. It was a catchy tune and they were told it could easily be a hit. 'A hit?' they said, still not taking it seriously. 'What? Do you mean people will actually buy it?'

After recording it in a London studio, it wasn't easy to find a record company willing to take it on board. Not surprisingly, most companies shied away from the idea of a footballers' record. But as luck would have it, sitting in the Tottenham stand one Saturday afternoon, Geoff Weston, a record company man, over-heard Waddle and Hoddle's wives talking about the record. He volunteered to take it on and 'Diamond Lights' was thrust upon an unsuspecting public.

A few weeks later it was number ten in the charts, and two England international footballers, slightly embarrassed but giving it their best shots, appeared on *Top of the Pops*. Next, they were introduced to the London Palladium audience one Sunday night by Jimmy Tarbuck. They had been used to big crowds and coping with every kind of football pressure, but this was something different. However, Glenn in particular threw himself into the new project. As someone said, when Glenn got on stage he gave it plenty.

Waddle adds: 'Because of the success of "Diamond Lights" we made another record, called "Goodbye". It was better, in my opinion, than the first. Then Glenn was transferred and didn't think he could promote the record properly from Monaco. We had taken a whole day making a video but with Glenn on a new career it was impossible. It was a pity because we were also due to make an album. I've still got a few of the singles in my garage.

'We always said that if we made a record it would be a proper one. We didn't want to just do a "here we go" number. It's more than ten years now since we made "Diamond Lights" and people still mention it. We get it out now and then and play it for someone's birthday! I certainly don't regret making it because I'm one of those people who will do something rather than live to regret it. What's the point of going through life and thinking, I wonder what might have happened if we had done that?

'I'm certainly not embarrassed about making the record, or worried about the stick that came with it. Too many people don't have the courage to do what they really want to.'

When Waddle signed for Marseille in France he made another record, this time with French international Basil Boli. 'It was an African rap and did well. It got high in the charts over there.'

Hoddle loves music and some will say he is a frustrated singer. The story goes that when he returned from France and was looking for a house, he fell in love with one in Ascot, Berkshire, because it already had a sound system installed with superb speakers in every room. Frustrated singer? He was certainly a frustrated footballer. So off he went. Not for the money or fame, but to win things, to find out more about himself, and to leave behind a game and a country that had not brought the best out of him.

5 The Making of Glenn Hoddle

David Pleat kept his promise to Glenn Hoddle and helped him find a club abroad.

After the Oxford match at White Hart Lane, when Hoddle scored his sensational goodbye goal in his last home game, Pleat, Hoddle and Irving Scholar met representatives of Paris St Germain at a London restaurant.

Pleat says: 'We did the deal at that restaurant. The Paris coach was a lovely man called Gerard Houllier, who had been at the game in the afternoon to watch Glenn. He was excited about signing him because he knew that he was about to get a rare talent. As far as I was concerned I had done my part, as promised.

'Towards the end of the season we had let it be known to the European market that Glenn Hoddle was available and Paris St Germain were positive and quick in their response. They were the first to come in, at that stage, and made it clear to me that they wanted him badly.'

Pleat still doesn't know why the deal collapsed. 'I know that at some stage Hoddle's agent Dennis Roach became involved with Scholar and I was not involved. I felt sorry for Houllier, who had done everything right. He was devastated when he realised that things were not moving smoothly.'

The deal seemed so certain that Roach and Glenn's wife Anne went to France to look for houses. Roach says Hoddle had accepted the conditions laid out by Paris St Germain but the clubs could not agree. News to Pleat, who was led to believe that the deal had been thrashed out over dinner after the Oxford game.

The key to Monaco eventually getting Hoddle was Mark Hateley, an England centre forward with Portsmouth and AC Milan and another member of the Roach camp. Hateley had just signed for Monaco and told the coach, Arsene Wenger, that Spurs were selling and that if he was looking for real quality in midfield then he must go for Hoddle. A telephone call to Roach from Wenger discovered that Hateley's tip was true but that the player was on the verge of signing for Paris. Talks and negotiations had been going on for ten weeks, Wenger was told.

Wenger persisted. 'If there is still a slight chance in me signing Hoddle, please let me know,' he told Roach. It is at this stage that things became grey to Pleat. Wenger was allowed to talk to Scholar and the deal with Monaco was done over the phone in ten minutes. According to Roach it was one of the quickest deals on record. Paris had been negotiating for ten weeks whereas it took Monaco ten minutes!

But the South of France suddenly became a marvellous opportunity for the English footballer with a young family. It was a transfer that set him up financially for the rest of his life, because everything he earned was tax free. And it was a transfer that was to change him as a person and a player. It was the making of Hoddle, the man and the manager.

Playing abroad had been at the back of his mind for some time before he eventually took the plunge, and on more than one occasion he had had the chance to sever his love affair with Tottenham.

The first came while he was still an Under 21 player and living at home with his parents in Harlow. There was a knock on the door one evening and a strange little man called Felix, who claimed that he had helped Kevin Keegan sign for Hamburg, asked to talk to Hoddle about a possible move to Germany.

Hoddle, at that time without the services of an agent, listened open mouthed as Felix reeled off clubs and figures of money that spilled into telephone numbers. Felix promised that German clubs would be in contact, and sure enough, at the end of that season while on a tour in Germany, Hoddle was contacted. Two clubs, Schalke and Cologne, the club Arsenal's Tony Woodcock eventually joined, wanted to sign him, and Hoddle negotiated at the team's hotel in Austria under the noses of the English reporters on the trip. By some miracle, it was kept a secret – not something that would happen today.

The Cologne deal fell through because Hoddle woke up one

morning and thought, It's too early. Sign another two-year contract with Spurs, establish yourself in the England team, and then think about abroad.

Other opportunities were to come along before Monaco. Naples' representatives watched Hoddle play for England in Paris and then travelled to London to take a last confirming look at him during a home game at White Hart Lane. Talks had advanced some way down the road when Hoddle suffered an Achilles' heel injury that put him out for five months. The Italians are not that patient and pulled out of the deal.

And so to Monaco. After the Cup Final against Coventry, this was it. Scholar, who loved Hoddle as much as he loved the club he had supported as a boy, was strong with the other Tottenham directors, telling them: 'He wants to go, the offer is good and I don't believe we can stand in his way. He has given us great service and now he wants to play abroad.'

Monaco turned the boy into a man, and he went from a player to management material in his own mind. It was during his time in France that he made the decision to put something back into the game after he was finished with playing. After all, he had his twelve-year-old dream to fulfil.

Pleat adds: 'He had to go. As a player in England he had not fulfilled what he had been born with. He was one of the best I have handled. Yet, significantly, he did not want to be King Kong off the pitch; certainly not in front of me. He had his say in the dressing room. He was very astute and made his points. He was a little shy but always respected. He contributed to meetings and tactic talks without being forceful.

'I certainly didn't see him as management material at that time. Even when he came home and went to Swindon and I was asked about Hoddle the manager I had to admit I wasn't sure. He had enough awareness and the ideas, I knew that. But did he have the personality? That was a doubt. Did he have the personality to dominate situations and players? To my mind he was a thinking man's manager.

'Today I think man-management is almost more significant than coaching. The one thing Glenn Hoddle had of course was respect – respect from all the players – and that helps tremendously. If you were a better player than them, or still are, then you're

Early days. Hoddle's hair on
England duty in 1975 (Sun)

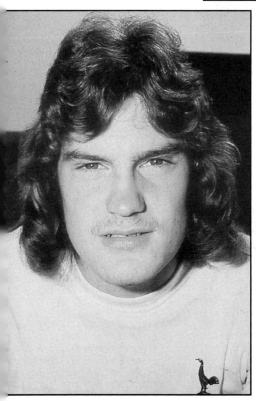

A year later at Tottenham with a more
subtle cut (Allsport)

Hoddle celebrates scoring with Chris Waddle, Ossie Ardiles and Paul Allen *(Sun)*

The mercurial Hoddle at his best *(msi)*

Celebrating with Steve Archibald as Spurs win the FA Cup in 1982. Hoddle scored in the final and the replay *(msi)*

The midfield maestro; Glenn Hoddle with Micky Hazard *(Sun)*

In action against Everton at the start of
the 1985 season *(Allsport)*

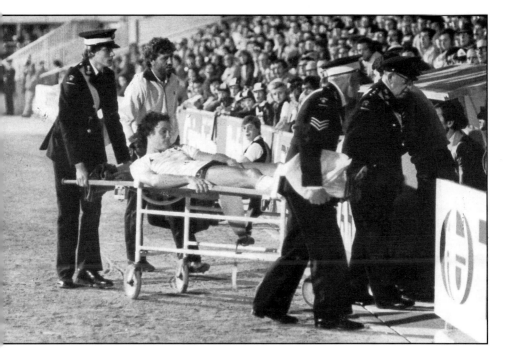

Not another injury. A stricken Hoddle is carried off at Spurs helped by physio Mike Varney
(Sun)

Glenn Hoddle with daughter Zoe
at his testimonial against Arsenal
(Sun)

Hoddle signs for Monaco *(Sun)*

Relaxing with Mark Hateley
(Sun)

The master at work *(Allsport)*

Hoddle for England *(Allsport)*

one step ahead. When he went to Monaco I wished him all the best and meant it. I admit I didn't have a clue what the future held for him.'

Pleat made a big mistake in trying to replace Hoddle with the same style of player. He signed Johnny Metgod from Nottingham Forest, a big balding Dutchman with a lovely touch and a range of passes. He thought Metgod would drop into Hoddle's shoes. He was wrong.

'Never replace a star with the same,' Pleat says. 'I learned that. You should give him a different shirt number or create a new system. Hoddle has gone and it was unfair on Metgod to try and recreate him.'

Yes, Hoddle had gone. Why? Because he finally made up his mind that English football did not appreciate him enough. It had been a long time coming and it took the axe from the Spurs team on 8 November 1986 to finally persuade him. 'Being dropped then was the best thing to happen to me. From a negative situation, something positive, very positive, emerged. I realised that I was bending over backward to play the way the manager wanted instead of concentrating on my game. I asked myself, Why should I change? I went back to concentrating on passing and creating chances instead of the defensive side of football.' It's significant that Hoddle already seemed to be thinking like a manager.

It was Hoddle's determination and inner strength that forced Pleat to change too. It was Hoddle's fierce battle with himself that persuaded the manager to change the system and create the formation that allowed him to be a free spirit in the side that eventually chased the treble. Hoddle, however, has an interesting theory about that. When he was dropped for a game at Norwich, he believes that had Spurs won that match that he wouldn't have been brought back in and the system might never have been changed to accommodate his unique talent.

Hoddle sums up what frustrated him most about English football and what eventually made him quit when he says: 'People talk about character. But what is character? Is it tearing around at a hundred miles an hour? Yet it seems that is what satisfies a forty thousand crowd on Saturday afternoons. It makes me laugh. If I thought defending was that important I could improve my game by fifty per cent. But it isn't.' With that Hoddle quit Britain, eventually returning to try and change the game. He is still trying today.

Chris Waddle was sorry to see him go but realised it was inevitable. 'He went abroad to be appreciated,' he says. 'It's as simple as that. Isn't it strange that you have to do that? Why does the English game not appreciate what they have? You can only blame the coaches at that time. All of a sudden Glenn was world class, because he was playing abroad. It's crazy – but a quirk of the English game.

'When he made up his mind to go he was so frustrated with the English game. The long ball was coming to its peak and teams were playing the high ball, using the offside and launching sixty-yard passes to a big front player. It was not for a lot of us and Glenn made it obvious that he had had enough. It was physical and horrible to watch. Like Glenn, I detested it. When you have to play in a game that's not using the ball as you would like, you become disillusioned. Midfield players were not encouraged to get the ball down and under control; they were simply told to help the ball on, over the top.'

Before Waddle, Garth Crooks saw the signs of frustration building up inside Hoddle. 'Glenn was a victim of a soccer philosophy in the country at that time. What some people tried to do to him was criminal. They tried to change a rare talent. Isn't it ironic that, after Terry Venables, the game is now asking Hoddle to continue the change in England for the good? If only they could have encouraged him before, we might, just might, not have been so far behind the continentals.'

Paul Miller also knew the time had come for Glenn to go. 'So many times he had spoken of his desire to play in a side, even a country, that wanted him for what he was,' says Miller. 'In private, in the rooms we shared or even in the Spurs dressing room, you could sense that in his mind he knew that English football was not what he wanted. He reached a period in his life when he needed a new challenge.

Clive Allen puts it slightly differently. 'He needed a new direction and he found it in Monaco.'

Glenn Hoddle had never heard of Arsene Wenger, let alone met him, when his agent Dennis Roach told him that Monaco, and not Paris St Germain, were now favourites. The fee had been agreed between the clubs and the choice was Hoddle's. Glenn had already thought long and hard about French football and was attracted to it, although Roach and his advisors were surprised that a giant like AC Milan had not entered the race. Had Hoddle gone to Italy there is no question that he would have become a legend in the world of football.

However, Wenger's reputation had been growing in France. He had not been an outstanding player but his knowledge was second to none and, significantly, his ideas were advanced and exciting. Hoddle was immediately impressed with this tall, studious man.

Discussing Hoddle's skills and strong points, Wenger told the player that he wouldn't have to defend at Monaco. 'I want you to do the things you are good at,' he told him. 'I want you to play in their half of the pitch and do damage in that area. I do not want you to chase back and tackle; that would just be a waste of your talent.' It was music to Hoddle's ears. He knew at last he had found a football soulmate.

'Monaco was tailor made for Glenn,' says Hateley. 'Glenn always gave the impression that he could play with a cigar in one hand and a glass of champagne in the other. It was style all the way. And if Wenger was going to use him properly, I knew that Glenn would enjoy himself.'

And it wasn't just Wenger's ideas that impressed Hoddle. He and his family fell in love with the South of France. They liked the weather, the lifestyle, and the fact that they would have superstars like Boris Becker as neighbours. A bank balance being bulged by tax-free money was also an attractive proposition.

Wenger speaks with only affection for his working relationship with Hoddle, which soon blossomed into friendship. They still keep in touch today, often meeting for dinner to discuss – what else? – football. It brought them together and from the start they had so much in common.

Wenger explains: 'I had seen Hoddle on tapes and he had caught my eye as a very skilful player. Then when his agent Dennis Roach offered him to us I looked closer and thought he was the right man to provide the passes for the strikers. Every game I watched him play, it was always Hoddle who provided the best passes for the attacking players. I spoke with Mark Hateley and he was adamant that I should buy him. After that it was easy.'

The first thing Wenger advised Hoddle to do was lose weight. It was a surprise – most people considered him to be a skinny beanpole of a player without enough muscle or power. But Wenger saw different things – he wanted more pace from him. So out went the steak and kidney pies, the burgers and chips and the pints of lager, and in came grilled chicken with no skin, pasta, rice, fish and salads. Hoddle soon lost a stone, increased his stamina and became the player that Wenger wanted.

It is a mystery as to why a player has to go abroad to discover how to eat and live properly. Why can't the English game look after their players in similar fashion? It is only now that Wenger, Ruud Gullit and other European coaches and players are working here that our game is changing. Even when players like Hoddle, Ray Wilkins and Liam Brady returned from Europe years ago with their stories of life abroad, still we did not respond. We are always having to catch up. Why did it only take Wenger five minutes to ask Hoddle to do something that a manager in England never saw?

Clive Allen, who left Spurs for Bordeaux, says: 'Playing abroad had a big influence on me, as it did Glenn. English football has been a law unto itself and thank heavens it's now changing. When you're eating the right things and living properly, it seems obvious. I did all those things ten years ago and yet we're only just coming round to the European way of thinking.

'When you sign for a foreign club they take over your life completely. They pay you well and you become their property. You don't do a thing without them knowing about it. I recall a knock on our front door one evening and the Bordeaux coach, president and other club officials were standing there. "What have I done wrong?" I asked. But they didn't want to see me – they'd come to visit my wife and make sure she had settled in well. That's typical of what happens. They invest heavily in you and do everything they can to guarantee a successful return.' (Allen's wife still couldn't resist a football question. She asked the men from Bordeaux why Clive was continually substituted towards the end of each game.)

Hoddle's repayment to Monaco was immediate. In his first

season, 1987–88, Monaco won the French Championship. It was the start of a great career in France, with the country's own playing legend, Michel Platini, giving Hoddle this tribute: 'He is undoubtedly one of the best players to have played in France. Had he been French he would have won one hundred and fifty caps.'

In Hoddle's second season, Monaco finished third in the League, as well as reaching the quarter finals of the European Cup and the French Cup Final. Hoddle was a hero, and the only frustration for him was the size of the crowds he played in front of. Monaco's lack of real tradition in the football world meant that sometimes his skills were only appreciated by around 3,000 people.

In his last season, before injury drove him back home, Monaco again finished third in the League and were semi-finalists in the European Cup Winners' Cup.

By the time Hoddle returned to England, he had changed completely as a person. Wenger's influence was massive, as he himself recognised. 'When a person is young his outlook and perspective on life can be influenced, hopefully for the good. This is what happened to Glenn in Monaco. It was a good move for him for many reasons.

'When I was a young player, a man called Hild at Strasbourg influenced me a great deal. He was a passionate man about football and he taught me a lot. I like to think that Glenn Hoddle and I had, and still have, that kind of understanding. After I left Strasbourg I felt more fulfilled and my head was full of ideas and new challenges I wanted to carry out. When a player like Glenn has a strong communication with his manager it makes him feel stronger and more confident.

'It's good for the team when a player can transmit the ideas of the manager to the side. That happened with me and Hoddle and it had a good consequence for the side. From the start we had a good relationship. He was good at analysing situations and he was always ready to speak up about tactical problems. When Glenn was at his best for Monaco, George Weah came into the side, finding Hoddle mentally stimulating as well as a wonderful player to play in front of. In every game Weah was given at least five chances of scoring by Hoddle. That is a very high ratio. The two of them got on and Weah had confidence in Hoddle – that too is important.

'When Glenn arrived from England I could sense he wasn't happy. He was frustrated at not playing regularly in the England team and had become disillusioned with the English game.

'Most worrying for him was that he had a small doubt in his mind about whether he could actually perform at the highest level. We had to eradicate that. Thankfully, it disappeared quickly.

'Without doubt he is the most skilful player I have ever worked with. His control of the ball was superb and he had perfect body balance. His skill in both feet was uncanny. He received close marking in France but two men on him was never enough. He was an expert at protecting the ball and his opponents never knew which way he was going to go.

'I couldn't understand why he hadn't been appreciated in England. Perhaps he was a star in the wrong period, years ahead of his time. When I looked at the teams he played in and the players around him I thought he must have enjoyed it, but he clearly did not.

'The obvious thing for me to do was build the Monaco side around him. The other players were happy to play for him, to run for him and give him the ball. They knew that with one pass he could win them the game. He was also a prolific scorer and scored eighteen goals in our Championship year. He was a superb finisher of chances. Much better than people appreciated; much better than I realised.

'He was a better player than I expected; a better player than the one I thought I had signed. He was a marvellous bonus. He also became sharper physically. We made him conscious of eating the right foods, but in the South of France you do become more aware of your body anyway. The weather is so good that people walk around in shorts, half naked. You look upon your body differently because everyone is looking at you.

'The culture and way of life had a big effect on him. I got the impression that he had found what he had been searching for. It's interesting to pick up ideas when you're abroad. I'm doing it now in England – it opens your mind and makes you stronger mentally.'

Hoddle had never seriously considered becoming a manager until he went to France. Slowly the idea formed in his mind. He had fulfilled his ambitions as a player – Monaco and Wenger had seen to that. He had proved to himself and hopefully a lot of other people that football could be played the Hoddle way. Management? Putting his ideas into practice through the minds of others? Perhaps. It was again Wenger who influenced him.

It was after training one day, while Hoddle was having treatment, that Wenger strolled up to him and talked about management. 'I had known for some time that here was management material. He had so much to offer, so many ideas to put back into the game,' says Wenger.

'While he was having treatment I said to him that now was the time for him to start considering coaching and management. He laughed. But I knew it was right because there were signs that he was not going to produce his peak for Monaco again because of injury.

'We joked about it many times although he knew I was serious. Perhaps it was this conversation that Glenn recalls when he remembers a turning point for him. For me it was obvious but I don't think he decided to take the plunge until he realised that injuries over the years to his back, Achilles' heel and knee had really taken their toll. He went back to England ready for a new challenge, just as he had arrived in France looking for answers.'

Hoddle admits that without Wenger he would never have taken over at Swindon, gone to Chelsea and then on to England. At his first England press conference he said: 'Without Arsene Wenger I would not be here today. I owe him a lot. Monaco was a vital part of my life. I will never forget it and am grateful for what I learned there and what I discovered about myself.'

After three seasons away, Hoddle returned to England, strong, confident and with no doubts in his mind. He had proved everyone wrong, especially those coaches who had tried to change him. Now he was ready for the next challenge. And Wenger was right – it had to be management.

6 Into Management

Glenn Hoddle peered across the shiny Swindon board-room table and admitted: 'I have never done anything like this before. I know nothing about it.' He was halfway through his first interview for a manager's job and was talking to the then Swindon chairman Ray Hardman. What Hoddle didn't know was that Hardman was hardly listening. He was gobsmacked, hardly believing that he was sitting at the same table as the great Glenn Hoddle, let alone on the brink of getting him as his manager. It was not a question of the job being offered to Hoddle. It was his if he wanted it.

And yet Hoddle's innocent comments to Hardman perhaps sum up this whole story. As a player, Hoddle was magnificently skilful with an inner determination, but he was never one hundred per cent confident. He was admitting that he knew nothing about managing, or how to go about asking for the job. It was honesty in the extreme.

Other applicants would have told lies and built themselves up. There would have been some good old-fashioned bullshit. But not Hoddle. He may have been a superstar, but as he spoke with Hardman and the other Swindon directors, he was a vulnerable figure wondering whether he was capable of doing the job.

When Hoddle returned to England he received treatment and trained at Chelsea, using their facilities and even turning out for a reserve game. There was speculation about him playing again, for Chelsea, but Hoddle had made up his mind. He wanted to start a new chapter of his career. He would try management and start to put into practice all those things he had thought about and preached about during his brilliant but often frustrating playing career.

Hardman recalls that first interview with pride: 'First, you have to appreciate that to a club like Swindon just the name of Glenn Hoddle was something special.

'We never thought we had a chance of getting him. Then there he was, the great man, sitting opposite me. I recall thinking, He's actually talking to me. I'm having a conversation with Glenn Hoddle.'

The only other time Hardman had met Hoddle was on a plane flying to Monaco for a business conference. 'The directors of the company took their wives and families and there were about a hundred and fifty on board on this particular occasion. Plus Glenn Hoddle, who must have been returning to the South of France after a quick visit back to England. We were all excited that he should be with us. We queued up for his autograph and I took my menu and lined up with the rest. When I got to him I said politely, "Will you sign this, please?" I never dreamt that six months later I would be saying to him, "Will you be our manager, please?" – or that he would say yes. When he took over I reminded him of the incident on the plane and he actually remembered . . . he actually remembered.'

The instigator of Hoddle's arrival at Swindon was Peter Day, the former Spurs secretary who was then Swindon's chief executive. The club had lost Ossie Ardiles to Newcastle and were looking for a replacement. One Saturday lunchtime in the Moat House, West Bromwich, as the Swindon directors were discussing a new manager over a snack and drink, Day mentioned that Hoddle was back in the country. Hardman adds: 'Peter said he had read that Hoddle was looking for a manager's role. Peter also said that he knew Glenn quite well.

'I have often been asked why I went for Hoddle. It was simpler than that. As soon as his name was mentioned by Peter there was no one else as far as I was concerned. But it was not a question of whether we could get him – it was more why would he want to come to Swindon? Peter said he would contact him that night and we went off to the game in the afternoon with me thinking to myself, Nice try, but we'll never get him.'

Hardman was wrong. Hoddle was interested, receptive and willing to talk. The bonus for Swindon was that they learnt via Day's conversation that Hoddle was keen to start his managerial career as a player-coach. Things moved quickly. Hoddle was soon being interviewed, but it wasn't him who had his fingers crossed under the table – it was the Swindon board.

'Never once did we say to Glenn, "If you are offered the job . . ." because we desperately wanted him there and then,' explains Hardman. 'It was not your usual interview. There was no short-list. It was Hoddle or nothing for me by the time he walked into the club. I can't tell you how I felt when he said yes. People asked me at the time, "Why did you give the job to someone who didn't have a clue about management?" and my answer was simple. Because it was Glenn Hoddle.

'It was a great moment for this club when Glenn Hoddle signed on the dotted line. The first time I saw him play in the red shirt of Swindon we knew we'd made the right choice. It was the start of a magical, marvellous period in our history.'

Swindon paid Hoddle £100,000 a year: £70,000 as manager and £30,000 as a player. 'It was peanuts but big money for us,' admits Hardman. Swindon had been paying Ossie Ardiles fifty thousand a year before he went to Newcastle. Hoddle also insisted that a clause be inserted in his contract that would release him if a big club came in for him and he wanted to talk to them. It was a clause that was to later cause a rift and be significant in his exit to Chelsea.

'We didn't blink at the money because how much would you have paid for Hoddle the footballer? At least a hundred thousand a year. We were getting a player and a manager for that much.'

And Swindon needed him, after coming through a terrible period. The club had won promotion to the old First Division under Lou Macari, but had then been punished by the FA for illegal payments and relegated to Division Three. It was reduced to the Second Division on appeal, but the old regime at Swindon had still left scars.

Hardman recalls: 'The club got itself into a trap because we paid our players too much. Some of them were on sixty thousand a year and that was a long time ago. When Swindon got promotion we gave the contracts out on the advice of Ossie Ardiles because he wanted to keep the players and sign others. He offered them incredible contracts. But then three weeks later there was no First Division. We were relegated and yet stuck with a huge wage bill. I arrived in 1990 and the Hoddle signing was like the dawning of a new era. After what the club had paid for some players in the old regime, giving Hoddle a hundred thousand a year was nothing in comparison. If someone had said we could have Hoddle the player and not the manager for that much we would have snapped him up.'

Hoddle's first move as manager was to introduce more discipline at the County Ground by issuing a code of conduct that saw players fined if they were late or didn't carry out his orders. The players were told they had to wear blazers and flannels on all club business, and Hoddle encouraged them to have more get-togethers, especially before matches. He also supported family involvement. 'I think his managerial skills came out quickly because of his reputation and influence as a player,' says Hardman. 'Not only was I in awe of him, but so were other players, and the supporters. They still talk affectionately about him now. We had three super years with Glenn Hoddle.'

In Hoddle's first game, Swindon used the system that he has carried with him right the way through to England. Three defenders, two markers and a spare man, and two wing backs. It was a system he had discussed with Wenger many times and formulated in his own mind over the years, and a system he was comfortable with. Hoddle used himself as the spare defender, spraying those big passes around and having time on the ball to do what he wanted. He was not only the manager but the sweeper – the role that makes the system work. Confidence soon started to ooze through the team.

One player who was in that first Swindon team was Micky Hazard, an old team mate from Spurs and a player, like Hoddle, who always insisted on playing the game the right way. Skilful and entertaining, Hazard was delighted to see Hoddle at the club. He was a fan of the person and player, and he soon became a fan of the manager.

Hazard remembers Hoddle's first day in management. 'Glenn gave a first-day speech as if he had been a manager all his life. Often people on their first day in a new job are nervous. Glenn called a team meeting and said what he had to say. The other players were in awe of him. He told us how we were going to play and what he wanted from us. He told us that we were going to

play football, pure football. I had discovered, and had it confirmed, that Glenn never talks without saying something worth
listening to. At that first meeting he got the immediate respect of
all the players.'

Hazard often recalls the first day Hoddle made an impression
on him – the first time he saw him play. Hazard was a young
schoolboy from Sunderland on trial to Tottenham. 'I was fourteen
and Glenn was sixteen and playing for Spurs reserves. I sat in the
stand and from that day he was my idol. I went home and told a
school mate Kevin Hilton: "Kevin, I've just seen a superstar." I
knew from that day that Glenn was destined for the top. He was
born to be a footballer.'

I could have dedicated this whole chapter to Hazard's glowing
praise of Hoddle, such was the impact he made on him, but the
following shows the impact Hoddle had, and has, on people.
'When I joined Spurs Glenn was in the first team. Even up against
more experienced, hardened professionals he did everything with
such grace and style. No matter how the ball came to him he
didn't have to readjust to bring it under control and master it. He
kept the same flowing movement and it was marvellous to watch
him and then play alongside him.

'As an apprentice I used to go and watch games simply to see
Hoddle. In Keith Burkinshaw's first season in charge, when the
club was relegated, Spurs played Leicester in an important game.
I can still picture this piece of skill in my mind today. The ball
was played into Glenn and he caught it dead on his instep. As a
defender flew in to challenge, Glenn lifted the ball over his
opponent's head and caught it on the other side. It was so
unbelievable I stood up in shock. For a boy of eighteen to have
such skill, confidence and awareness in a pressure-cooker relegation situation was incredible.

'There is no doubt in my mind that Glenn should have been the
greatest footballer in the world. I have never seen anyone with
such God-given talent. Why wasn't he the greatest? He suffered
because of the period in which he played. There was such a
decline in the want for his type of player in that time. Sadly, there
weren't enough people at that time who appreciated him. They
would knock what he had rather than appreciate and use it. I am
sure there were managers who didn't want to use him and only

did because of his skill and because they thought they should. It was tragic.

'I made my debut against Everton and I admit I was in awe of Hoddle. I was so star struck that I took a back seat in the team and did for a few weeks. People have said to me that I played my best football when Glenn was not in the side. I dispute that because in my first season we won the FA Cup, got to the Cup Winners' Cup semi-final, the League Cup Final and were third in the League. I know I was similar to Glenn in style and I could read what he was doing. I could even read what he was going to do. What a team that was to play in – Ossie, Glenn, Ricky Villa and the rest.

'I have so many special memories of him. My fondest are when I sat in the stand and just watched him. Seriously, it was an education, a pleasure just to be there when he was playing. He was also a fantastic goalscorer. The volley against Manchester United when he was off the ground. The goal when the ball didn't touch the ground from when Barry Daines kicked it out to it landing in the back of the Forest net. There was not a better finisher around. No one could finish like Glenn. He could score with either foot and he made it look effortless.'

Hazard left Spurs for Chelsea a few weeks before Hoddle's own departure to the South of France. 'When he came back I was already at Swindon,' recalls Hazard. 'I was delighted. Ossie had set a trend at Swindon with good football and Glenn carried it on to a different wavelength.

'I certainly didn't want a long-ball manager and Glenn couldn't have been a better choice for me. I was there for his whole period, the three years, and we played some wonderful football. You used to wake up on match day mornings and think, Great, I'm looking forward to this.'

Hoddle's best line-up at Swindon saw David Kerslake and Paul Bodin as his full backs – 'They were too good for that division,' says Hazard – Hoddle as sweeper and Colin Calderwood and Shaun Taylor his markers. In midfield Hazard lined up alongside John Moncur and Martin Ling and up front Duncan Shearer and Dave Mitchell were the strikers. 'It's the same system he now uses with England, and certainly did at Chelsea,' says Hazard. 'Just substitute the names. At Swindon, at our level, they were the perfect players to make it work.'

Without a doubt, Hoddle made Swindon more professional. He introduced a masseur (Steve Slattery, now working with him again with England), and a faith healer was made available to the players. 'What Glenn did was make things available to us. Then it was our choice,' says Hazard. 'It was very professional. The only thing he forced on us were his football beliefs. Nothing else. He had standards that we had to live up to and the other things, like a masseur and faith healer, were optional. If we wanted them, great, if not, he didn't order us.'

But there is a tougher side to Hoddle – a much tougher streak than most people realise. Hazard caught it face on during a Monday morning inquest into a Swindon defeat. Hoddle had his say and, as always, encouraged the players to respond and put in their own reasons and comments. Hazard has always had an opinion and has never been afraid to say what he thinks, and on this occasion he wasn't impressed at being singled out for criticism. He had a go back and the exchange between player and manager became heated. 'It got more than heated, it got naughty,' admits Hazard. 'We said things we regretted. I swore and it was a mistake. There is a time and place. Had it been just the two of us in his room then it would have been different but this was at a team meeting and as a player I shouldn't have gone as far as I did. I had so much respect for the guy – after all, I had known him for years – although on this occasion familiarity bred over-familiarity. I felt I could say what others could not, and I was wrong.'

The meeting over, a furious Hoddle pulled Hazard aside and told him he would be dropped for the next game. It was a tough step to take, but Hoddle knew he had to set a precedent for the other players, who had all heard the outburst. Hoddle did add that it would only be a one-match ban, and he stuck to his word, despite Swindon winning the game Hazard was axed from.

'It was a big decision for him and it took a strong man to do it,' says Hazard. 'Especially to recall me regardless of the result in the game that I missed. It meant that he was, and I know still is, prepared to stand up for what he says and believes. It only added to my respect for him because he did exactly as he said he would.'

Hazard's discipline story is supported by Peter Shreeves, his number two at Chelsea: 'The players knew who was the boss.

There were disciplinary measures taken that people didn't know anything about. Glenn had standards and they had to be maintained.'

Hazard adds: 'Glenn is tough but often comes over as relaxed, probably because of his beliefs and feelings for other people. Nothing phases him. He got criticism as a player but it didn't alter his thinking or his determination to succeed. He is going to get criticism as a manager and nothing will stop him going about the job his way.

'He is also very flexible in his thinking. I recall being four-one down once and he changed things around on the pitch. We discarded the sweeper system and went to a flat-back four with Glenn coming into midfield. We won six-four and it could have been ten. The dressing room afterwards was pure elation. We knew we had been involved in something special.'

It was inevitable to Hazard and Hardman that Swindon could not hang on to Hoddle for too long. Chairman Hardman hoped that it would have been longer than three years although he is grateful for the experience and the memories. 'What was his greatest achievement?' asks Hardman. 'He lifted our football on to a different plane. I can still hear the screams of delight from the fans at some of the passing we produced and some of the passes he hit.

'Here was a man influencing a team just by being out there on the field and making a huge impact on a community. Yes, he made a huge impact on a lot of people's lives in Swindon, connected to the club and otherwise. People talked about Hoddle wherever you went. There was a buzz about the town and it was down to one man – a legend that had come to Swindon.

'His final act was to take us to the play offs at Wembley when he scored and we beat Leicester to go up. Ossie had done the same but the football we played under Hoddle was so much better. There was also a much bigger expectancy.

'The people of Swindon are grateful for Lou Macari and what he did before the controversy, and for Ossie Ardiles, but they will never forget Glenn Hoddle. Never. Had he not gone to Chelsea after the play offs then I'm sure we wouldn't have been relegated straight away. Hoddle would have kept us up, even on a shoestring. He would have done a Wimbledon for us.

'To sum up Hoddle is easy – he's a winner. He's a super guy and a sound man with strong family values. I think these help him in what he does in his life. We got to know his wife Anne and the kids – he made sure they were involved. In whatever he does Glenn will carry those family values with him.

'As the chairman I had a different relationship with him than other people at the club, even the other directors. They saw him as the manager; I knew him as a person. We travelled together and talked many times. He had strange ideas about certain things, and very strong religious beliefs which you have to respect.

'The moment he came through the Swindon door he was never pompous; he never lived off his name. One of the first things he said to me was, "Let's get Swindon on the straight and narrow." He was always straight with me from day one and never tried to pull the wool over my eyes.

'The annoying thing about being chairman is that I couldn't treat him as a real friend, because there has to be a different working relationship. I worked with him every day for three years.'

The end, when it came, was messy, and Hardman regrets it. The day after Swindon's play-off victory at Wembley, Hoddle and John Gorman led the players on an open-top bus celebration around the town, and were greeted by thousands of fans holding up 'Don't go Glenn' banners because the rumours of a switch to Chelsea had already started circulating. The day after the tour Hoddle and Gorman asked to see Hardman and handed him their letters of resignation.

Hardman recalls: 'They must have spoken to Chelsea before Wembley but we were polite enough not to want to know. Swindon had had enough trouble in the past. I was extremely disappointed, but never said anything publicly. I accepted their resignations because I had no option, although I certainly didn't want to.

'They were still around the ground when my phone rang fifteen minutes later. It was Ken Bates, the chairman of Chelsea. He asked if he could see me – he was in a chauffeur-driven car about twenty minutes from the ground. He said he would buy me lunch if I had the time.

'Over lunch he asked for permission to approach Glenn Hoddle about becoming manager of Chelsea. I looked at him and said, "Well, that's a coincidence. Glenn has just resigned." "Really?" he said. I remained diplomatic.'

Hardman and his directors later made a decision not to stir up trouble. While they could have made it embarrassing for Chelsea, Bates and particularly Hoddle, they chose not to. Hoddle was lucky, because if Hardman had accused him of negotiating with Chelsea before playing for Swindon at Wembley it would have triggered a long saga of controversy.

Hardman admits: 'We could easily have stirred up all sorts of things. We all know what Ken's like. There is no question that Glenn had spoken to Chelsea behind our backs and a lot of clubs would have kicked up a fuss.

'We took a lot of stick in the papers, nationally and locally. We were accused of being naive and so many times we were asked, "What the hell is going on at Swindon?" The facts are, we didn't want another fuss.'

Hoddle, of course, had that get-out clause in his contract, the one that allowed him to talk to another club. But Chelsea never approached Swindon before he resigned, and what hurt Hardman was that he felt he'd been stitched up. 'Ken would never have known about the clause; how could he?' says Hardman. 'Technically Glenn didn't do anything wrong. I'm convinced Bates had been told of the clause. Who told him? Maybe an agent. I have no idea. Maybe Glenn himself, although I can't believe that.'

Maybe it was Hoddle. Did he handle it well, or should he have been more open with Hardman? Did he discuss the Chelsea job with Bates before resigning from Swindon? Should Swindon have kicked up a fuss? Perhaps most likely is that Hoddle did something that has been going on for years in football. He or his agent probably talked to Bates, who wanted Hoddle to take over, and the deal was no doubt struck and copper bottomed long before the play offs. Hoddle had made up his mind to quit behind Swindon's back and they were too naive to see it happening until it was too late. End of story.

They were powerless to stop him and their credibility remains intact because they didn't expose what they believed to be some dirty tricks.

But there was one more twist in the tail. To his embarrassment,

Hardman discovered that his Swindon directors were determined to have the final say. They demanded a £1 million transfer fee for Hoddle the player. They could do nothing about him walking out as a manager but they held his playing registration. 'Glenn was bitterly disappointed,' recalls Hardman. 'He thought it was unfair after what he had done for the football club. I had sympathy with him but I represented the Swindon board and had to back their wishes. I was torn.'

It was left to an FA transfer tribunal to discuss the matter and set the fee for Hoddle the player. They ordered Chelsea to pay £75,000 plus £2,000 for each game he played up to 50 appearances. Chelsea were delighted while Swindon weren't quite so happy. Hoddle and Hardman spoke to each other at the hearing before parting company to start new chapters in their lives. However, Glenn Hoddle did leave a part of the Hoddle era, because Swindon persuaded John Gorman to stay and take over. But it proved to be a mistake on Gorman's part, and the bouncy, confident Scot took Swindon down in his first season. They played some good football but couldn't cope with the pressure of the non-stop slog of the big time. Eventually Gorman resigned and had to be replaced, beginning another search for Hardman, now a director and no longer chairman.

There was no star gazing this time, although the comparisons with Hoddle were inevitable. 'With Glenn it wasn't a discussion. We just said how much we wanted him to take the job and that was that,' says Hardman. 'After Gorman it was different. The people we interviewed after him *wanted* the job. With Hoddle we desperately wanted him.'

Two of the first people they interviewed were Steve Nicol, the former Liverpool and Scotland star and a former Footballer of the Year, and Steve McMahon, another hugely successful international from Liverpool. For Hardman, their differences proved very interesting. Under Hoddle and Gorman, Swindon had a settled backroom staff in place – all loyal, good people. Hardman explains: 'We asked both Nicol and McMahon the same question: "We have a stable backroom staff. Would you want to change it?"'

'Nicol said he would want everyone out; that he already had his people lined up to come to Swindon with him. He said he had an assistant manager, a physio, a youth development officer, an assistant coach all waiting. The cost to us would have been around seven hundred and fifty thousand a year. The board weren't happy at all.

'McMahon was different. He said, "Why should I change it?" – and that probably convinced us to give him the job. There were a lot of good people at Swindon after the Hoddle and Gorman eras and we were reluctant to break it up.'

However, McMahon *has* made changes since becoming player-coach. He fell out with John Trollope, a Swindon man through and through, and there have been others moved in and out. 'I'm sure we've more scousers now at Swindon than they do at Liverpool,' says Hardman sarcastically.

Hoddle will never be forgotten – and that's a problem for Swindon. Hardman, who resigned as chairman in 1995, leaving a profit of over £1.3 million, is proud of what he achieved for the club. He is still around, watching carefully, and he doesn't like all he sees about McMahon – but that's probably because he will always compare him with Hoddle.

'Glenn was a gentleman, whereas Steve is sometimes too cocky. For example, Glenn didn't have a fridge in his manager's office. It was one of the first things Steve demanded and it was always filled with six bottles of the best Chablis.

'Steve also took over one of the executive boxes. It holds twenty people and would represent a large commercial gain on match days for sponsors or business entertainment. Steve put twenty of his family and friends in it and drank on Swindon until the cows came home. Once they went on until one in the morning and drank it dry. It may sound petty, but Swindon could have done with that income.

'I know it's easy, and perhaps wrong to look back, but Glenn would never have taken liberties like that. If we could use the box for making money then he would have said that was the best use for it. Steve takes advantage over certain things, while Hoddle always put the club first. He would never have considered giving him family drinks on the house.

'Is Steve popular at Swindon? Yes and no. He is certainly not on the same street as Glenn as far as popularity. We just have to look back at Hoddle's period as a fantastic three-year era. I was proud to be chairman at the time because we achieved so much, on and off the pitch. I suppose if I put my hand on my heart I knew it couldn't last.

'Glenn and I are still good friends and we speak occasionally. He's a lovely man and I'm his biggest fan. I just wish he could have stayed with us a little longer. I would have loved to have seen him with us in the Premiership – to keep us there and get us established. But he couldn't, for his reasons, and we have to understand that.

'When he was with us we played football from a different planet. He was keen and ambitious and it shone through. People were bitter for a spell after he left and he got a hostile reception when he brought Chelsea back to the County Ground for a Premiership match. It was unfortunate and yet it's a fact of football. It was frustration more than anger.

'Technically, Glenn walked out on us and deserted the ship. People felt let down. He felt that he had accomplished what he set out to do. He had given us three years, taken us to the Premiership, and then he had the call to go on to bigger and better things.

'Local people said he left because Swindon had no money. It was far from that. We could have kept him financially, but it never came to that. He didn't ask for a new contract. He just said it was time to go. He knew what he wanted and we had been a stepping stone. We should be grateful and certainly not bitter.'

The players could see it coming a mile off. Hazard explains: 'The moment Glenn realised that he could be a manager – and I suspect it was pretty early in his Swindon career – he would have been thinking of the future. He was never going to stay for long at Swindon, was he?

'It was written down somewhere that he would reach the top as a player. Everything he touches turns to gold. And he will be a success right at the top as a manager. The bloke has got a gift. A gift to be a success with style.'

There was one more twist to this particular chapter – Hoddle was approached by his old club Spurs. They wanted him to take over from Terry Venables, who had been controversially sacked by Alan Sugar. It was tempting for Hoddle, who has always wanted to manage his former club, and there were discussions, but two things worried him.

First, Hoddle had given his word to Chelsea chairman Ken Bates. Second, Sugar and Venables were at war, and he didn't want to become stuck in the middle of a crossfire that was sure to go on for a long time.

Hoddle was torn apart for a few days. Spurs were his club and saying no to them wasn't easy. It was the fact that he had said yes to Bates and shaken hands with him that was the biggest influence. If Hoddle is anything it is loyal. And if he makes up his mind to do something, he does it. He also felt that Chelsea was right for him. He is a man who has gut feelings about things; something inside tells him what is right.

He knew it was right to play abroad when he did. He felt that Swindon was the correct job, the next challenge for him. Now that little voice inside him was telling him that he had to go to Chelsea.

There were other factors too. Spurs had won things under Venables, while Chelsea was a sleeping giant. It was the ideal platform for him. His reputation could grow with the west London club who for years had been searching for the old glory days. No, he would go to Chelsea. Deep down he knew it was the right decision.

He was also looking to the future. He knew what he eventually wanted – the England job – and believed that his reputation and stature as a manager would grow faster at Stamford Bridge than back at White Hart Lane. The only question unanswered in his mind was how long it would take.

It would take exactly the same time as he stayed at Swindon. Three seasons.

7 The Enemies Inside Stamford Bridge

Glenn Hoddle spent three seasons at Chelsea. He arrived from First Division Swindon Town in the summer of 1993, the man to finally bring the glory back to Stamford Bridge. Here was a figure the fans would respond to and the players would respect and, surely, someone chairman Ken Bates would allow to manage 'his way'. He left to take over England in May 1996. His record, on paper at least, looked extremely impressive.

In Hoddle's first season, Chelsea reached the FA Cup Final, their first final since 1970. They lost 4-0 to Manchester United but this was only the start of good things to come, everyone thought, including the directors. The defeat was not as emphatic as the scoreline suggested – Gavin Peacock hit the bar in the first half with the score at 0-0 – and to reach the Cup Final at the end of Hoddle's first season was an impressive initial adventure. It meant getting into Europe the following season and Hoddle looked at home as he pitted his wits against continental coaches and players, and proved that he was by seeing Chelsea to the semi-final of the Cup Winners' Cup before losing narrowly to Spain's Real Zaragoza over two legs.

In Hoddle's last season at Chelsea, with Ruud Gullit and Mark Hughes signed, the club reached another semi-final, this time in the FA Cup again, which they lost 2-1 to Manchester United at Villa Park. Close again. Interestingly Gullit put Chelsea ahead but did not celebrate his goal. Why? 'The game was young,' he explained. 'We had not achieved anything.' That, sadly, has been a Chelsea motto for too long. It was a clinical approach by Gullit. You win nothing, you do not celebrate. You can't survive on dreams alone.

At that stage no one at Chelsea knew that Hoddle had already been approached by the Football Association and asked whether he would be interested in taking over from Terry Venables. He had been contacted, without permission, by the FA's Jimmy Armfield. Hoddle was the only manager approached at that time who didn't dismiss the job out of hand. Others, like Kevin Keegan and Bryan Robson, gave Armfield a 'no way' verdict immediately.

Hoddle's record of a Cup Final and three semis in three seasons had pleased everyone at Stamford Bridge, and they would be sad to see him go. Well, almost everyone. One man was not sure because, basically, he was not sure about Hoddle, the man or the manager. In those three seasons Chelsea finished fourteenth, eleventh and eleventh. Not bad, but not good. Hoddle, however, left with his head held high.

On the day he was unveiled as England coach, Hoddle admitted that he would not have left Chelsea for any other job than England. 'I'm sad to leave Chelsea because I believe that the job is only half done there. I would have stayed if the England job had not come up. It's been offered to me and I don't believe that I could have turned it down.'

Across London, Hoddle's comments provoked a wry smile from Chelsea chairman Ken Bates. He didn't believe a word of them.

By the time Hoddle left Chelsea, Bates had changed his mind about the man he employed and enticed from Swindon, and certainly wasn't broken-hearted to see him resign. Bates, in fact, found Hoddle self-centred, aloof and only interested in two things: himself and his bank balance. In addition, Bates wasn't particularly impressed with the job Hoddle did for the club. The Premiership is what managing is all about, and not finishing in the top ten in three seasons was not Bates's idea of progress. The fact that Chelsea still hadn't won anything didn't escape his notice either.

If Bates is one thing it's tough. He's a fierce opponent, and far more intelligent than people give him credit for. 'I simply do not suffer fools,' he says.

Bates, of course, *is* Chelsea. Without him there would be no club. He took over in 1982, buying the club for a penny and inheriting the debts and aggravation that has gone with being chairman. In his first weeks in control he told supporters that his vision was to give Chelsea the best team and best stadium in Europe. He meant it.

The fans respect him. They know he took over when the club was on the edge of disaster and will never give up the fight to make Chelsea great. All along he has wanted people with him – not beside him or behind him. 'With me means just that,' he says. 'Anyone who is not with me can get out. And I mean that.'

Bates thought Glenn Hoddle was with him, but by the end of Hoddle's Chelsea career the two men were hardly talking. You were lucky if they said 'Good morning' to each other.

So what brought about the erosion of friendship, if their relationship could be called that. What brought the downfall in communication between the chairman and his manager? The answer is simple. The late Matthew Harding. Bates didn't like Harding and was aware from early on that Harding and Hoddle were becoming too close for his liking. Harding wanted power and Hoddle wanted money to buy players – and the chairman felt there was conspiracy in the camp. He believed he had enemies inside Stamford Bridge.

It made him fight even harder, trusting neither of them. It is impossible to say what would have happened had Hoddle not taken the England job or Harding not been killed so tragically in a helicopter accident in October 1996. Would Hoddle have signed a new contract at Stamford Bridge? Would Harding ever have become chairman? I doubt if Bates could even answer those questions.

In the beginning Hoddle seemed like the obvious choice to Bates. During that 1992–93 season, Bates had sacked Ian Porterfield and asked former Chelsea hero David Webb to do a rescue job for him. Chelsea were in danger of being relegated. Webb, out of work and running bicycle shops in Southend, readily accepted. He would have cycled into London for this particular job.

Webb had thirteen matches to keep Chelsea up. He won five, drew four and lost four. It was enough to see Chelsea survive but not enough to keep him in the job he wanted. Webb, now manager of Brentford, recalls: 'I knew before the end of the season that Ken Bates wasn't going to offer me the job. You get a feeling don't you? Our last match was against Sheffield United and I had cleared my desk before I met Ken on the Tuesday.' Characteristically, Bates didn't beat about the bush. He simply said to Webb that he had decided not to give him the job. Webb didn't hang around and said that if Bates ever wanted another rescue job to give him a call. 'Fancy yourself as a Red Adair, do you?' joked Bates, and it was the end of another era at Chelsea.

Bates, however, likes and respects Webb. When the Bates v. Harding war was at its fiercest I did an interview with Webb, and the next morning his girlfriend Suzanne rang Webb to thank him because the article showed a vulnerability about Bates that has never been exposed in public. Two weeks after Harding was killed, Bates flew to Dublin to visit his family and grandchildren. He just wanted to see them and be close to the people he loves. Despite his antagonistic working relationship with Matthew Harding, he was shaken and saddened by his sudden death, and understandably, he felt vulnerable. He is often too easily dismissed as 'Bates, that hard bastard from Chelsea'.

Bates went for Hoddle because he knew that Chelsea had to move on to the next stage of their dream; his dream. If Chelsea were to go forward they needed a modern-day approach; they needed tomorrow's man. Bates liked the look of Hoddle. He knew all about him, of course, as a player with Spurs, Monaco and England, and he had admired the sophisticated football played by Swindon. Webb had no idea whether Hoddle was approached before the end of the season, even though he expects that Bates decided on Hoddle long before he had kept Swindon in the old First Division. Swindon chairman Ray Hardman believes that his manager played and scored in the play-off finals at Wembley knowing that it was his last game for the club, but he could do nothing about it.

Bates was not in awe of Hoddle as the Swindon directors were but he believed he had found the right man for a new dawn and Hoddle signed a three-year contract.

Hoddle lost his first game as manager, a 2-1 home defeat by Blackburn, then drew at Wimbledon and lost at Ipswich. He had to wait until 25 August for his first victory, a 2-0 home win over west London neighbours Queen's Park Rangers. Gavin Peacock, a £1 million signing from Newcastle, and Tony Cascarino scored the goals. It was that kind of in-and-out season for Hoddle, and a disappointing fourteenth place in the Premiership was hidden by the club's journey to the Cup Final.

In the third round they were lucky to draw with Barnet, even though the game was played at Stamford Bridge, with Barnet waving home advantage. Coincidentally, Hoddle's brother Carl was in the Barnet side. In the replay, again at Chelsea's ground, Chelsea won 4-0. In the fourth round they again did it the hard way, drawing at home to Sheffield Wednesday and winning the replay 3-1. They won at Oxford in the fifth and Peacock's goal beat Wolves at home in the sixth. Peacock was again their hero in the semi-final, scoring both goals in a 2-0 victory over Luton at Wembley.

All the time Bates watched with interest. Of course, he was happy to get to Wembley – the money helped and it put Chelsea right back in the big time. But there was a doubt beginning to grow at the back of his mind. Earlier that season he had invited Matthew Harding, a fanatical Chelsea fan who had become a millionaire in the City with the Benfield Insurance Group, on to the board. Harding was not, on face value, a similar character to Bates. More than twenty years his junior, Harding was a new breed of director, who liked enjoying himself and would get drunk with the fans before going into the boardroom.

Harding boasted openly that one day he would become chairman. It was dangerous talk, especially in public, because Ken Bates has ears everywhere. Bates began to worry, which eventually grew into deep concern, bitterness and finally hatred.

Harding loved Hoddle. He courted him like a man chases a woman. Bates was the fatherly figure, Harding was the starry-eyed new kid on the block who liked to be liked. He also had millions of pounds to offer Chelsea and knew that the club needed his cash.

Harding christened Hoddle 'Saint Glenn' while behind Bates back he slagged off the chairman. It was a delicate situation that grew over the years. Bates was once asked if he felt sandwiched between Hoddle and Harding. 'No way,' he answered. 'I'm not in the middle. They're on one side and I'm over here on another.' Bates tolerated them both.

Bates knows that without Hoddle there would be no Ruud

Gullit at Chelsea today, and he is grateful for that. He also knows that Hoddle would never have been able to capture the world stars currently lining up in the famous blue shirts, such as Gianluca Vialli, Gianfranco Zola, Robert Di Matteo and Frank LeBoeuf. But how does Bates afford it without Harding's financial clout? 'Mind your own business,' he says. Gullit has taken the club on to a different planet.

Bates wants to reach for the sky on and off the pitch and he was never convinced that Hoddle could take him there. He liked Hoddle's more professional approach to training – eating habits, lifestyle, discipline – and he knew the players had respect for him. He also backed Hoddle's massive changes to the training facilities at the team's Harlington HQ near Heathrow Airport. Hoddle thought the changing and canteen facilities were a joke, and the club rebuilt on his say-so.

But there were also a number of things he didn't like. The Harding relationship was always at the back of his mind. He didn't much enjoy widening the pitch because Hoddle thought Stamford Bridge was too narrow, and then seeing Chelsea win more away from home than in front of their own fans. He was certainly not impressed with Hoddle's transfer market wheeling and dealing, and believes Hoddle has left the club with a lot of dead wood that can't be sold on.

Players like David Rocastle, Mark Stein, Paul Furlong and Andy Dow were not good signings in his mind. Furlong was purchased from Watford for £2.3 million and eventually sold to Birmingham for £1.2 million. Bad business, said Bates. Rocastle and Stein were either playing in the reserves or on loan at smaller clubs at the time of writing, with little chance of first-team football with Chelsea and no chance of them being sold on at any kind of profit. Hoddle will argue differently about his transfer dealings. What about Dan Petrescu, a highly intelligent, overlapping full back signed from Sheffield Wednesday, perfect for the system that Hoddle and now Gullit play. A good player, admits Bates, but he was told by Hoddle that Petrescu would cost £1.4 million and the club ended up paying £2.3 million. Bates believes he was conned.

Below is a list of all Hoddle's incoming and outgoing transfers in his three years at Chelsea:

Incoming:

Andy Dow (from Dundee)	£175,000
Gavin Peacock (from Newcastle)	£1.2 million
Jakob Kjeldbjerg (from Silkeborg)	£400,000
Mark Stein (from Stoke)	£1.5 million
Paul Furlong (from Watford)	£2.3 million
David Rocastle (from Manchester City)	£1.2 million
Scott Minto (from Charlton)	£775,000, increasing to £1 million
Ruud Gullit (from Sampdoria)	Free
Mark Hughes (from Manchester United)	£1.5 million
Dan Petrescu (from Sheffield Wednesday)	£2.3 million
Terry Phelan (from Manchester City)	£750,000
Total spent:	£12,325,000

Outgoing:

Andy Townsend (to Aston Villa)	£2.1 million
Graham Stuart (to Everton)	£950,000
Ian Pearce (to Blackburn)	£300,000 down and increasing to £500,000 after 60 matches
Steve Livingstone (to Grimsby)	£130,000
Damian Matthew (to Crystal Palace)	£150,000
Tony Cascarino	(released on free)
Mal Donaghy	(released on free)
Neil Shipperley (to Southampton)	£1.2 million
David Hopkin (to Crystal Palace)	£850,000
Robert Fleck (to Norwich)	£650,000
Darren Barnard (to Bradford City)	£75,000, rising to £175,000
Gareth Hall (to Sunderland)	£300,000
Andy Dow (to Hibernian)	£25,000
Total recouped:	£3,380,000

The figures were not lost on Bates. Nor was the fact that Hoddle had signed three left backs in Dow, Minto and Phelan. But it is likely that even this would have been tolerated had

Hoddle not been so close to Harding. The chairman simply didn't like what he saw developing in front of his eyes. He was grateful for Harding's money although he never went along with the argument that it was an investment as big as some people made out. 'The Co-Op bank loaned us more than Matthew. His financial commitment to the club was not as big as some people imagine,' says Bates. 'He bought twenty-four million shares for ten million, of which five million went towards the North Stand. He also gave us a bank guarantee for a five million loan. We pay interest on that and have to repay it. That was his total involvement in the club.'

There was also a transfer fund which Bates repaid at a stormy meeting between the two men on 26 June 1996. Bates and Harding's lawyers were trying to do a deal which would see Harding become vice-chairman and perhaps add to his investment. Bates was growing impatient with the saga and wanted an answer. He was unhappy that the 'goalposts were being changed' every few days. So at that meeting he handed Harding a cheque to repay his transfer fund loan and told him in no uncertain terms to 'fuck off' if he didn't want to be involved long term with the club.

Harding was visibly shocked. His eyes, says Bates, almost popped out of his head. A deal was struck a few weeks later – a paper partnership for the good of the club. It is clear that Harding wanted to become chairman, and there is no doubt that he wanted Bates out of the door eventually. Bates knew that, and treated his vice-chairman like an upstart who was trying to run before he could walk. When the war was raging, he banned Harding from the director's box, VIP areas and the car park, even though Harding owned the freehold of the ground. Harding responded by laughing his way through it, although all the time plotting a way to eventually take control. He contacted other clubs so that he could sit in their directors' box alongside Bates. It was confrontation between two strong, rich, proud men.

Bates is now determined to prove that, following Harding's death, he can run the club his way and be even more successful.

Hoddle liked Harding much more than Bates. The two men enjoyed a much closer relationship than Bates had with either man, and when Harding and Hoddle talked in private, Bates thought Harding was using Hoddle to help plot his downfall. Rumours abounded that Hoddle and Gullit would quit if Harding did not win the battle, but Bates knew they'd been planted and he proved it.

Along with other Chelsea officials, he would tell Harding about players they were interested in knowing that the club had no intention at all in making bids. Bates waited for the stories to break in the media. They did and he knew that he had an enemy.

Bates was once asked to draw a picture of himself. He drew a spider. He was the creature in the middle and around him there was a huge web with all the strings returning to the spider in the middle. 'I know everything that is going on,' he boasts. 'People tell me and I cannot understand how those against me do not realise that I know.' Bates, for instance, knew that Hoddle had been approached by England long before it was admitted by his manager or the Football Association. The FA had not asked for permission and yet Bates knew where and when the conversation between Armfield and Hoddle took place. The first official approach from the FA to Chelsea came in May, 48 hours before Hoddle resigned. The approach was made by Graham Kelly. Bates was not available and Kelly spoke to Colin Hutchinson, the club's chief executive. Hutchinson's answer was simple. 'We can't stop you speaking to him; Glenn is out of contract in a few days.'

Bates knew that it had been planned for weeks, even months. He had a new contract on offer for Hoddle but he didn't fight the FA for him. He was not unhappy to see him go to England.

The question of Hoddle's contract negotiations with Chelsea, before he said yes officially to England, are also clouded in mystery. Hoddle insisted all along that he would not sit down and discuss a new contract until the club had sorted itself out 'upstairs'. Hoddle claimed that he had to know who was going to run the club and what commitment there would be to the signing of new players. He also wanted to know how much money there was. He asked through the media if Chelsea's ambition was as big as his. Bates's public answer was that Hoddle always said that it would be February before the board sat down and talked about his and the club's future. Privately he claimed that Hoddle never asked him for details of the club's future or what the Chelsea strategy was going to be, suspecting he was getting all his information from Harding.

Not once, claims Bates, did Hoddle request a meeting with him to get the answers he said that he wanted. By that time, in Hoddle's last months at the club, the relationship between the chairman and his manager was at an all-time low. England gave Bates a get-out, and he won't answer the question about what would have happened had Terry Venables stayed with England and the FA not offered the job to Hoddle. It is hypothetical, he says.

England probably averted a massive blow up arising at Stamford Bridge. Hoddle's agent Dennis Roach had negotiated a huge new pay deal for his client – a £300,000 a year contract that would have made Hoddle one of the top earners in the Premiership. How long would it have taken for the strained relationship to reach breaking point? It's impossible to say, but doubtless it would have ended in tears.

Bates did not like Hoddle and the feeling appears to have been mutual. When Bates was ill with pneumonia in the winter of 1996, he didn't receive one get-well message, card or phone call from his manager. That hurt him, proving that there was no love lost. So much for the caring, God-loving, forgiving public image of Hoddle, Bates told friends. 'I could have been dead for all he knew,' said Bates.

But let us not forget that Bates can be a vicious opponent. Did Harding know who and what he was taking on? Did Hoddle realise that his chairman did not like him? There are unconfirmed stories that Bates had already approached George Graham with a view to him taking over from Hoddle before he resigned. Also, Swindon chairman Ray Hardman believes that Bates poached Hoddle from him before permission was granted. 'Bates,' says Hardman, 'is a loveable rogue who gets what he wants.'

Bates says that in 2002 he would have handed over the chair to Harding, happy to retire after having seen Stamford Bridge rebuilt completely both on and off the pitch. But what would have happened before then, had Harding not been killed? Surely the relationship would never have lasted the distance? And surely the same goes for Hoddle had he stayed.

Peter Middleton is the latest to be seen off. 'Another Johnny Come Lately from the city,' said Bates. Middleton wanted to become chairman of Chelsea Village, the company which owns

Chelsea Football Club. The former monk, who rides motorbikes and only wears sandals, was certainly an oddball and Bates couldn't understand him. He welcomed him on to the board of Chelsea Village and then forced him to resign when he discovered that Middleton, it was claimed, was plotting to oust him. Bates called an emergency meeting soon after Harding's death because, as he says, 'No sooner than Matthew had died than they were all coming out of the woodwork to unsettle me. The rumours about people taking control from him had started and I found the whole thing goulish and distasteful.'

One of the people Bates blames for the unrest behind the scenes is Paul Miller, a former Spurs player and close friend of Harding and Hoddle. Bates believes that Miller was working for both Harding and Hoddle in trying to stir up trouble. 'He knows I know what has been going on,' said Bates. 'Well, Mr Miller, I am after you.' Bates even released a statement denouncing Miller and confirming that no statement from Miller should be taken as an official one from Chelsea Village. Miller naturally denied all links. 'These are crazy allegations,' he said. 'I have never worked for Mr Bates and never will. What he says is completely without foundation.'

Middleton does have a letter from Bates in his safe stressing that Bates would hand over the chairmanship of Chelsea Village, but in the right circumstances and at the right time. Once Bates discovered the behind-the-scenes plot then Middleton was finished. No friend, no deal.

It always bugged Bates that Harding was often quoted as saying that his dream was to see Chelsea be the best team in the best stadium, with Hoddle the manager coaching the best players. 'It wasn't his dream, it was mine,' says Bates. 'And it wasn't a dream, it was a vision. I started this in 1982 and I am bloody well going to finish it, my way.'

Ruud Gullit, of course, fell into his lap. The fans liked and respected Hoddle, but they were mesmerised by the dreadlocks and reputation of the Dutch master Gullit. In Hoddle's last game, a few days after resigning, at home to Blackburn on Sunday 5 May 1996, the crowd sang and chanted for Gullit. They made it clear that this was the man to continue the playing dream, and Bates was moved by the Gullit backing, as were his directors. A few days later they offered Gullit the job. Within months, players from all over the world had started to arrive and the memory of Hoddle was swamped. The Chelsea board backed Gullit with millions and Bates was a contented man, although nobody knows for how long.

Chelsea have reached the stage when they need to win something. The expectancy level has never been higher and the dream has long gone. The fans have woken up to the fact that this is more than a dream. If Chelsea do not qualify for Europe in the 1996/97 season, it would be a disaster for financial reasons, the morale of the fans and the standing of Gullit and his team of foreign stars.

Bates is a remarkable man. You can't help admiring him but like many others, I have something of a love-hate relationship. At the start of the 1996/97 season, I met him for breakfast at the Park Lane Hilton one Sunday morning at his request. We exchanged stories and he recalled his youth in London before coming to the point of the meeting. 'I am not putting up with any more shit,' he said. 'The last year has been one long round of aggro off the pitch. There are people behind the scenes plotting against me and I'm not putting up with it. You know what I'm talking about.' He was, of course, referring to Harding. 'I haven't liked everything you've written, but I've let it go,' he told me. All I want you to do is check things with me because there are always two sides to a story.'

It was a warning – a friendly one, but a warning. Bates meant business. We left on good terms and he even bought the scrambled eggs.

There was another run-in with him years ago. He had been pestered late at night by the *Sun*'s news desk. They had woken him up and because at that time he got up early each morning for work on his farm in Beaconsfield, he did not appreciate it. Two days later the phone rang at my home at four in the morning. My wife Linda answered and Bates roared: 'Tell Brian that if they're going to wake me up, you can get up too.' The fact that my wife screamed that she was a teacher and didn't appreciate the call before plunging down the phone was lost on Bates. He had made his point. He had had the last say. We have met many times since and laughed about it. You know where Bates is coming from. He hasn't changed much down the years.

Will both Bates and Hoddle get what they want? Bates will certainly not stand down until he has sat in the best seat in the house overlooking the best team and best stadium that money can build. Until he has moved into the penthouse he has ordered at the top of the huge Chelsea Village project being erected behind the old Shed End. Until he has completed his vision. Hoddle wants to win the World Cup. That is his vision. I wouldn't be surprised if both made it happen.

Both men are stubborn and both men know what they want. They go about it in different ways but they both crave success and glory. But Hoddle and Bates were never going to do it together. It was a partnership that could never have lasted.

8 Harding's Story

Seven days before Matthew Harding was tragically killed in a helicopter crash returning from a Coca-Cola Cup tie at Bolton in October 1996, he and I met for a few beers because I wanted to talk to him about Glenn Hoddle for this book. He and I had become friends and we often met for a drink or lunch. It was not uncommon for him to ring and say, 'Wooly, I'm thirsty, fancy a few beers?' He was on good form on this occasion, and opened up about Chelsea, Hoddle, his relationship with Ken Bates and his plans. It was his last interview.

Harding, I know, would have wanted the interview to be used. It was a football interview and one that emphasised his love of Chelsea and admiration for Hoddle. We stood at the bar because when Harding was drinking – and he drank a lot – he never sat down. At his favourite Chelsea watering hole, the Imperial Arms in the King's Road, he was always on his feet, exchanging pints of Guinness and stories with the Chelsea fans who loved him.

The pub in Wimbledon was almost empty when we arrived just after five. By the time we left, shortly before eight, he had baited the barman about the difference between Chelsea and Wimbledon, spilt a lot of his beer, as he always did as the stories and conversation got louder, and said goodbye to anyone who was interested in listening.

Matthew Harding was a larger-than-life character who loved Chelsea. He would have done anything for them.

'On October 15th 1993 [Harding was a man for dates and detail] I read an advertisement in the *Financial Times*. It had been placed by Ken Bates and was about a quarter of a page. The advert said that Chelsea were going places, that they had just appointed Glenn Hoddle as their manager, and that they were the club to invest in. It also mentioned Chelsea Village and the plans to develop Stamford Bridge. It caught my eye. As a Chelsea fan it made interesting reading. I logged it at the back of my mind.'

Harding was chairman of the Benfield Insurance Group but still a Chelsea fan at heart. Not for him the top hat and tails, or the city pinstripe; he was a torn jeans man with an earring, a blue Chelsea shirt he wore with pride, a drum, a favourite scarf and a flag bearing his club's name. On the Intercity train up from Brighton to Victoria Station, he would lose his city reputation completely, swilling beer with his friends and other Chelsea fans, often going behind the buffet to help himself to more refreshments. No one knew, at that stage, he had a tab with British Rail.

When Harding eventually became a Chelsea director he would arrive at Victoria, go straight to the Imperial Arms for more Guinness and then skip over to Chelsea, where he would change into a suit in Bates's office in order to mingle with directors from other clubs.

His obsession with detail and punctuality would often see him jump on to the platform if the train waited too long in a station. He didn't like the thought of missing out on his match-day ritual, and was seen on more than one occasion rushing up to the driver, shouting 'What's wrong? Don't you know I'm a very successful and important business man?' Unsurprisingly, the driver took a lot of convincing as he looked down on this small, tubby man wearing usually torn jeans and a Chelsea shirt. But that was Harding.

A few weeks after the *Financial Times* advert appeared, *Business Age* magazine ran a list of the top 500 wealthiest men in England. Harding had leapfrogged up the list into the 60s. Crucially, it also said in the article that he was a Chelsea fan. Someone pointed the article out to Ken Bates and a few days later Harding received a phone call at his city office. 'I'm told you are richer than me. I've rung to see if it's true,' said Bates. He arranged to meet Harding a week later at the Imperial Arms. Bates claims this was the first time Harding had visited the place. 'I went there first and Harding didn't know of the pub until I took him there,' Bates has rather childishly told friends.

Guinness and oysters, Harding's favourite combination, were on the menu. The conversation soon got round to money and

Bates's plans for the club. Harding told me: 'At that stage I had met neither Bates nor Hoddle. My lunch with Ken was the first time we had clapped eyes on each other and Hoddle was simply the manager.' Bates told Harding that he wanted to build a new North Stand but didn't have sufficient funds. 'How much do you need?' Harding asked him. The reply was £7.5 million. Harding said he would love to help and would talk to his people before getting back to Bates. The two men had some coffee, shook hands and went their separate ways.

Harding's love affair with Chelsea began in 1962. At the age of eight, his father Paul took him to watch Chelsea play against Newcastle. Harding was hooked. His favourite player was Bobby Tambling. 'I was the kind of fan who arrived five minutes before kick off. I never purchased a programme because I wasn't interested in the opposition. I knew who was playing for Chelsea and that was good enough for me. If they didn't wear a blue shirt they weren't a member of my family.'

When Harding left the Imperial Arms on that first meeting with Bates, he had already decided to sign a cheque for Chelsea. He spoke to his financial backers but it was only a token conversation. 'They said I was mad,' he recalled. 'I had the money, so why not? I rang Bates back and told him I was in and that it was OK. I made five million available, with no interest.' That was the start of his relationship with Bates and the start of his climb towards the chairmanship. When we met it was three years to the day since he had signed that cheque. 'This is something of a celebration,' he chuckled. 'An anniversary drink. Isn't it fun being me!'

Harding called Stamford Bridge his spiritual home, but he quickly added that it was a football ground with disgraceful facilities. 'When I met Ken he spoke enthusiastically about the ground and it was about time. The club needed a new North Stand and the West Stand was long past its sell-by date. Do you know, Chelsea even had weeds poking through the terraces and other parts of the stadium. That's appalling for a Premiership club.'

Bates had asked Harding on what basis he would make the money available. 'I told him that given my love for the club I would effectively give it to him for nothing. My money was given to Chelsea as merely convertible loan stock which at some stage could convert into shares in Chelsea Village, which at that stage was a private company. I was told by my people that for a private individual to put money in and get nothing back, not even a coupon, was crazy. There was also a grey area with the shareholders of Chelsea Village. Outside Ken, no one knew who they were, or even if they existed. I was warned but I went in because of my love of the club. No other reason.

'My total commitment was also helped because I knew that Glenn Hoddle was at the club. His arrival had nothing to do with me, but as a fan I was delighted. I felt it was the most positive thing to happen to Chelsea since the days of Dave Sexton. Apart from a couple of seasons when Eddie McCreadie built a good team, nothing had happened for twenty years. I, like all Chelsea fans, had been saying "If only, if only" ever since. Chelsea can become great; we have the potential to be this and that. The arrival of Hoddle actually gave us supporters a lift because here was a big man in every sense of the word. It was a declaration of the club's intent.'

Harding didn't meet Hoddle until November of 1993. 'My first impressions of him were of a decent man, a man who listens and talks only when it is important. I liked him although our friendship didn't grow straight away. I am four years older and more outgoing than Glenn. He recognised my unswerving devotion to the club. He also, more than anyone, recognised my financial contribution to the club. He knew that his job would have been impossible without me.

'That appreciation drew me closer to him. Without my financial contribution where the club would be, or how long Glenn would have stayed, God only knows.'

Harding's first game as a director was at home to Oldham on 3 October. Harding raced from the pub, did a quick change in Bates's office and watched Chelsea lose 1-0. He would rather have been in the crowd with his mates, swearing and banging his seat, like he always did. When Bates banned him from the directors' box area it was, the chairman said, partly because of Harding's war with him and also because of his bad manners in the box. Once a fan always a fan, said Harding, and he just couldn't stop himself shouting, singing and dancing in front of other directors. That was him, take him or leave him.

In his first eight games as director, Chelsea only picked up two points during a disastrous run that slumped them towards relegation.

He got his first win on 28 December, at home to Newcastle, with Mark Stein scoring the only goal. Chelsea then won five of their next nine games, drawing two more, with Stein getting ten goals in that run. Harding added: 'Glenn has been criticised for buying Stein but I believe his goals kept us in the Premiership. Those goals and that run saved us and also lifted the season. We went on a run that took us to the Cup Final.

'Another player Hoddle was criticised for buying, Gavin Peacock, scored the goals that took us to Wembley. People have short memories. They should appreciate what Hoddle did for this club.'

Harding will not have a word said against Hoddle, or 'Old Saint Glenn' as he always called him. 'Glenn did for Ruud Gullit what Tommy Docherty did for Dave Sexton,' said Harding. 'I have said to many people that all of Hoddle's best work was unseen. It was the behind-the-scenes stuff that was to bear fruition. The day Glenn left he told me: "I have got you there, now take it on." He knew. I knew. He was leaving the club in my hands. Certainly the long-term future.'

Harding loved to look back. When Peter Osgood, a real Chelsea great, joined him in the Imperial Arms for a pint, Harding used to shout 'Here comes the king' as he walked through the door. Harding recalled: 'When this club was on its uppers, relegated, Ted Drake sacked and everything falling apart, along came Tommy Docherty. He took over and built a fantastic side. It was all English, you know, not a lot of people realise that. We were the first to wear the all-one-colour strip – it was dashing football and great days.

'Like all great people do, the Doc pressed the self-destruct button. But under him we won things. Until Glenn arrived this club was going nowhere. I'm telling you that had he stayed we would have been great again. We have to keep his legacy going. Thank God we had Gullit to replace him because to find a manager for Hoddle without Ruud would have been thankless.

'I don't go along with this criticism of Glenn, especially about his signings. David Rocastle was unlucky with injuries and Paul Furlong did a better job than people gave him credit. Good old

Furs. And you can't put a price on the fact that Glenn attracted Ruud Gullit to our club. And what about Dan Petrescu, one of the most intelligent footballers you will see in the Premiership? The trouble is that people are never happy. They always want to knock and be negative.'

Harding's friendship with Hoddle didn't blossom until after that first season. 'Glenn had told the board that to move forward the club needed to buy a big centre forward and another defender. 'But the club were still financially embarrassed. There is no point saying it wasn't, because it was. I made two point five million available in a transfer treasure chest and from that point became more involved with purchases and sales. It developed from there.'

With the money Hoddle bought Furlong ('You don't get many top name centre forwards for two point three million') and Minto. They were the first deals with Harding's cash and his relationship with Hoddle grew stronger over the next two seasons.

Harding added: 'The more I got to know him I felt that his heart was really in the club, and still is to this day. Anybody that smells Chelsea from the inside will tell you the opportunity that's there. Glenn knew that. He realised that we could be bigger than anyone. Look at the facts. We have the most valuable football pitch in the country, situated amongst the most valuable square miles in the country. Go into the next century with the best ground and the best team on that site and Europe beckons. He recognised that. He came to Chelsea because he saw it as a significant stepping stone from Swindon. Had he not been offered the England job he would still have been at Chelsea. I would have made sure of that.

'He isn't an easy man to get to know. I believe I know him as well as anyone who doesn't know him, if that makes sense. He's a man with his own agenda, a man who commits himself to something that he wants to do. He felt that Chelsea had to go in certain directions to achieve what needed to be done.

'He wasn't able to convince himself that, as a football club and as a business, Chelsea was going in the right direction sufficiently quickly to enable him to sign a new contract for another three years before England came in. Had he signed that contract he would have turned the England job down. I know that. It is fact.

Had he signed the contract he wanted then England would not have him as manager. Fact.

'I fully understand why Glenn hadn't signed his contract. I was disappointed; the club was disappointed. But I believe that it was the right thing to do. He couldn't sign an extended contract until he knew where the club was going. I wasn't vice-chairman then, I was a director. I couldn't speak for others. I think he felt he needed more comfort. There was a lot going on upstairs and that was reflecting on what might have happened on the pitch. He knew that. So did I. He waited because he had to.

'If the FA hadn't approached him I believe he would have signed a new deal, but only for a year. I expect he would have signed for twelve months to enable the club to move in the direction they were destined for. He would have signed for twelve months to also allow him to continue to search for answers about the club, to see what happened.'

I then asked Harding, as we refilled our pints, whether the club could have done more to keep Hoddle. He mulled the question over in his mind. He took a sip of beer and said carefully, 'My hesitancy to answer the question probably gives you the answer.'

Here lies the crux of the Hoddle years at Chelsea. Harding believed that Hoddle was lost because the Chelsea board dragged their feet. He blames Bates for not reaching an agreement with him and consequently unsettling him. Bates will have none of that. He blames Harding for prevaricating and not getting into bed with the club until handed an ultimatum. He also says that Hoddle had no interest in discussing the future with the board, and never asked him for a meeting.

Bates believes Hoddle was simply waiting for the England job. And one thing is certain, Bates would never have let Hoddle sign a one-year contract – he would have insisted on more commitment than that, despite the long-term uncertainty in his own mind.

Harding went on: 'I'm not going to criticise Ken over this. We all have different talents; we all come to the party from different positions carrying different bags of booze. The facts are that Ken arrived in 1982 and I was not around to help, financially or emotionally. I got involved in 1993, which, I believe, is just as important as Ken arriving in 1982. I would never say that Ken's input has not been valuable. I will say that mine has been as valuable. In his heart Ken knows that too.

'Glenn was a victim of the world in which we live; the times we find ourselves. All progress involves pain. Ken and I had our differences and it was a shame that so much went into the media. The fact of the matter is that it did, and that caused Glenn some concern. He was worried that things were not right upstairs. At Christmas he was uncertain, which was a pity because as a manager he was ready at this stage to sign. But he just felt that as a business and a football club there were too many grey areas. The truth is that the board were also uncertain where it was going.

'Glenn had a five-year plan for Chelsea. There would have been money available. But he wanted to know who owned what, who owns who, and was there a positive future? Had he got his answers he would have signed a contract and not broken it, not even for England.

'But life must go on. The great thing is that he managed Chelsea Football Club. It's there in the records. He managed for three years and in those three years he did what had been neglected for the previous twenty. He gave the club its self-respect back.

'He made the world take us seriously again. Since the debacle of Sexton's exit, what had happened? The Osgood rows, Hudson going, the nightmare of the stand, relegated, losing at home to Carlisle, the Mears family losing control, the whole thing from the late seventies through the eighties was a nightmare. Chelsea, one of the great names in football, had done nothing. What had we achieved for twenty years? Micky Mouse Cups; what was it, the Full Members. It's like discovering your best friend from school is in charge of the prison library. I'm pleased for you but what are you doing there in the first place? Chelsea in the Full Members. Who cared?

'Since Sexton there's been two outstanding teams. McCreadie's with Ray Wilkins as captain. And the Kerry Dixon and David Speedie team. Then came Hoddle and we went up a notch. The work behind the scenes was immense, and the quality would have come, as would the trophies.'

Harding then recalled the day that Hoddle rang him and told him officially that he was considering quitting for England. It was an emotional twenty-four hours for Harding and, he says, Hoddle too.

'Glenn rang me because he had always promised that he would never leave Chelsea without ringing me first. He told me that Tuesday that he was in a terrible dilemma. England had offered him the job. I asked for forty-eight hours and Hoddle, true to his word, passed that message on to the Football Association. He told Graham Kelly that he would like two days to consider his future. When Glenn rang me I still had hopes that he would stay. I asked if we could meet and we arranged to see each other the following morning. It was ironic that I was due to do a BBC Radio Five Live interview with Gary Richardson. It had nothing to do with Hoddle leaving but it did fall into their lap.'

Bates doesn't believe this. He thinks Harding set up the BBC and Richardson for publicity over his relationship with Hoddle.

Richardson, in fact, followed Harding around the whole day and did regular updates for his radio station, adding weight to Bates's belief that Harding organised the whole thing as a publicity stunt. He is convinced that Harding wanted to be seen as the man from Chelsea doing more than anyone to keep Hoddle at Stamford Bridge.

While the FA claimed it knew nothing about Hoddle being offered the job, Glenn himself was confirming the offer to reporters camped on his doorstep at his Ascot home. He travelled to meet Harding at a nearby hotel and the two men spent five hours together. Harding said: 'For me it was not a question of it being the right time or wrong time for Glenn; all I was interested in was the right outcome. I also wanted to make sure that Chelsea did all they could to keep him; to make sure that we could do no more.'

So, picture the scene. Hoddle and Harding locked together over lunch, Chelsea's flamboyant director, and soon to be vice-chairman, desperate for Hoddle to stay. But it seems likely that Hoddle had made up his mind to say yes to England long before he met Harding. He was not going to lose the chance of fulfilling a dream.

When Harding admitted that he had lost his fight, the two men talked about Chelsea's future. Harding recalled: 'We discussed how far we had come in three years and how far the club could go. All along Glenn kept emphasising, "I've done the hard work, the difficult bit. I've got you there, now take it further." It was emotional and he said he didn't want to leave. I respected that. Glenn felt it was in his destiny to manage England. Who was I to argue with that? I made one last effort and said, "Please, Glenn, stay for three more years and finish what you started." But he felt it was meant to happen. He told me it would be arrogant of him to say no to his country.'

Many times in the conversation Hoddle reiterated that he had done the bulk of his work at Chelsea. He clearly felt that the platform had been built and the foundation laid, and that the club could now move on with stability. It was at this meeting that Hoddle first mentioned Ruud Gullit as the obvious coach to take Chelsea into their next era of development. 'At no stage did I mention money to Glenn,' said Harding. 'The meeting was not about money and offers. It was about me trying to persuade him to stay with us. I was about gut reactions, not pounds. His gut reaction was to go to England. I understood because I am someone who has gut reactions. At the moment I'm supporting the Labour Party and have given them a million pounds. I'm doing it because I feel that Tony Blair is the right man to run the country. In five years time I may feel that he is not.

'Glenn felt that he was the right man at the right time for England. It was his turn and he knew he would regret it for the rest of his life if he said no. There was no way I was going to stand in the way of that kind of thinking and ambition. I wished him well and we went our separate ways. I had no idea at that stage what Ken, the board or Denis Roach was doing as far as the future was concerned. I knew that I had done my best. I had failed. But I am just grateful for the three years that Hoddle gave to my club.'

Before Hoddle joined Chelsea, Harding hadn't given him a thought. 'I couldn't have cared two bob,' he confessed. 'If players don't wear a blue shirt then I'm not interested. Hoddle, Spurs, who are they? But if they join my family then that's different.' Harding's affection for Hoddle was demonstrated in his new support for England, something he had never shown an interest in. 'I didn't like the football they played, and only watched on TV if Germany or Brazil or one of the big countries was playing. I am ashamed to say that I wasn't disappointed if England lost. The last time I saw them play live I was fourteen and Bobby Charlton scored.'

His interest lifted with Hoddle. 'The man had a big impact on me,' said Harding. 'He made me look upon football differently.' Harding, in fact, went to Wembley for Hoddle's second game in charge, the 2-1 home victory over Poland. He was like a little boy lost after the game, not the 45th richest man in England, as he was introduced to players like Paul Ince ('Oh hello, I haven't met you before'). It was a fan wandering about. A Wembley official stopped him entering a Polish beer company's private reception, even though he had an invitation and I had arranged to meet him there. The company was embarrassed and sent him an invitation to travel to Poland next May as their guest. 'We will show you how to entertain,' they told him. And Harding planned to go; to make his own way to Poland to watch England play, and no one but Hoddle would have persuaded him to do that.

Harding related what Hoddle did for Chelsea to what he had achieved in his own business. 'It's not a million miles away,' he said. 'Building from the bottom, making sure everything is in place before you go for the big hit. Too many people, you know, look at me when I'm in a pub drinking and shouting and singing and think, How the hell can he run a successful business? Those people don't know me. Let me say this. Show me a foolish millionaire and I will show you a liar. I'm a funny old bugger, really. I'm a nutty Chelsea fan, that's all. Some people play fantasy football, I don't have to. I'm not an anorak or anything like that. I'm a successful businessman with a love of football and particularly Chelsea. When I go to Wembley now I think to myself what a dreary place this is to get to. There's no buzz about the place when you're walking up. Chelsea is alive with people and atmosphere. You have to have a buzz in life, don't you?'

When I asked Harding for the highlights under Hoddle he didn't have to think twice. The greatest moment for him was winning at Newcastle in an FA Cup third round replay in January 1996. 'We came from behind twice – I think we were the only team to score twice at St James's Park – and we won on penalties,' he recalled. 'I was in Marakesh with Richard Branson that day – I'm an official project partner for his round-the-world balloon enterprise. Nothing, however, was going to stop me watching Chelsea. I caught a plane to Morocco, refuelled at Beirut and arrived at Newcastle fifteen minutes into the game. Wonderful.

'Twelve days before, we had conceded a goal in the fourth minute of injury time when dear old Dimitri Kharine fluffed his five iron and allowed Les Ferdinand to equalise. After each Chelsea home game I tried to go and see Glenn in their dressing room. It's a thing I enjoyed and one I believe he appreciated. I went to see him as a mate and a fan, not as a director. After that Newcastle equaliser I popped in and we had a beer and a sandwich. I told him that if we won the replay we would only be back where we were, so head up and let's go and win it. And we did bloody win it, we bloody well did. It was a great occasion.

'I had a private plane waiting at Newcastle Airport but their chairman Sir John Hall insisted on us having dinner first. He's Mr Newcastle and he kept the airport open for me. He eventually packed me off with a carrier bag full of wine and Newcastle Brown and I got on the plane for the return journey. We had to refuel again and I got out for a stretch. There I was on the tarmac, sipping a coffee and looking up at a clear sky. The stars were out and I thought to myself, A few hours ago we won at Newcastle; here I am on my own looking up at the sky in another corner of the world. This is heaven. It was one of those great moments. Everything had gone right. It was exciting. My adrenalin was pumping. It was great to be alive. A few hours later we were in Marakesh and I had no sleep before going up in the balloon, with Branson. Magic. Magic moments. It's great to be alive, you know!'

Another highlight for Harding came in Hoddle's dressing room after Chelsea's infamous FA Cup replay with London rivals Millwall. 'There was an awful undercurrent of menace in the air and around the ground,' recalls Harding. 'You smelt trouble. We scored first through Mark Stein, they equalised late on and then we lost on penalties when John Spencer missed. If that was not bad enough the Millwall fans wanted to fight and there was trouble inside and outside the stadium.

'When the calm, albeit uneasy, had settled, I popped down to see Glenn. I always knocked and this time there was no reply. I put my head round the door and spotted him.

'Glenn was sitting on his own, his head in his hands. The television was off, that funny old fridge in the corner of the room was closed and no one had touched the plate of sandwiches. We didn't exchange a word that night. We simply hugged each other. I could have cried.

'It was a very special moment for me. He knew how much winning and losing meant to me. I knew exactly how he felt. Glenn Hoddle and I had a special relationship at Chelsea – don't let anyone tell you otherwise. He loved Chelsea more than people know, and more than he can bring himself to say.

'I wonder how many managers have that relationship with their chairman or vice-chairman? A special relationship with someone who's running the club they manage? Glenn knows how much he means to me, and I know how much Chelsea means to him. He knew he could talk to me privately, and he did. I understand Glenn more than most. He isn't shy, and he has enormous self-confidence. He's an achiever. He does appear to border on seeming arrogant, but he is far from that. He's a self-starter who doesn't suffer people he doesn't like or admire. He has little smalltalk and doesn't waste his time. He certainly knows what he wants. He wanted England at the wrong time for us. He had to take it, didn't he?'

All this will make interesting reading for Bates, and it will confirm what he suspected – that Hoddle and Harding were closer than anyone knew. They met privately, yes, but were they conspiring to oust Bates? Harding wanted to be chairman, there is no question about that, but Hoddle simply wanted the best, and when England came along he saw an opportunity that he had dreamt of since he was twelve years old. Nothing was going to stop him.

Matthew believed that two people saved Chelsea, and neither of them was Ken Bates. 'Ken criticises Glenn but Glenn and I have saved Chelsea together, and one day that will be a matter of record. I'm not cross about Ken any more. I am happy and relaxed. I am confident about the future.

'But all this is a long race, you know. Life is a long race and Chelsea is a long race. I am planning long term. It wouldn't surprise me if one day Glenn was back at Chelsea.' As manager? 'No, it wouldn't surprise me if he was back at Chelsea one day,' is all that Harding would repeat. There is no doubt that Harding's long-term plans involved him becoming chairman and Hoddle being invited on to the board when and if he was ready.

It emphasises the problems that would have occurred if Bates and Harding had continued to work together. It would not have worked, that is obvious. There would have been clashes, far nastier than the club had already experienced. A 'him or me' confrontation would have been inevitable.

And yet it is impossible to say who would have won. Bates is the street fighter, the experienced heavyweight, the man who has been around for years. He has taken a few blows on the chin but never gone down. Harding was the new challenger and he had one major thing on his side. Money. Loads of money.

'I put the money in with no interest. My friends said I was mad. They said it was like throwing an electric fire into the bath. I did it because I wanted to and I was able to. Do you know an interest-free £5 million is like £12 million of someone else's money? Shall I tell you why I gave Chelsea money? Commitment. Commitment to my club. Chelsea will become great, you know. I can tell. I know we'll do it. It's just a question of getting the right ducks on the right road. When we get there the principal person to thank will be Glenn. Saint Glenn. He gave us the starting point and when all this is history his arrival will be significant. I have said that getting Hoddle was the best thing this club did for twenty years, and I mean it.

'I will make it my business to see that Chelsea is never denied the opportunity to aspire to the greatest club side in Europe. Yes, better and bigger than Manchester United and more successful. The ceiling can't be touched at the moment. But we will – and we won't need a ladder.

'Look, where do all the best players in the world want to play? In London. In SW6. It's the place to be. The buzz is here. It's all very well saying we're getting there. You have got to get there. Got to. I am proud of what I've already done. They say the North Stand is one of the most attractive in the League; I'm proud of that. One day soon people will say, "My God, this club is going places." And we are.'

Harding believed that within five years Chelsea would be the most successful club in England, up there with Manchester United and competing in a European League. And everything he wanted for Chelsea was because he was a fan, and he remained a Chelsea Blue despite mixing in different circles. 'I don't bang my seat when we score, or swear so much in the directors' box, but the feeling is just the same when we score or win,' he chuckled.

'I enjoy meeting the other directors and I particularly like away games. When you're a fan, away games mean a bad seat with a poor view, stuck in the corner with last week's stale meat pies. I get a decent view now when I go away. Benfield is my eight days a week life; football takes up a lot of the rest.'

I last saw Matthew Harding on the evening of 16 October 1996. I dropped him off at his new home in Wimbledon and he jotted down his new numbers, at home and his office, before saying goodbye and going in to have a Scotch and some supper while watching Newcastle in Europe on television.

Seven days later he was dead.

What did Matthew Harding leave behind? A hugely successful business, a king's ransom and a family at odds with each other. His wife Ruth still loved him passionately, even though he had left the family home and lived with Vicky, their baby daughter and her child by a previous relationship. Harding's teenage daughter Ella never spoke to him and his twin boys were bemused by him living away. Then there was fourteen-year-old son Luke 'Greavsie' Harding, called after the one and only Jimmy Greaves, who scored goals for fun for Chelsea. Luke and his father were very close.

'He is one of my best mates,' Harding told me once. 'Vicky is the other.'

They all came together in Ditchling, Sussex, for his funeral. The twins and daughter sat with Ruth in the front row, who laid a Chelsea scarf on his coffin. Luke sat near the back with Harding's sister Grace. Towards the end of the service Vicky burst out of the church because their love together had not been recognised.

Glenn Hoddle, Ken Bates, Ruud Gullit, Steve Clarke and Gwyn Williams were there from Chelsea. Ah yes, Chelsea, perhaps his greatest love of all. Harding left Chelsea behind. In three years he did so much for them financially, not to mention emotionally because he was a larger-than-life character and a real man of the people. At 42 years old, Harding had so many plans for his business, his family and his football club. He believed that one day the club would be his. Chelsea fans can only hope that the dream – or vision, as Bates prefers to call it – is possible without him.

9 The Chelsea Revolution

t is a fact that professional footballers in England are a rare bunch. They have tremendous character, a never-say-die attitude and are great when the chips are down. They also have an enormous capacity to change. For Chelsea in 1992–93 the Hoddle era was waiting to happen.

During that season the Chelsea players had three managers. Ian Porterfield was replaced by David Webb, who kept the club in the top division by raising the spirits and getting vital results. All the Chelsea players assumed Webb would get the job. They were wrong.

What the Chelsea players didn't realise was that a football revolution was imminent: the era of the Premiership, Sky television, bigger sponsorship and foreign players. Bates knew big changes were around the corner and came to the conclusion that he needed a new-age manager.

Bates had met Hoddle when he was using Chelsea's facilities on his return from Monaco, and when he took over at Swindon Bates kept an eye on him to see if the master footballer could be a master manager. He liked what he saw.

He liked the football Swindon played, with a Europe-style three-man defence and two wing backs, and he made up his mind that when the time was right he would offer Hoddle the job of taking Chelsea into a new era. He considered him when he decided to sack Porterfield, but Swindon were pushing for promotion at the time and he knew he wouldn't win any friends if he poached him. So he called in Webb to do a rescue act, knowing that Hoddle was the man he really wanted.

When he did finally arrive, Hoddle began to plot what he could do for Chelsea. He studied the players, knowing this was the opportunity he had been waiting for. The player who was never appreciated as a player was damn well going to be appreciated as a manager.

A man who played right the way through the Hoddle era at Chelsea was Nigel Spackman, a vastly experienced midfield player who started his career at Bournemouth before moving to Chelsea, Liverpool, Rangers and Queen's Park Rangers, then back to Chelsea. Spackman, as they say in football, was his own man; a sensible, intelligent footballer who spoke when he felt it necessary. 'Glenn clearly felt Chelsea was right for him,' he says. 'By the time we reported back for pre-season training I had spoken to him. He had contacted me because I was injured and he wanted to know how I was getting on. In our conversation he made it clear what he wanted. He came across as a very determined and single-minded person.'

Hoddle asked John Gorman, his assistant manager at Swindon to move to Chelsea with him. Gorman was a left back with half the ability of Hoddle, but they laughed at the same jokes and there was a chemistry there. Hoddle, as many people have discovered, does not forget. If he likes you and you remain loyal, you are a friend for life.

So he was disappointed when Gorman decided to stay where he was, and instead turned to Peter Shreeves, who had been his coach and manager at Tottenham. Shreeves is one of the most popular men on the circuit. Always available and good for a chat, he is very well respected, both by players and reporters. However, it was Hoddle's friendship with Gorman that was to be eventually significant.

The one thing that Hoddle immediately had on his side, of course, was respect. With Swindon, Chelsea and eventually England, he was the most skilful player out on the training pitch, and it helps tremendously if you can ask a player to do something and then show him how it is done. Spackman recalls: 'In training he did magnificent things with the ball. You could see how gifted he was. I had certainly admired him as an opponent. He was the kind of player you enjoyed playing against because he was so skilful and you knew it would be a good game of football.'

Hoddle's team plan was the same as he had introduced at Swindon. He would play sweeper, with two overlapping wing backs, two markers and the same attacking shape. He saw this as the only way forward and he instructed his staff to make sure that every player, from the kids of twelve upward, played the same way. He wanted every player to know what to do if and when he was called upon to step up to the next team.

He wasn't, however, quite so good at delegating, as Spackman explains: 'Glenn started as sweeper but when he wasn't fit he was reluctant to play that system and let anyone else do the job. If he wasn't sweeper he didn't think the team functioned properly. We had David Lee but at the start Glenn was reluctant to play him as the spare defender. If Glenn wasn't fit we often used to revert to a diamond midfield with a flat back four. His principles were there although he knew he needed the players. That was often a frustration. He knew how he wanted to play and knew how successful it would be but deep down I suspected that he believed that the players weren't good enough for what he wanted to do.'

That frustration of the quality at his disposal was always in the background. Chelsea never set the world alight in the Premiership, despite success in Europe and in Cup competitions. 'Players can't take everything on board overnight,' reasons Spackman. 'There is so much you can learn and put into practice in the space of a season. Revolution takes time.'

It was not only the playing side that Hoddle was determined to change. He was appalled at some of the facilities, particularly of the training ground. Although there were magnificent pitches and training areas, the showers, changing rooms and canteen facilities were shocking. Again Spackman was impressed with the new manager's attitude. 'Before Hoddle arrived there was no real togetherness among the players. The players came from different areas and we used to shoot off after training. Harlington is a freezing place to be in the winter and there was nothing to keep us there after training. A quick shower and home.'

Hoddle ordered the showers, baths and dressing rooms to be refurbished while the canteen was transformed into a proper restaurant serving pasta, grilled chicken and rice rather than sausages and burgers. He also asked that the players arrived a little earlier for training so they could eat breakfast together, and that they stayed afterwards for lunch. He wanted to create a warmer, more family-like atmosphere. He introduced a masseur

(Terry Slatery, who is now with England), a reflexologist, a dietician and a faith healer to the players, if they wanted to use them.

'There was no pressure,' Spackman explains. 'It was introduced slowly and Glenn simply said that if we needed a massage or if we wanted to go to see the faith healer then do it. He is a great believer in alternative medicine. Some players took it seriously, some didn't. You're never going to get a bunch of footballers agreeing anyway.'

Hoddle's ideas and ideals of management were formed in Monaco when he worked with Arsene Wenger. Indeed, he changed as a person while living in the South of France and brought his thoughts back to England. He was not alone. Most players who have played abroad have been influenced in some way – just ask Trevor Francis, Ray Wilkins or Graeme Souness. After his first training session for Spurs, Jurgen Klinsmann asked Alan Sugar where the masseur worked from. 'What masseur?' asked Sugar. Tottenham did not have one. They do now. What has been commonplace in Europe is now, finally, operating in this country. Spackman adds: 'Glenn told the players who were thirty or over that a masseur helped fight off injury. Again it was advice, not an order.'

Everything Hoddle did had the professional touch. He changed many things behind the scenes and this is what Harding referred to when he talked of Hoddle laying the foundation. 'I have got you there,' he told Matthew. 'Now go on and finish it.'

The groundwork behind the scenes, however, is not always obvious to fans – or the chairman in the front row of the directors' box. A new bath is all very well, but what about winning a couple of League matches? In that first season there is no question that Hoddle's reputation was on the line. The Cup run to Wembley held off criticism – the club and the fans were grateful for a slice of glory – but what were the highlights of that first season, apart from the Cup? A double over Manchester United, with Gavin Peacock scoring the goals in two 1-0 victories. Home wins over Liverpool and Newcastle, but not much else. From the start of October to the middle of November, Chelsea lost six successive matches and at one stage looked to be heading for relegation. They did improve, but what a dreary season it would have been had it not been for Wembley.

'At times it was hard work and I thought he kept us out in training for too long when we were struggling,' says Spackman. 'We usually trained from 10.30am to 12.30pm, but often under Glenn it went on till 1.30 and then again in the afternoons. Players found that hard. It wasn't what they were used to.

'When the team was going well it was a pleasure to be in the side. Fantastic. I think Glenn achieved a lot in his three years although I accept that it was more evident off the park than on. He was getting it right from the first rung of the ladder and the best was definitely still to come. He only half finished the job he started.

'People will point to the table and say that we finished no higher than when he first came, but these things take time. It takes time to blend the right system, it takes time to get what you want and it definitely takes time to find the right players. If you don't have a bottomless pit then there's going to be frustration. Look at Manchester United and Liverpool. They buy the best players for the system they use. When I went to Liverpool I was signed because they believed I was right for the system. Had I been a full back I wouldn't have gone to Anfield, because they didn't need a full back then. Glenn waited until his last season to get the two full backs he believed were right for what he wanted. Dan Petrescu arrived from Sheffield Wednesday and Terry Phelan from Manchester City. That's the point. No doubt he had been searching for his wing backs, but it took him two years to get them. It takes time.'

Most people thought Glenn Hoddle was a bit of a soft touch when he first arrived at Chelsea. He had that reputation as a player and the word soon spread. Glenda, they called him. Hod too. How wrong they were. Hoddle is more determined than most, not to mention single minded, and the Chelsea players never got close to the manager. Hoddle is not that kind of man.

'He is a very private man,' says Spackman. 'He knows what he wants and will do it his way. If he is a success, great. If he fails, OK, and he will take the criticism. A lot of managers will listen to senior players and take things on board; even be flexible with advice. Glenn isn't like that. He didn't do that with us and I don't believe he sought and used Peter Shreeves in that way.'

Hoddle's high standards soon became evident to the Chelsea

players. He insisted on punctuality. 'You normally got a warning the first time and a fine if you were late again,' says Spackman. 'If you went out when you were supposed to be in your room, then that was an automatic fine. Fair enough; players need rules and regulations. Most footballers like a leader.'

The really tough side of Hoddle emerged when he stripped Dennis Wise of the captaincy. Wise had been warned about his on-pitch conduct and then got sent off again at West Ham. He had also been involved in an unsavoury incident outside Terry Venables' club, Scribes West, in the early hours of a Sunday morning, when he had attacked a taxi driver. He was sentenced to jail but the ruling was overturned on appeal. Wise did get the captaincy back from Hoddle, but not for a long time. 'I believe it was more for the sending off than the taxi incident,' says Spackman. 'Glenn had given Dennis a warning and felt let down. He does his discipline in his office, rarely in front of other people.

'I have seen him get cross, at half time or at the end of a game. He is not a tea cup or a hairdryer thrower like Graeme Souness but Glenn has his moments. He will have a go. Maybe he should have been even stronger with us – he perhaps would have got even more respect. He preferred to do it in a quiet way though. He felt it had more effect doing his rollicking in a controlled way. Maybe he was right, but I'm not sure. Footballers need to be told "You were useless" at times. Glenn got his point across without effing and blinding. Souness was a screamer. He would have a go at individuals in front of the team. Hoddle was never like that. Hoddle rarely loses his temper in public.'

He did once with Scottish international Craig Burley, who didn't like being substituted. He made his feelings known and he and Hoddle had a heated exchange on the touchline. It was a row the manager had to win, and he did. He later fined Burley for lack of control.

Spackman, who one day wants to become a coach or manager, has taken on board a host of experience from the managers he has worked with. 'I've been lucky,' he says. 'Alec Stock at Bournemouth was a lovely man and at Chelsea John Neal put together an outstanding team. The team spirit under Neal was superb. John Hollins was the coach who stepped up and he found the manager's job too difficult. At Liverpool Kenny Dalglish was a bit like Glenn – his man-management was good and he would pull you into his office if you needed a ticking off. You rarely needed it at Liverpool because we won all the time. Kenny had Ronnie Moran and Roy Evans at his elbow and the right staff is important. There has to be hard and soft in charge of players. Walter Smith at Rangers does not get upset that easily. When he does you really know about it.'

In his second season Hoddle began with a first-day victory over Norwich, with new signing Paul Furlong scoring on his debut, always a relief for the manager. Then they won at Leeds after being two goals down and eclipsed Manchester City at home 3-0. Hopes were high. Defeat at Newcastle and a home loss to Blackburn, Hoddle's bogey side, brought everything crashing back to earth. When they won at Crystal Palace on 24 September, they were fifth – the highest Chelsea got. The highlights? They were all in the Cups again and this time Europe. In the domestic competition they got past Bournemouth in the second round of the Coca-Cola Cup before going out at West Ham. In the FA Cup they beat Charlton in round three, before losing to Millwall in that infamous fourth-round replay at Stamford Bridge.

The Cup Winners' Cup was exciting and, once again, helped ease the fans' frustration at more disappointment in the League. In the first round they beat Viktoria Zizkov over two legs, Russian goalkeeper Dimitri Kharin saving a vital penalty in the return. In the second round they drew at home 0-0 with FK Austria before Scottish international John Spencer put them through with a fantastic goal. He ran the length of the pitch before going round the goalkeeper and netting the winner.

On to Belgium for FC Brugge in the quarter-finals, which saw a 1-0 away defeat but goals from Mark Stein and Paul Furlong at home on a wildly exciting, emotional night at Stamford Bridge. There is nothing like Europe to capture the smell of glories past, and that victory meant a lot to Hoddle. In a rare public show of emotion, Hoddle threw his arms around Peter Shreeves at the end of the game. But Chelsea were just too inexperienced for Real Zaragoza in the semis, and they were torn apart in the first leg, losing 3-0. The second leg was amazing for more reasons than one. Chelsea almost came from behind before going out 4-3 on aggregate, and then, after the game, Hoddle – who had replaced

Erland Johnsen for the last twenty minutes – announced his retirement from playing.

Hoddle had treated us to a marvellous cameo display for those last twenty minutes. During that time he was the best player on the pitch, hitting passes, opening up the Zaragoza defence at will and almost scoring. But the injuries had finally taken their toll and the master passer said that it was the right time to go. He would concentrate on managing.

Spackman looks back at Hoddle's last game: 'The way he played that night was perhaps an indication of his own frustration. He wanted to change things quicker than his own players allowed. For the last twenty years the Championship in this country has been won by sides using a four-four-two formation. That is the way the game in England has been played, like it or not, and it has been successful. OK, Liverpool might play one up, with one trailing slightly behind, but it is mostly a basic four-four-two. Glenn was trying to change that and is now doing it at international level. With England at least he can hand pick the players he believes can do the job for him. At Chelsea, he needed more quality for what he wanted to do. He will never change, that's for sure. His ambition will never die and he won't be satisfied until he has achieved completely.'

At the start of his third and last season Hoddle got some of that quality he was looking for. Ruud Gullit, one of the great players of the modern era, was available. Gullit needed a new challenge, it was said in reports from agents in Italy, and Hoddle was ready to provide that challenge. Gullit had admired Hoddle from afar, had played against him for Feyenoord in Holland and for the Dutch national side and knew that Chelsea would play his kind of football. English football was on the up and Gullit happily signed for a free transfer but with a yearly salary of £1 million. It was the next stage of the revolution for Hoddle. With Gullit he made people sit up and take notice, and he knew that Gullit's name and presence would rub off on the other players. Next he signed Mark Hughes from Manchester United, and there was suddenly a new buzz at Stamford Bridge at the start of the 1995–96 season.

The optimism proved to be unfounded, however. The season began with a goalless home draw with Everton, then a goalless away draw at Forest and a 2-0 defeat at Middlesbrough. Three games, no goals, two points. Not good enough. A 2-2 home draw with Coventry was not good enough either, before, at last, victory at West Ham. But Chelsea proved again that they were too inconsistent, and the highest they got in the Premiership was eighth, three times. They only scored 46 League goals.

Once more the Cup saved the season from being a complete disaster. In the third round came the wonderful victory in the replay at Newcastle, then a 2-1 victory over west London neighbours QPR. Then followed a replay victory over Grimsby and another replay in the sixth round, this time with Wimbledon – a 2-2 home draw before an impressive 3-1 victory at Selhurst Park. Gullit put Chelsea ahead in the semi-final against Manchester United before Andy Cole and David Beckham scored. So near, yet again.

Spackman says: 'Ruud started that season as sweeper. Glenn believed he had found the player to take over from him as the spare defender. He had been searching long enough. But Hoddle as sweeper was better than Ruud in a defensive role. Ruud would come out of defence with a flourish, join in and then not go back. I played the holding midfield role and ended up playing sweeper more than Ruud. Many times I screamed at him to get back. The trouble is that all over the world Ruud had played with wonderfully gifted players, the best that money could buy. If he went off on a run others would simply slot in. They filled in until it broke down and he went back. It wasn't like that at Chelsea. We didn't have the players.'

Ironically, the right balance wasn't struck until Gullit was injured. David Lee was moved back into the sweeper role and was a revelation for the rest of the season. 'Ruud returned in midfield and that gave us a better balance. He took people on, ran at defenders, just like Steve McManaman does at Liverpool, and we were a better side for it. Ruud gave us an attacking option and Dennis Wise and Gavin Peacock were better for it, and happier, too.'

But it still didn't bring the kind of success Chelsea needed, Bates craved and Hoddle wanted. Many will say that Hoddle was extremely lucky to be asked to become the coach of England. His record, certainly in the Premiership, did not warrant the invitation, but the FA saw in Hoddle what Bates had seen three years earlier – someone to continue the revolution.

They believed that the handover from Terry Venables to Hoddle would be smooth – the same type of football, European thinking and someone the players respected. And, perhaps most importantly, here was a man who was desperate for the rise to the biggest job of all. Spackman, who left Chelsea soon after Hoddle on a free transfer to Sheffield United, says, 'I always felt that Glenn would go. When the England thing started it was obvious to me that he would take it. He had a great ambition to manage his country.

'He does regret not finishing the revolution at Chelsea. He started it but it was still unfinished when he left. He knows that, but he felt that if he turned down England he would never get the chance again. England came too quickly for him but he had to take it.

'Now things have developed even further at Chelsea. The stars are there and a lot is going on at an electric pace. It is the next stage and Ruud must blend the stars with the players that are already there. Good luck to them; I hope they are a success. I hope Glenn is a success.'

For Glenn Hoddle there was one last task. He had been with Peter Shreeves all the way through and a lot of people expected Glenn to take him to Lancaster Gate. But Hoddle went back to John Gorman, and Shreeves had the news broken to him in a short, curt phone call from Hoddle. Shreeves is too much of a gentleman to go public on his true feelings about the way he was treated, but his disappointment was clear when he told friends, 'The manager gets the England job, I get the sack.' Shreeves is now working alongside David Pleat at Sheffield Wednesday.

That's football. Hero one day, villain the next. Chelsea manager one moment, England coach the next. Loved one minute, hated the next. When Ruud Gullit arrived in this country to sign for Chelsea he had no idea that less than a year later he would be the coach of one of the biggest clubs in the country, being asked to finish what Hoddle had started.

10 Goodbye Glenn, Welcome Ruud

uud Gullit signed for Chelsea because of Glenn Hoddle. No other reason. OK, the million pounds a year salary helped, but the Chelsea board should always remember that Gullit wouldn't have agreed to play for someone he didn't respect. Matthew Harding was never convinced Ken Bates realised the significance of the Gullit signing.

Without Hoddle there would be no Gullit, without Gullit there would be no Vialli, Zola, Di Matteo and the other world superstars sure to arrive. It has been a snowball effect, and all thanks to the Hoddle groundwork, as Harding liked to call it.

Gullit didn't know Hoddle before he met him for the first time at their meeting about playing for Chelsea, and the only reason he went to the appointment was because he had watched, played against and marvelled at Hoddle's skill and performance. He knew that here was a man after his own heart, and that was important.

Hoddle and Gullit joked about playing against each other with club and country and then they discussed Chelsea's future and how Hoddle wanted the team to play. Hoddle's plan was to sign Gullit as his sweeper, and use him as a teacher and inspiration to the other players. Gullit didn't take a lot of persuading. He was ready for a new challenge, especially in a team that wanted to play such sophisticated football. He spoke fluent English, and here was the opportunity to live in London and learn a new culture. For an intelligent man like Gullit it was an ideal opportunity, especially at an advanced time of his career. However, the fact that he was 32 didn't worry Hoddle in the slightest, not least because the Europeans, especially those who have played in Italy for so long, are known to look after themselves. 'Not a gamble,' said Hoddle. 'He will become Chelsea's greatest signing.' That was certainly proved right.

How many times has the word skill been used in the same sentence as Gullit? Not so when you talk to the great man. 'I was never very skilful,' he admits. 'I could not do the ball tricks of Glenn Hoddle. He can keep the ball up for hours. That is not me. Today I still cannot do great tricks. My skill is the vision of the game. Also, I could always run; I developed a technique of speed, not skill. Everything I did revolved around speed. Glenn Hoddle can resolve a game on a square yard. I do not have that. I need more space.'

The two men shared an early love of football, their fathers having introduced them to the sport. 'First you are born with talent. Then you have an interest which allows the talent to develop. I loved the game from as early as I can remember. I was prepared to learn. Glenn was certainly born with more ball skills than me. I have asked him many times, "Are you right footed or left?" You cannot tell. It means he was gifted with extraordinary balance. You are born with that. You cannot develop wonderful balance. You either have it or not.

'My father made it easy for me. He loved football and saw that I too had caught the bug. I can recall always being interested in the game and how it developed on the pitch. The more coaches I played for, the higher standard I played at and the more interested I became. The faster the game the quicker the solution has to be in your head. Many times when I was young I said to myself on the pitch, "I can't get out of here" and then you see it, the solution, and you are free on the pitch. It gives you tremendous satisfaction.

'I felt the more I understood about the game, the more I could tell it to others. I was lucky. I played alongside Johann Cruyff and Vanhanagan. Wonderful players. They were good teachers and I watched closely and carefully, and learned quickly.'

Yet despite their many similarities, Glenn Hoddle and Ruud Gullit still hardly know each other. They have met, talked, played on the training pitch, been in the same dressing room, embraced after goals and disputed decisions, but they have never become close. They are certainly not friends and have never mixed socially. Gullit didn't need that kind of relationship with his manager, which is still a surprise because Gullit and Hoddle seemed to go together. Of course they did, but football was their marriage, nothing else. They had one thing in common – how the game should be played.

Gullit first remembers hearing about Hoddle when he was playing for Feyenoord in Holland and Hoddle was making a name for himself at Spurs. Gullit adds: 'We saw all the English games on television in Holland and when you watched or thought of Tottenham you thought of Hoddle. They went together. You admired his technique from afar, his skill and how he handled the ball. When one of my teams played against him we talked about him because he was the danger.

'The Dutch players could never understand why he was not appreciated more. Had he played in Holland he would have been a huge world star. Glenn Hoddle would have got into all the great Holland sides. He would have been mentioned along with Cruyff, Van Basten, me, if you like; all the great Dutch players. In Holland they believe in their players. That helps you mentally and physically. Footballers are no different; they like to be liked. What means more to a player than anything is to be appreciated.'

So the two men had never really met when Hoddle and Chelsea chief executive Colin Hutchinson flew to Italy to open transfer negotiations. There was simply admiration and respect when Gullit entered the hotel room. Gullit says: 'I had seen him play, played against him and knew of his record in Monaco. He wanted me, and so that was a good starting point. We talked about football, of course, and he said how he wanted Chelsea to play and would I join and play as sweeper. It was a compliment and I felt flattered. It didn't take long for me to make up my mind and say yes.'

From the outside you would be forgiven for thinking that the two men would become friends and form a close relationship, but it was far from that. It was purely a football relationship. 'Respect is the key word here,' says Gullit. 'You have to have it. It is not vital that the player and the coach like each other. If the player thinks he knows everything then there is a problem but with vision you have to listen and learn. Glenn and I had a huge professional relationship. We talked although the conversation was not in depth, apart from football. We exchanged opinions and he was the decision maker.'

Gullit's impact on Chelsea was simply the way he played. The crowd turned up to see him just because he was Ruud Gullit. If respect was the key word, as Gullit said, the Chelsea fans had it for both these men. Although Hoddle was not hugely successful, there was an underflowing feeling that the good times would come under his control. The expectancy was such that Hoddle's name was enough to carry it through. Gullit's arrival only helped the good feeling factor.

It is hard to gauge Gullit's impact, but it certainly wasn't found in trophies during that first season. He was ... well ... just Gullit. A big man, dreadlocks bouncing around his forehead, all swagger and pace, wonderful passes and goals. Perhaps the biggest gauge is yet to come – the influence he has and is having on the other Chelsea players, especially the young ones. If they do not learn from Hoddle and Gullit, they never will. They should count themselves very fortunate to be part of a club hitting a revolution.

During his first season at Chelsea, Gullit could often be seen hanging his head in disappointment and frustration. The hands would go up and flop down to his side. When you've been the star of AC Milan and a great Holland side, playing for Chelsea is no doubt a culture shock, but Gullit never allowed any negative thoughts to dominate him. He enjoyed his first season in English football, and knew the football suited his style: 'I made my reputation playing my way. Had Glenn said that he was going to play long then of course I would not have come. It would not have been worth it.'

Gullit only started to think about becoming a coach when the rumours linking Hoddle with the England job began. They went on for weeks and the stronger they got the more Gullit toyed with the idea. He now admits: 'I asked myself what I would say if they asked me. Did I want it? And if they did ask me and I said yes, how would I do it?'

Yet when Gullit arrived in England, he had no thoughts of coaching or management. He loved playing too much and wanted to extend that side of his career for as long as possible. 'To play is all that matters to me,' he said at the time. Similarly, Glenn insisted that he didn't want to manage until he went to France and met Wenger.

The family man. Wife Anne and daughters in 1990, as Hoddle returns to English football from Monaco *(Sun)*

Hoddle proves he's still got it *(msi)*

The first steps into management at Swindon Town *(Allsport)*

Hoddle moves on to become player-manager at Chelsea *(Allsport)*

A warm reception. The Swindon fans let Hoddle know what they think of him *(Sun)*

Mark Hughes signs for Chelsea from Manchester United in 1995 *(Action Images)*

Hoddle with Ken Bates *(Sun)*

Ruud Gullit and Hoddle
discuss tactics *(Sun)*

Glenn Hoddle tries to restore order at his last match as Chelsea manager *(Allsport)*

Terry Venables hands over the reins of international management
(PA News)

The man has arrived. Hoddle is installed as the new England supremo *(msi)*

Hoddle's first training session *(ASP)*

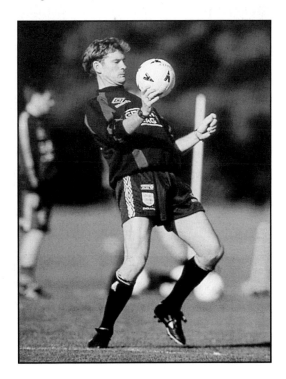

Hoddle leads by example at
Bisham Abbey *(Allsport)*

The highs and lows.
Above: The bench celebrates during
England v. Georgia *(Empics)*
Right: Dejection after Italy *(msi)*

However, it wasn't one person who convinced Gullit, it was thousands of people standing and chanting his name. 'Ruuuudie ... Ruuuudie, we want Gullit' screamed the non-stop chorus from Chelsea supporters at Hoddle's last League game. 'It touched me,' admits Gullit. 'It was perhaps the moment when I made up my mind to say yes if Chelsea wanted me to do the job. I have always loved supporters and had a special relationship with them, all over the world. This was something else. They wanted me as their manager. How could I say no?'

The board were also impressed with the fans' attitude, Bates and Harding for once seeing eye to eye. A board meeting was hastily called and by the Friday, five days later, the club announced that Gullit was Chelsea's new player-coach. On with the revolution and this time it was going to be bigger than ever before. One of Gullit's favourite phrases, along with 'lovely boy', which is how he addresses players, colleagues and friends alike, is 'You must wait for the moment in your life'. This was undoubtedly Gullit's moment.

Gullit had his own ideas. In principle they were similar to Hoddle's but he did make early changes. He didn't believe that the Chelsea players were fit enough, mentally or physically. He introduced a physical conditioner trainer Ade Mafe, something that, surprisingly, Hoddle had not considered. 'Mental stimulation is important,' says Gullit. 'This game is not just about fitness. The mind reacts with fitness. I have to say that the players who want to be part of Chelsea's future are responding.'

Gullit also decided that Chelsea's squad was not big or strong enough in depth. 'It is impossible to play in the English League with its demands with only a squad of sixteen or eighteen. I also believe that it is impossible for a player to be ever-present in all these games. How does he do it? I hear managers in England saying all the time, 'I can't play without him, what are we going to do?' At Blackburn earlier this season I did not have LeBoeuf or David Lee, who had broken his leg. So for the spare defender I had to improvise. But if you have the squad there is someone to play there.' On this occasion it was Craig Burley, switching from midfield to sweeper.

'If a player plays every week, and he knows he is going to be in the team, then he must get complacent. If there is a stick behind him, or the manager punching his fist into his palm, then he reacts. My attitude is this. If you do not perform, you are not in the team. Ajax have this, Milan have this, United have this. Why not Chelsea?'

Gullit's biggest change was, of course, the introduction of three Italian players. He signed Gianluca Vialli before the season. Vialli, who captained Juventus to their European Cup triumph in 1996, is one of the biggest names in Italian football. Then came Roberto Di Matteo and then, in November 1996, Gianfranco Zola. Add the Frenchman LeBoeuf and it's no wonder the expectation at Stamford Bridge rose with the building work being carried out at the famous Shed End of the stadium.

The Italian connection, however, brought Gullit's biggest problem. Players who had been established in the team were overlooked. Stars like Scottish international forward John Spencer, a member of his country's European Championship squad, could not get a kick in the first team, and began to complain in the media. Skipper Dennis Wise had a showdown with Gullit after complaining about his role in the side. But Gullit was determined to go his own route, even if it meant upsetting the players who had been established under Hoddle.

Gullit, who admits that the change from player to coach and decision maker has been hard because of his relationship with players, says: 'Since becoming a coach I have found things out about myself. I have to be tough. It is not something I enjoy because I am not a tough person. But I know that I must. I am getting harder, at least on the outside, although there are times when I do not like myself for it.

'The so-called problems for a country when foreign players arrive is not new to me. In Italy, when their revolution started, there were the same arguments. Too many foreign players; too old; it will stunt the growth of homegrown players . . . there was an outcry. It took Italy five years to change and everyone to realise. Now look. Times change. England does not have to change a lot but all this, all these new players, is being done to make English football better.

'Glenn knew what he wanted. He became frustrated, you could see, because he did not have the proper materials to do the job he had in his mind. That was his greatest frustration. He loved the job but he knew he needed extra quality, better players.

'What he did with the players was good. He wanted them to change more quickly, however. It happened too slowly for him. The players were learning and improving. He wanted it now. In life that is not always possible.'

Ironically, the Chelsea board backed Gullit with more money than Hoddle ever had available to him. At the meeting, when Gullit discussed the job with Ken Bates, Colin Hutchinson and Harding, he laid down some ground rules. It was basically this: 'I will continue the revolution but you must back me.' At the time of writing, Chelsea have five players on their staff earning more than £1 million a year: Gullit, Vialli, Di Matteo, Zola and LeBoeuf. Gullit was not interested in how the club afforded it or what the other players were earning.

What Gullit had was the best contacts book in football and a mobile phone that could pluck anyone from around the world. He was a star and he knew them all. He had one phone call with Vialli and captured him. It was a similar story with the rest. 'I told them that the club was ambitious, English football was improving and London was a great place to live. That was it. I left the negotiations up to Colin. I am not interested in how much my players earn. I do not want to know. Are you coming? Yes. Then it is up to the club.

'I have had no complaints at all. The nicest thing for me is that the Chelsea people trusted me. I can see that with Colin and Ken Bates. Trust. They gave me the job and there has been no interference. We talk, of course, but they keep their distance. They are good at business and I can play football and run the team. For me that is ideal. It works well.

'I bought three Italians because they can help each other, and they can help me in what I am trying to achieve. Age is not important. What I needed first was an example. If I do not have an example how can I teach the others? The rest will come and learn. Just as I was taught. If a teacher in the classroom is the same age as the pupils, how can he have respect? If my Chelsea players look and learn from the players I have brought in they will be better for it. They will find their level. At the moment, some of them are down there [holding his hand towards the floor] and soon they will be up there [raising his hand above his head]. It takes time, it is part of the process. Glenn would know what I was doing.

'In Italy new coaches, new players and new ideas arrived. The outcry died down and the success began. Surely that is what English football wants? The English game can be stronger. You must not, however, lose your identity in the change.'

Gullit also slightly changed the Hoddle playing system. 'Glenn played two men behind the front man, who were usually Mark Hughes and John Spencer. I prefer three across the middle of the pitch and two strikers.' With the arrival of Vialli there had to be casualties. Hence Spencer's frustration and eventual annoyance. 'Tough decisions had to be made and they were mine,' said Gullit. 'I was playing golf with the players one season and telling them they were dropped the next. At the beginning they did not understand or want to accept it. They had to accept it.

'At Milan Capello was tough. He screamed and shouted at us. We hated him at times but we respected him. That is the key. Then at Milan there was Oscar Tabarez. They say that he is a nice guy but look at the results. In society if the boss is nice the employees see that as a sign of weakness. So at Milan now again there is Saachi. You have to be tough. And I cannot explain my decisions all the time to all of the players otherwise I would be talking, talking all day long.'

Gullit knows he cannot keep all his players happy. Even Vialli voiced his frustration at not being in the side all the time, telling Italian television that he wasn't happy. Gullit told him to be patient.

The changes at Chelsea in the last three years have been incredible. At the turn of 1993 Ian Porterfield was the manager. Then David Webb for a few weeks. Then Glenn Hoddle, the start of the biggest thing to happen to the club since Peter Osgood headed that marvellous winner in the 1970 FA Cup Final replay against Leeds. Now Gullit. Plus a huge multi-million complete redevelopment of the stadium.

What next for the club that has been searching for past glories for so long? Hoddle was exciting, Harding gave them a feeling of stability, and Gullit has lifted dreams towards that ceiling that Harding talked about. It is still not within touching distance because, whatever the team you put out, winning is the bottom line. As Osgood said when he mixed with fans at the Imperial Arms four days after Harding's death, 'This bloody club is cursed. We are not meant to be successful.'

But Bates will not rest until they are, and he is far more confident with Gullit. He did not like Harding and Hoddle, but he admires Gullit. He likes the system that sees the manager manage and himself run the club.

Hoddle will certainly want Chelsea to be successful while he attacks the biggest challenge of his career. He didn't have the players to carry out his dream at Stamford Bridge, but now he can choose anyone he likes and has the best at his disposal. Funnily enough, he wouldn't mind the quality of one or two players Gullit has signed for Chelsea.

11 The England Mystery

Glenn Hoddle was 22 years old when he made his debut for England. He was 31 when he played his last international nine years later. In that period he won just 53 caps.

Why did English football waste such talent? Everyone who watched him or played against him, at home and abroad, said that he was the greatest England player to have been produced for years. Here was a rare talent, a player way beyond his years. They all thought the same, it seems, except Keith Burkinshaw, his manager at Spurs for an important period, and his two international managers, Ron Greenwood and Bobby Robson.

Of course, they knew he could play. They knew he had the touch of a butterfly, the pass of a genius and the on-pitch knowledge of someone twice his age. But, they said, he could not defend, tackle, work in his own box or head the ball.

The more they said it, the more disillusioned Hoddle became. He was proud to pull on the white shirt of England but he never really enjoyed his international career because he never had that feeling of great satisfaction he craved. He never felt wanted. He was never an automatic choice. He was right, of course, because both his England managers would ponder, pencils poised, and ask themselves, Is this a match for Hoddle?

No one could really understand it. Michel Platini, the great French midfield star who later managed his country, says: 'If you have a talent available to you like Hoddle then he must play in every game. You must create from him. Had I been his manager he would have been my first choice, not my last. To play for your country for almost ten years and only get fifty-three caps is a nonsense. Someone, somewhere, was misguided.' Those were

Hoddle's thoughts. He often felt bitterness and more than once contemplated turning his back on his country.

Paul Miller spent many hours persuading Hoddle not to quit on England. He recalls: 'His biggest frustration was at the 1982 World Cup in Spain. He went to the finals as the best midfield player in the country. He had been brilliant that season with everyone talking about him. But he played just once in the World Cup, against Kuwait when England had already qualified. He returned really cheesed off and adamant that he would never play again.

'It was always the same when he went off on England duty. He would often come back unhappy. When we roomed together for a Spurs away game the Friday nights were always dominated with the same conversation. He would say to me, "That's it, I'm not going any more. What's the point of travelling all the way round the world for seven minutes as a sub? The whole thing's a waste of time. I don't need it. So many people say I should play but I'm in and out and not appreciated."

'It was a pity for Spurs, because on returning from England he always had to be lifted as a person. His morale was on the floor when it should have been sky high because he was so good. There was a lot of bitterness in him where England were concerned. He always felt deep frustration against Greenwood, Robson and Burkinshaw. Glenn would cite Maradona and Platini and argue that teams were built around them. Glenn and Keith often used to have rows with Glenn shouting: "This is what I'm good at, this is what I do. Why do you want to change me?" Hoddle was only appreciated at Spurs by Peter Shreeves, who took over from Burkinshaw, and then David Pleat built a side around him, almost by chance.'

Hoddle would love to have worked with Terry Venables, the man, ironically, he took over from at senior level with England. He felt on the same wavelength as Venables when they met at Under 21 level, and Hoddle is on record as saying that he discovered more about tactics and football working with Venables in a week than he did with anyone else. This was before he met Arsene Wenger at Monaco, however.

This is a key to Hoddle as a player, man and manager. All through his life, professional and private, he has only really been accepted by people on the same wavelength as him.

This chapter of the Hoddle story is more about the England games he *didn't* play, rather than the ones he did. Even on the day he was named in his first squad for a European Championship qualifier against Bulgaria at Wembley in November 1979, he was met with these comments from Burkinshaw: 'It has been a real battle to make him change but it has worked and everyone at the club is delighted for him. The other players must take credit too. For a long time I could sense that Glenn felt he was unable to do all the work we required. He probably felt that he was not good at it but now is eager to have a go and try winning the ball back. He looks a better player all round and there is more snap to his game. His attitude has definitely changed.'

Burkinshaw didn't realise the damage he did with that kind of comment. What Hoddle wanted to hear was: 'It is a great selection for the English game. Glenn is one of the most skilful players we have produced and can go on and win a hundred caps.' But it never happened and the tone of Burkinshaw's comments haunted Hoddle throughout his career in English football, certainly with the national side.

But Hoddle's love of England was always there. Indeed, in 1966, when he was eight, he and a friend, Andy Jessey, made a huge 'England for the World Cup' banner and marched around the streets of Harlow. It is one of the game's great ironies that we should ask the player we did not appreciate to manage us through a vital decade.

Hoddle first discovered that he had been picked to play for England on the coach returning from training on the Tuesday before the Wednesday game against Bulgaria. Manager Ron Greenwood stood up at the front of the bus and read out the team, Hoddle's name included. Strangely, the manager had given him no clue, and there was no arm around the shoulder to ask him how he was feeling. You can't imagine someone like Kevin Keegan not telling a player he is picked before reading out the team.

It was the next morning in training that Greenwood said to Hoddle, 'I want you to go out and do what you do for Spurs.' That was a joke. It was exactly what Greenwood didn't want.

The game on the Wednesday night had to be postponed for 24 hours because of thick fog encircling Wembley. Having qualified for the finals already, England released skipper Kevin Keegan back to Hamburg, and Greenwood replaced him with Kevin Reeves, also for his debut.

Hoddle scored a spectacular goal on his debut. Trevor Francis pulling the ball back and Glenn volleying it into the top corner with his instep from twenty yards. 'It was one of the great moments of my career,' he said. 'I didn't know where to run and celebrate, to let off steam, because Wembley is so big.'

England won 2-0 and the media were full of glowing tributes to Hoddle, predicting how long he could stay in the side and how many caps he would win. For a short time Hoddle was on cloud nine, brought crashing back to earth by Greenwood for the next game, against the Republic of Ireland, again at Wembley. Greenwood approached Hoddle in training and told him, 'I'm going to leave you out of this one. Don't worry, you're still young and time's on your side.'

It was again a terrible piece of man management by Greenwood, forcing Hoddle's career to go backward instead of forward at a stage when he wasn't strong enough mentally to cope with such pressures. He didn't even make the senior squad for a victory against Spain in Barcelona. In and then out; it was the story of Hoddle's international career.

Hoddle always felt that Greenwood was too cautious in throwing bright young talent into the senior side. He also thought his impact on international football and the England set-up was held back by inconsistent team selection. Hoddle was not given a run in the side and too often found himself playing in important matches with not enough experience behind him. The disastrous World Cup defeat in Norway was only Hoddle's tenth game for England but he hardly played in two successive matches. Top-class players should be able to adjust, but how can they, Hoddle argued, when they are unsure of their place? It is an interesting theory that he must take into his international managerial career with England.

The fire burned within Hoddle all the time, and he never doubted that he should be playing. When he sat and watched England lose at home to Denmark from the Wembley stands, his frustration was clear: 'I've got more ability than most of the players out there. What am I doing sitting up here? I ended one season in the England side and now I'm back in the grandstand. Why? I wish someone would pin me up against a wall and say, "Glenn, this is why you're not being selected." I have never been sure that Ron Greenwood and Bobby Robson believe I am a great player. Why, why, why? I want ten games on the trot, a run in the side to feel an England player and to convince people. Every time I play I feel I'm on trial.'

He still feels the same way now. 'International football demands that everyone in the team has a clear idea where and when colleagues will be in any given situation. That comes only from having a settled side. I spoke to Ossie Ardiles about this. When the Argentinians were preparing for a World Cup they kept the same side together for a long period and they played as a unit all the time, often behind locked doors against college and minor sides. They lost games but every time they were together something was added to the unit. It made sense.

'There are frustrations inside me at not having been able to play how I wanted to play for England, or as many times. Perhaps England managers now regret it. After all, we didn't have real success in that period.'

So why didn't they pick him? Why did England have such talent and waste it? Or did they? I first went to Ron Greenwood for the answers, and he gave a completely different insight into Hoddle the player.

Greenwood, manager between 1977 and 1982, says: 'He was a gifted, talented player who stood out above anyone else at that time. The only problem that I could see he had was his own personality. Glenn never realised how good he was.

'It was related. He didn't realise how brilliant he was. I found that there wasn't enough belief from the player himself. That held him back. I know it has been said that in his era the skilful player was not encouraged but I don't think that was true. It was whether he imposed himself on the game, with his own belief. Too often Glenn didn't.

'He was a retiring type of person, rather shy, and that reflected in his personality. Obviously it also reflected on him as a footballer. Glenn didn't feel he was *that brilliant*. He was certainly not a flamboyant character, which would have been more fitting for him as a player, especially with the skill that he had. It is often

down to the player himself about how many caps he wins. People
say he should have got more but they should also look at the
character of the player as well as the ability.

'He was gifted. Yet his belief was not prominent at Spurs. It
was only when he went abroad that he blossomed. He changed,
and that was it for him. It's a pity he didn't have that confidence
in his early years. The only thing that always stood out for me,
that emphasised the inhibitions in himself, was that he was what
I call a toe tripper. He had a habit of drifting along and dragging
his boot toe behind him. I thought that was a clear indication of
his lack of belief in himself. It was a give away for me.

'He was a lovely lad to deal with and he never gave me any
problems. I just felt that he could be offering more because he had
the ability to do so. He lacked that real belief in himself. He was
never a tactical man at that early stage. He was like most players,
they like to play and show off their talents. He was no different.
Glenn never struck me as a deep thinker about the game.

'That's reflected in his later years, with him becoming more
confident as he matured. He only got that real belief when he met
Arsene Wenger at Monaco and that period in his life must have
been quite enlightening for him. Wenger, I am sure, changed his
thinking and outlook on the game.

'I would not have envisaged Glenn being a manager and a top
coach in those early years. He was a gifted player without the
flamboyancy. People throw at me that he should have won a
hundred and fifty caps. I think that's reflected in what we're
talking about. Belief. He didn't develop in his early years, not as
well as he should have done.

'Glenn was way above the players from his era in ability, that
is not an argument. For me he didn't have that real belief. Not
when I had him.'

The picture changes all the time with Hoddle. A graceful player
with more ability than anyone else around in his era, but now,
according to Greenwood, a person who lacked real belief. He
knew he had the skill and yet something held him back.

Greenwood's comments are perhaps the most significant of all
regarding Hoddle the player. The former England manager has
been heavily criticised for his mishandling of Hoddle. Now he
reveals that he wanted to pick him more but it was Hoddle

himself who held back the caps and the right to dominate
international level. We knew he was shy but thought it was lost
once he crossed the white line of a football pitch. Not so,
according to Greenwood. At the highest level Greenwood believes
that it was only Hoddle's personality which held him back.

So what makes the perfect player? The skill of Hoddle, the
sheer determination of Bryan Robson, the power of Alan Shearer
. . . you can go on. Perhaps it is impossible to find him. But it is
now apparent that Greenwood and Robson, did look hard at him
and there was something holding them back. Had they pinned
him up against that wall and delivered a harsh verdict, it would
have been something like this: 'Glenn, have more belief in
yourself. You can do it. It's not us holding you back, it's you.'

Greenwood gets total support from Don Howe, the coach who
worked for England under Greenwood, Robson and Terry
Venables. Howe, often criticised as being too defensive-minded,
says: 'Glenn got fifty-three caps and it's not fair for anyone to say
that Ron and Bobby did not have the football intelligence to give
Glenn Hoddle more caps. Glenn as an England player worked for
two of the top coaches in the country. Ron Greenwood was noted
for the football academy he built at West Ham. He brought
through wonderful players like Bobby Moore, Martin Peters and
Geoff Hurst. He knew a good player when he saw one.

'I would argue strongly against the case that Ron didn't give
Glenn Hoddle enough caps. Bobby Robson took England to the
semi-final of a World Cup and has had tremendous success in
England, Holland, Portugal and Spain. If anyone says that these
two men did not have the appreciation of Glenn Hoddle, I would
say not on your nelly.

'They used him when they thought he could be used. It was up
to Glenn. You only get the caps you are worth. People say he
should have got more than a hundred. I'm saying that they did
appreciate him but used him when he was worth using. They
never once said to me, "We'll use Glenn here, but not there."
They looked at what he was producing for the country and
selected him accordingly.

'The other argument is that the team should have been built
around him. That is not on. You always get dominant players and
Glenn was dominant because of his quality. But France didn't

build their side around Platini and Germany wasn't formed around Beckenbauer – they were personalities that deserved to be in the team. I simply do not go along with the case that said get Hoddle in and pull the others around him. It doesn't work like that. It's nice to dream and there's a lot of romance in football. I'm telling you that building a team around one player is not the real world.

'Glenn didn't win more caps because it was down to him. Players win caps because they impress the manager in charge, not because other people think they should be in the team. The player's personality and the way he plays is the influence, nothing else. No manager would cut off his nose to spite his face to leave a player like Hoddle out if he thought he was the right man for the job. It is up to the individual. Glenn – and I have a lot of respect for him – can say what he likes. He was appreciated as a player. Anyway, why are we sniffing at fifty-three caps? That's a lot.

'Ever since football began there has been an argument about players who should be in the England side – Matthews, Finney, Mannion, Hudson, Currie, Le Tissier – right the way through the ages. The point is this: it is in the player's hands, no one else. Every England manager will pick the player he thinks will bring the country success. And the player has to make the manager pick him.

'I have had criticism as an England coach too. People levelled at me that I was too defensive and didn't appreciate the skilful player. Nonsense. I have never said we can't afford to play him, nor have I ever ordered a side to be defensive. I've had to grin and bear this criticism, as have Greenwood and Robson over Hoddle. It's easy to blame the coach and the manager.

'Terry Venables got heavy criticism over Matthew Le Tissier. It was ridiculous that he should be criticised because Terry has always been looked upon as one of the brightest and most free-flowing coaches. But he didn't pick Le Tissier, a player so many wanted in the European Championship squad. Why? Simple. Because Le Tissier did not impress him. Terry didn't think Matthew could do the job he wanted. Had he impressed him, he would have been in.

'There's a lot of rubbish talked in football. Players play for their country because they are good enough. Players play because they are the right character. Do we honestly believe that a manager would not select a player for any other reason than he did not believe that he was the right man for the job?'

Howe was one of the men axed by Hoddle when he took control of the England side after the European Championships in June 1996, but he isn't bitter and has a high regard for Hoddle. He gets angry about the complaint that Hoddle was overlooked as a player but he is backing him all the way as England coach.

Howe adds: 'I want to emphasise that Glenn as a player had more technical ability than most others. He stood out. I can always remember playing possession games in training, when a group form a circle with one player in the middle. The players on the outside have to pass the ball – one touch – around without the spare player gaining possession. If he does the last player to pass the ball goes into the middle, and so on. Glenn never went into the middle. In the end people would slam the ball against him, just hoping he would make a mistake or lose control. He never did.

'He had this knack of being able to control the ball at whatever angle it was hit at him. And he could control it with different parts of his body. It was uncanny. He was born with a gift, an instinct for the ball. If you're lucky you have a feeling inside that tells you that whatever happens, you can control it. It's a lovely feeling to have and very few players enjoy it. Having got the ball under control Glenn could knock the ball anywhere on the pitch. If you put down a circle of plastic or anything like that, he would drop the ball into it, from sixty yards.

'Glenn is without question the best passer of a ball I have worked with, bar none, and he was nonchalant with it. He would just give this lovely impression of getting the ball to wherever he wanted it. And he did.'

So why didn't he play more, Don? Again, it is the same answer – it is down to the individual to impress the manager. We can only assume that there was something missing in Hoddle's make-up as a footballer. There certainly was in the eyes of Burkinshaw, Greenwood, Robson and Howe. They appreciated his skill, his passing and his balance, but there was something wrong with his work rate, his tackling, his attitude.

Howe also dismisses the argument that Hoddle played in the wrong era – that he was unlucky with the game being so physical and the tackle from behind not having been vetoed. 'It isn't an argument,' says Howe. 'What about Puskas and Maradona? They coped. What about Law and Charlton? They coped. You must not make excuses for Glenn as a player.

'I don't think he would be looking for excuses either. He was always a student of the game and talked tactics. He looked at the game from all aspects and he was clearly interested in the skilful side of it and its development. He was the one who wanted to talk football until midnight when we were with the England players as a group, although at that stage I didn't see him as a manager.

'His ideas were often refreshing. He would come up with an idea for a free kick and I would think to myself, Bloody hell, that's brilliant. Why didn't I think of that?

'Now he's got the chance to put all those ideas into practice and good luck to him. I'm certainly not bitter at being left out of his backroom team. That's part of football. Someone new arrives and wants his own staff. No, I had some great years with England and working again with Terry Venables in the build-up and during the European Championships was a wonderful bonus for me. Glenn is very much his own man and knows what he wants. Good luck to him. I'm supporting him from the outside.

'It's interesting that he's been thrown into a World Cup qualifying situation. He has to pick sides and players to win matches. That is exactly what he experienced as a player, from the other side. Managers looked at him and thought to themselves, Is he the player for this job? and made the decision. Now Glenn is looking at players and making the same decision. Perhaps when his career is over there will be players who thought they should have won more caps under his control.

'It's very important for him to be single-minded, and I know that he's very much that. You listen but the decisions have to be yours. He is very open about his ideas and he and I had a long chat once at a youth coaching seminar. I'll tell you what, there were people on that course who were in awe of him. He came over as a relaxed, confident, single-minded person. He is also a realist. He knows his job is to get England to the World Cup finals.

'Qualifying for major tournaments is interesting. You pick sides and get results to get you to the finals and then when you have qualified you relax briefly before starting again to win the damn thing. No, I'm impressed with Glenn. He knows where he's going. He knows what he's doing and what he wants. There will be a few jolts along the way, but I get the impression he is ready and enjoying this job. Good luck to him. He has matured and grown up quickly.'

Burkinshaw, however, has changed his opinion somewhat. He now says: 'I suppose if people had believed in him more – yes, including me – he would have been an even better player. It was always this work rate thing, wasn't it? That was the stumbling block. In any other nation the team would have been moulded for him. We weren't prepared to do that.'

It's a great irony that when Hoddle finished playing, Swindon, Chelsea and then England really wanted him as a manager, but as a player people were not entirely convinced, especially with England.

When Hoddle returned from one England tour he was so fed up with English football he would have signed for a foreign club there and then had they been waiting at Luton Airport. He lived through the nightmare of the defeat in Oslo in 1981 and went to Spain in 1982 for his first World Cup finals. At one stage it looked as though the Falklands War would stop England travelling to play in a tournament alongside Argentina, but the government made a decision to play on and Hoddle went with Greenwood's squad of 22.

Hoddle was sub for the first game against France – a 3-1 victory which included Bryan Robson's fastest World Cup goal after 27 seconds. He made his World Cup debut in the 2-0 win over Czechoslovakia, coming on for the injured Bryan Robson at half-time. He played the full game against Kuwait, a disappointing match with England relying on a Trevor Francis goal for an unimpressive 1-0 victory. Next came Spain and West Germany. Two goalless draws meant that England went home without being beaten and having only conceded one goal.

For the first time at international level Hoddle experienced tears in the dressing room; grown men crying after the draw with Spain that meant the end of the adventure. Greenwood, in his last game before he retired, told his players to hold their heads high with pride. But it wasn't easy. Football is a wonderfully emotional game and players savour the highs and suffer the lows. This was a low that sticks in Hoddle's memory.

Hoddle had two more major finals to play in before it was all over. In the 1986 World Cup in Mexico when, at last, he was a regular, he started all the matches, against Portugal, Morocco and Poland in the group, then against Paraguay. After that came the 'Hand of God' quarter-final, when Maradona scored with his hand and then produced one of the greatest goals football has ever seen when he ran from the halfway line, beating five England players, before rounding Peter Shilton. 'It was just a genius at work,' says Hoddle. Hoddle returned to England a regular, he thought, but the doubts remained. The consistency still wasn't there for some people, including the manager Robson.

In the 1988 European Finals in Germany, Hoddle was sub against the Republic of Ireland when Ray Houghton's goal gave England one of their most embarrassing moments. I can still see Hoddle now, sitting on the grass, kicking his heels – he thought he should have been playing and his body language made that clear.

He started in the 3-1 defeat by Holland that saw Marco Van Basten produce a stunning hat-trick and then played against Russia in the game that was to send England home and prove to be Hoddle's last at international level. England lost 3-1 and it was a bitterly disappointing way to end. The team, just for the record, was Woods, G. Stevens, Sansom, Hoddle, Watson, Adams, Robson, T. Steven, McMahon, Lineker and Barnes. Subs used were Webb for McMahon and Hateley for Lineker. It was a shame-faced England who returned home, with the Russians declaring England were twenty years behind the rest of the world and the critics saying that Robson must go and the team be broken up. In many ways it was the end of an era. Robson survived for another two years, but Hoddle and others did not. So has Hoddle learnt from his and others' mistakes? Greenwood and Wenger have both revealed that as a person and player Hoddle lacked confidence, yet behind the mask there is a stubborn, single-minded person, which emerged when he was ready to manage.

Wenger was the key. He gave him the confidence he lacked, and the belief that others had failed to find. Hoddle found what he was looking for; not in playing for England but in going to Monaco and meeting Wenger.

Wenger had convinced him that he would make a good coach and had exactly the right credentials.

As he flew back from Monaco in order to find out, a million things went through his mind. Would he play again? He certainly had to get fit. And would anyone want him as their manager? After all, he had never done it before. He didn't have to wait long for an answer.

12 England Coach

Let's be perfectly honest: Glenn Hoddle is lucky to be England coach. His record at club level was not outstanding and he was only manager in Europe for one season. He was only 38 years old, the youngest man to get the job, and he was not the Football Association's first choice.

But he had two big assets in his favour: he was Glenn Hoddle, a name that conjures up pictures of magnificent football, entertainment and performance, and his image was perfect. The men who run our game had lived through two years of controversy with Terry Venables and they vowed never to experience it again. They'd had enough of looking over their shoulders and turning to the back pages of the tabloids with dread. No, they needed someone who could play the game properly and who had the right image. Enter Glenn Hoddle. He was a safe bet.

What the FA didn't realise when they made their decision was that there is far more to Hoddle than just pretty football and a clean-cut image. He is a tough man of great principle; a deep-thinking religious man who knows exactly what he wants. Neither did the people inside Lancaster Gate realise that Hoddle had been thinking about becoming England manager – or coach, as they like to call it – for a long, long time. He was, he knew, made for the job, and he had already been formulating plans in his mind.

Terry Venables' resignation before the European Championships was one of the great pieces of mismanagement in our football history. It was a typical FA cock up. There have been various reasons given for Venables' resignation, but they are all clouded in mystery. No one has really said why he left, not even Venables himself.

The reason that Venables gave was that the FA would not extend his contract, but the fact is that Venables signed a two-year contract on the understanding that it would not be reviewed until after the European finals. However, when his future was in serious doubt, he then said he had to quit to concentrate on the court cases against Alan Sugar, the *Daily Mirror*, BBC Television and *Panorama*. The argument was eventually changed. Whatever the truth, and there is always a grey area with Terry, he should still be in charge today.

Why did Venables deserve a new contract before the finals? What would have happened if Euro 96 had been a complete shambles and he had already signed another three-year contract? Of course he wanted security but surely he had to prove himself in a competition proper before he got it, especially as two years of friendlies had hardly convinced anyone that he was going to get it right on the night.

The man who gave him the job, and who helped choose Glenn Hoddle, dismisses Venables' claims that he was not offered a new contract. Sir Bert Millichip, who retired as chairman of the Football Association after the European Championships in June 1996, says: 'Despite what has been said and written, Terry Venables would still be manager today if he had ever said that he had said to me, officially, that he wanted to stay. But he never did. And that is a fact.

'In fact, I asked Terry for the last time, just twenty seconds before going into the meeting to rubber stamp his successor, if he would change his mind, and he said no. I could not do any more than that.

'The reason he left has nothing to do with a new contract. That is nonsense. Rubbish. I verbally offered him a new contract for two more years until 1998. I wanted him to stay.'

These revelations made by Millichip will no doubt shock a number of people. It was generally thought that the FA were happy to see the back of Venables. Not so, according to the chairman.

Millichip adds: 'The reason he left has to be over the court cases, it can be nothing else. We never got down to discussing a new contract because he never wanted to. He had made up his mind that he was going and there was nothing I could do to stop him.' Millichip is quick to point out that, as chairman, he carried a lot of weight. 'Had I announced to the committee that I wanted Terry to stay, and there were others who didn't want him, then I like to think they would have listened to me. But Terry didn't want to stay, and that was the end of the story.'

A sub-committee of the international committee – consisting of Millichip, chief executive Graham Kelly, Southampton director Keith Wiseman (elected FA Chairman after Sir Bert's retirement) and Liverpool director Noel White – was chosen to find Venables' successor. Once again headhunter Jimmy Armfield, the former Blackpool and England full back and former Leeds and Bolton manager, went out into the game to discover who the professionals wanted and, more to the point, who was happy to take the job on.

When Armfield asked managers, coaches, players, scouts and even media men who should manage England after the sacking of Graham Taylor, there was a unanimous vote for Venables. He was the best coach in the business, he was available and he was just right for the job, but because of his controversial business dealings the FA had to be persuaded. Indeed, when first told that the man the game wanted was Venables, Millichip said, 'Over my dead body.' This time Armfield found a different problem. No one really wanted the job, except, of course, Hoddle.

When speculation was rife, Hoddle stated that he had not had any contact with the FA or Armfield. 'Until I am asked I cannot comment,' he said. Hoddle, in fact, was approached in March 1996 by Armfield and asked if he would be interested in taking over from Venables. Hoddle said he would but was told to keep the conversation a secret and sit tight. He then waited patiently, knowing that Armfield was talking to other contenders, and reading with interest when other managers made it clear that they were not interested in the job.

Kevin Keegan told Armfield for the second time that he didn't want the job. Bryan Robson, the man who had worked under Venables for two years and the man Tel was grooming as his successor, said he wasn't ready. Alex Ferguson and Gerry Francis were discussed but Armfield got no encouragement. Frank Clark did not rule out the idea altogether, but he wasn't sure if he wanted the hassle that went with the job. Hoddle did. He knew he was made for it and he couldn't wait to start.

Chelsea knew their manager would be a candidate, but they didn't know he had been approached in March or that he had told the FA he was interested. Chelsea expected him to discuss a new contract with them even though Ken Bates was happy to see the back of him. It is impossible to know what would have happened to Hoddle had he not been offered the England job, but it was rumoured that Chelsea were ready to offer him a new £300,000 a year contract – £50,000 more than he gets with England. But would Hoddle have stayed, come the crunch, if Bates had remained in powerful control? The late Matthew Harding had his doubts while Paul Miller, his friend and former Spurs colleague, says that Glenn would definitely have walked away.

Bates said that Hoddle would be insane to take the England job. Swindon chairman Ray Hardman knew he would go and says: 'I thought to myself, It serves you right, Ken, because Ken was going through what I suffered at Swindon. We are both victims of Hoddle's ambition. The moment I heard that the FA wanted him I knew he would take it. It was not in doubt. We are talking about a very ambitious, strong-minded individual. His career has been on an upward curve ever since he kicked a football for the first time. We have all been just stepping stones to the job he always wanted.

'I believe it's a great choice. I'm sure Glenn will bring to the England team what no one has brought before. We hear so much about the continentals and under Hoddle we will catch them up and overtake them. Glenn played with the best and he wants the best from everything he does. He put Swindon on a new planet, he was building an era at Chelsea, and he will not be satisfied until England are world champions. I believe we will win the World Cup under his control.'

Hardman's confidence was not shared by everyone. Former England star Geoff Hurst, the only man to score a hat-trick in a World Cup final, said bitterly, 'Show us your medals,' and many others thought the job had come too soon for him. It was a case of déjà vu for Hoddle. As a player so many questioned his ability to play the modern game, and now as England manager they were giving reasons for him not getting the job long before he started.

His friend, Paul Miller, has no doubts. 'You only get offered England once and Glenn knew that. If he felt that it was too early he did not let that influence his decision because he knew that he had to say yes. He would have liked two more seasons at Chelsea because he was confident of getting it completely right and winning something. But Glenn Hoddle was always born before his time and had to take it. He knew he was destined and it was no real surprise to him when he got the call.

'He is the youngest manager to do the job, and the richest. He doesn't need to earn. He is, however, fiercely ambitious and very patriotic. He badly wants England to do well. He is also the most successful player to become England manager. I think that's significant.

'Glenn has also become a very serious thinker about the game. Sometimes I wish he would lighten up. If things go wrong he will simply draw ranks. He has good people around him and he'll do the job his way. He very rarely changes his mind. He knows that the press needs to be handled, especially when things go wrong, as they probably will at some stage. He was hurt by the press in the old days. He hated them. It's probably why he's so wary of them today. One thing, Glenn never forgets. He has got an elephant's memory. Cross Glenn and you have a problem.'

Garth Crooks, another former team mate of Hoddle's, reveals a story that emphasises Hoddle's determination and desire to become manager of England. Crooks was working for *The Sunday Times* when he told his editor that he wanted to write a story about Glenn Hoddle one day becoming manager of England. Crooks explains: 'I just had this feeling, a premonition if you like, that Glenn was destined to go right to the top as a manager. My editor asked me if I thought I could get him to talk about it. I believed I could and hot-footed it down to Swindon.'

Crooks was surprised at the reaction he got from Hoddle.

'I spoke with him at length and he told me, "Garth, you're right, it is a job I've always wanted." ' But Hoddle swore Crooks to secrecy and would not talk about it himself. 'Glenn said that he would be grateful if his dream remained out of the public. I begged him to change his mind. I tried for at least a year, but he was adamant. It was too early and I never got the story. I knew though that Glenn wanted the job, and he always believed he would get it. Mine was just a gut feeling. Having played with him and been close to him I felt that not only was this man capable, but if things went right, he could change the face of English football.

'Now he has got it there are many questions. Has he got the players? He caught a cold early on at Chelsea and his job was only half finished. Can players change for Hoddle? Can you teach an old dog new tricks? Sol Campbell is a new breed of centre half. Can he be comfortable on the ball all over the pitch at the very highest level? Sometimes players find answers about themselves when they work for a particular person. Terry Venables was very good at asking things about his players. He planted things in your mind that sent you away searching for answers. If Glenn can take the same approach, and I am sure he will, then he could find players doing things and producing form that they didn't think they were capable of. The opening of a player's mind is so important. To be responsive and flexible.

'Let's take Paul Gascoigne. Glenn inherits him at a time when so many people are almost ready to write him off. I suspect that Glenn will see a lot more in Gazza, and do his best to bring it out. The first position Glenn himself played in the system that he employs, and has always done through his managerial career, was sweeper. I believe that he can turn Gascoigne into an outstanding spare defender. If Glenn can get Gascoigne to mentally focus then sweeper could be the answer for him. It would be a new challenge for Gazza without the physical demands on him. Glenn will be looking forward to all these kinds of challenges.

'Isn't it ironic that the very men who want him to lead a revolution of English football are the same people who could not see his genius as a player? As a player he was a victim of soccer philosophy. Now the FA have turned to him to influence so many about how the game should be played. They are looking at the continent and how they do things and putting their faith in Hoddle. Their change of attitude is one of the jokes of the modern game.'

It was early evening one Tuesday night when Glenn answered the call from Graham Kelly that he had half been expecting. He knew the FA had still not named their new man, and Jimmy Armfield had not got back to him, one way or the other, as he had promised.

Hoddle asked Kelly for 48 hours to think about his decision. He wanted to speak to his wife Anne, his agent and close friend

Dennis Roach and he had always promised another good friend, Chelsea director Matthew Harding, that he would never say yes to the England job without consulting him first.

By the Wednesday morning the story had broken in the newspapers. The FA, however, had still not admitted that Hoddle was their choice. 'It is all speculation as far as we are concerned,' said an FA spokesman. But in a spectacular piece of mismanagement on the FA's part, Hoddle was simultaneously telling reporters that he had been offered the job and Matthew Harding was confirming Chelsea's end of the story.

Hoddle claims that he eventually made his decision in the early hours of Thursday morning after much soul-searching and talking with Roach. What seems more likely is that he had made up his mind to say yes the moment he heard Kelly's voice on the other end of the line.

Of course he had to say yes. Here was an ambitious young man who desperately wanted to manage his country. The money wasn't important, which is a great position to be in because it always gives you the option to walk away. It is fascinating that in this era of huge salaries that half of today's top managers are millionaires with no financial concerns. Hoddle, for sure, Trevor Francis, Bryan Robson, Ray Wilkins, Ruud Gullit, Arsene Wenger . . . the list is long and impressive. They can all say they have had enough whenever they want.

Sir Bert Millichip was impressed when, as chairman of the FA, he met Hoddle for the first time. In contrast, he had been extremely wary and worried when he had interviewed Venables two and a half years earlier. He had to be won over by the former England coach, but Hoddle was different and Millichip admits: 'I looked upon Glenn Hoddle as a gentleman, not necessarily a football manager. I found him very presentable and articulate.

'I admit that after a successful European Championship it seemed a shame and unnecessary to change the coach, but that was down to Venables. In Hoddle we had the ideal replacement. The general opinion of the committee was that it was essential that we went for someone with international playing experience, and it was a bonus that Hoddle had played abroad. I remember watching him closely as an England player and I admired his skill and appreciated him as a player.

'I have no idea whether everyone had the same opinion as me about Hoddle the player. That was a personal view. But we all agreed that he was the man to be given the chance of managing the team. He certainly played the type of skilful football all the committee appreciates and that we need at international level now.

'The game in this country is changing, and will continue to change. They have changed in Europe and if we don't continue to expand and open our minds then we won't keep up with what's happening abroad. Hoddle fitted into that plan, too.'

The image of the manager was vitally important for Millichip. He had been persuaded to employ Venables, but over the years had grown much closer to him than he had ever thought possible. He admired the England manager, and was extremely proud of the team's superb performance in the European Championships. But for Millichip there was always something in the background, even though Venables repeatedly told him there was nothing else to come out of the woodwork. There was also the worry that Venables would have to up and leave for some reason, be it a court case or problems with another business venture.

'When you appoint a new England manager you do it usually for two reasons: that the man in possession has come to the end of a successful career and wants to stand down, or there is an understanding between you and him, or that it has not worked out, like the situation with Graham Taylor. When we appointed Taylor I never dreamt that he would be my last appointment. It depended on his success, of course, but I never saw him lasting more than four years.'

And indeed he did not. Taylor was appointed in 1990 to succeed Bobby Robson and left, in controversy and shame, early in 1993. It begs the question, doesn't it, why he was given the job in the first place if Millichip wasn't convinced about his long-term lasting? Still, that's history, and another story.

'With Venables I didn't know; it was impossible to gauge,' adds the former chairman. We knew he had problems and we never knew about the extent they would interfere with him doing the job. I feel now that we are in good hands. Under Glenn Hoddle I am greatly optimistic and leave the chair encouraged that as a nation we can go forward confidently.'

Hoddle becomes England's ninth and youngest manager behind Sir Walter Winterbottom, Sir Alf Ramsey, the late Joe Mercer, the late Don Revie, Ron Greenwood, Bobby Robson, Graham Taylor and Terry Venables. Millichip adds: 'I was not aware that he was the youngest manager until you told me. It shows that age didn't come into it. We didn't want an old man and yet we never asked Hoddle's age, or sought it.

'We discussed several people and Hoddle's name was always right up there. Some were crossed off for various reasons and in the end it was a unanimous decision to give it to Glenn Hoddle.

'I like to think that under my chairmanship English football has achieved a lot of things. We have climbed a few problems, particularly hooliganism, and I go with our game catching up quickly with what is happening elsewhere. For someone like myself it's very difficult to tell the managers in the game how they should play football. Hoddle clearly wants to play the continental way. This I am sure will rub off on other clubs. That is important for our future.

'I know there has always been a problem about getting the players together for the England coach. I have sympathy and believe that the manager needs at least ten days with his squad to prepare for a game. It is, however, not easy to organise.

'The way Chelsea played under his control had a bearing on our decision. I thought Chelsea were the most improved team in the Premier League; they played some delightful football.

'One day I would like to see England play the same way, and with the same success.

'I hadn't spoken to Hoddle before we met across the table at our first interview. He came across well; an impressive, intelligent man with strong views about football. He clearly saw a long-term picture of what he wanted to achieve. We were happy to give him a four-year contract because that allowed him to qualify for the World Cup, and then beyond. It has been asked since why Venables was not, initially, given four years. Simple. Because he didn't ask for it, was not offered it, and – because of the problems that surrounded him at first – did not warrant it.

'Hoddle has been thrust right into the deep end. There aren't many managers who have to start with vital World Cup qualifying matches. It'll take a few games before we can judge him properly and yet the early signs are positive and good. He will bed down into the job. And he must do it with no friendlies, no get-togethers and hardly knowing his players. It's a big task and needed the right choice.

'There will always be respect for Glenn Hoddle because of the way he played the game. Unlike people like Kevin Keegan then and Alan Shearer now, he was never a regular with England, not enough for people to really appreciate him. It is much the same way as we look upon Matthew Le Tissier now. Very skilful but can he do it at international level? Hoddle was always looked upon as a very special player, better than the others, even if he was not selected that many times. To have that tag is a great way to start a managerial career.'

A glowing reference indeed from the outgoing chairman. Millichip says what he means, however, and he firmly believes that Hoddle is going to do a great job for England. He has admitted that Taylor was never long term in his own mind and that the FA were never sure how long Venables would last. Hoddle is different. 'I can see him staying ten years minimum,' says Millichip. 'Two World Cups, at least. If he stays that long then it will be guaranteeing England success and, significantly, stability.' And that, after all, is the bottom line. Success. Glory for the nation. To make England World Cup winners again.

Hoddle believes he will be successful. He would never go public with such statements, because he is not that sort of person, but he knows he is going to turn England into World Cup winners – maybe not in France 1998, but one day. He's got the kind of gut feeling that has followed him all of his career. When he went for his interview with the FA he knew he would get the job. He knew because something told him. From the moment Jimmy Armfield asked him how he felt about the job, he knew.

'Some people say that I am not experienced enough,' says Hoddle. 'But how do you gauge experience? By grey hairs? A certificate? I'm ready for this. I would not have taken it on if I didn't think I could do it, or that we would not qualify for the World Cup, and that is my first target.

'We have the players and the talent; everything is there. I am going to enjoy myself because for me this is the greatest job any footballer – any English footballer with ambition – can have. I can't wait.'

13 Game Two, Game Won

Wednesday 9 October 1996
England 2 Poland 1
Scorers: Shearer (2)

Glenn Hoddle has never looked completely relaxed at public functions. His body language suggests that he finds the media side of football a nuisance, and he certainly doesn't enjoy public speaking, giving press conferences, personal appearances and being at the beck and call of the men who have turned football into the huge billion pound industry it is today.

Even now, Hoddle would rather be playing. Who wouldn't with his skill? His personality on the pitch was vastly different to when he put on the manager's hat. On the pitch he was arrogant, loud and dominant, but when he became a manager that personality was never transferred. Certainly, if a prime quality the Football Association was looking for was media awareness, then Hoddle would not have been considered.

At Chelsea he could be difficult or unobtainable, then relaxed and informative. If he felt strongly about something then he would say so. With England he certainly handled the Paul Gascoigne affair magnificently, but there is no real consistency to his off-pitch performance – reminiscent of the complaint coaches made when he was a Spurs and England player.

That isn't to say that Hoddle doesn't have immense faith and confidence in his own ability, it's just that confidence is not displayed in public. But while results are, of course, the priority, football today is so big that Hoddle *is* public property, whether he likes it or not. And yet you get the impression that he would simply like to stay on the training pitch with his squad, and that he fears the media want something from him.

Of course, he had a hard act to follow. Terry Venables was a master of the media game. His personality was infectious and he was always available for public functions, weddings and after-dinner speaking. Sir Bert Millichip, at first so wary of him, finally admitted, 'Venables won me over with his charm and personality.'

Previous England managers have all found it hard to cope with the media, with the exception of Bobby Robson, who was a dream. You warmed to Robson because he was so honest, and you couldn't fall out with him because he wouldn't let you.

Graham Taylor tried to be far too clever. He employed a public relations advisor and carried out stunts simply to satisfy the thirst of the journalists who travelled everywhere with him. After a home draw with Holland, when England surrendered a 2-0 lead, he arrived at the press conference the following morning and sang a Buddy Holly song: 'Oh misery, misery, what's going to become of me?' Then he brought an alarm clock to a press conference because the journalists had complained that he had only given them twenty minutes the previous time. Taylor was the first to expose Gascoigne's drinking problem. Refuelling, he called it, and he spoke about it for the first time in Norway, when Gascoigne himself had just given a superb press conference. Next morning, the headlines had changed from good old Gazza to Paul Gascoigne the drunk. Taylor thought he was doing us a favour – and the copy was marvellous while it lasted – but all he did was help cut his own throat.

Before Taylor and Robson, Ron Greenwood was hopeless with the media, the late Don Revie was too tricky for his own good and Sir Alf Ramsey was legendary for his contempt for the newspapers. But times have changed dramatically. They call our national side 'Team England' now, and part of that team are the fans and the media. We are all in this showbiz era together. Including Glenn.

All this leads us to Hoddle's first home game as England coach, the biggest public appearance of his career. Wembley, packed full of expectancy, hope and glory on a mild October evening, all eyes on Hoddle. But it certainly wasn't a dramatic entrance from the new coach. Hoddle emerged a few minutes after his team, walking around the old dog track, waving occasionally and striding forth to get to his place. It was impossible to tell what was going through his mind.

His face showed no emotion but Hoddle was proud. He had desperately wanted the job and Wembley for his first home game was one of the special moments of his career. Nothing, however, was going to deflect his mind from beating Poland. He admitted: 'Image is important, I know that, and is part of the job, but it is not the number one in my eyes. Let's qualify first and then I will think about image. I hate wearing ties. Sometimes I have to do it. If I wear a tie at Wembley on match night it's not going to get me three points against Poland.

'I love Wembley. I have had a great relationship with the place and the fans since I was twenty-one. Nothing else matters to me except getting England to the World Cup. I want to win this game desperately. Style and how we play comes into it. First, I want to win.'

Hoddle slightly altered his squad and there were two interesting new names. Dominic Matteo, the young Liverpool defender so highly rated in the game, pushed through for the first time. It was a surprise considering his age and lack of experience, but Hoddle proved that age is not important to him. 'It doesn't matter how old they are. Over thirty or under twenty, I will pick them if I believe they are good enough and are the right players at the right time.' Hoddle has asked all of his backroom staff to watch Matteo, including his assistant John Gorman, and all the reports were glowing. Hoddle and Gorman, when they were together at Swindon, had tried to sign Matteo on loan. 'He was a left back then and all credit to the people at Liverpool who have helped develop him so well and quickly,' said Hoddle. He clearly saw Matteo as one of his players for down the line when England qualified. Matteo, however, reported with an injury and hardly trained with the rest of the squad. He was sent home after treatment and examination by the club doctor.

The other significant new face was that of Paul Merson, self-confessed gambler, alcoholic and drug taker. Merson was fighting back strongly, desperately trying to beat his addiction, and Hoddle liked what he saw. The old Merson was re-emerging, certainly on the pitch, and Hoddle's caring nature didn't allow anything to cloud his mind. It was a quality that was to keep Paul Gascoigne in the team for the match in Georgia, when many people wanted him dropped in shame.

Hoddle could see how hard Merson was fighting for his life and career and was happy to help him, as well as pick him. 'People need goals when they are going through a bad time in their lives,' he said. 'I have no idea whether you ever get completely over the problems that Paul is suffering with but he is proving a good example to anyone with similar problems. Those not in the public eye will use Paul as an inspiration. All credit to him, and those people who have stood by him.

'It takes a lot to come out and say things about yourself, as he has. In many respects you feel better about yourself and you are no longer living a lie. I suppose this is the start of his rehabilitation and I am sure being picked by England will help him. Paul has been selected for no other reason than he is a damn good footballer and I believe that he deserves to be in the squad. I am not a counsellor. I have no idea how long it will be if he ever gets over the other thing – if he ever does completely.'

Another player with problems, who didn't make the squad, was Merson's Arsenal skipper Tony Adams. Adams, England's inspirational captain during the European Championships, had just returned to playing after a knee operation but was not yet ready for international football. Until the eve of naming his squad for this Poland game, however, Hoddle hadn't spoken to Adams, which was a strange piece of man-management by the new England coach. Adams, surely, would figure in his long-term plans, so it was extraordinary that no contact was made.

A few days before Hoddle named his squad, Adams led Arsenal in their UEFA Cup journey to Germany, for the tie with Borussia Monchengladbach. On that trip Adams admitted that he had not spoken to Hoddle and the story got wide publicity. It was treated as a snub by the England coach, who ended the silence with a telephone call the night Adams returned from Germany. 'I have now spoken to Tony,' Hoddle explained. 'It was on the football front and there is no problem. This is no time for me to talk about his drink problem, that will come when I see him face to face. This game has come just too soon for him. He is not one hundred per cent yet. When he is he will be in the forefront of my plans.

'With people like Tony out it's an opportunity for others to come in and show what they can do. I can only repeat that Tony is right in my mind.'

But it was still a strange way to treat Adams, a hero in June and vulnerable after exposing his personal problems. Surely a consoling phone call before the eve of an international he wasn't picked for was the very least Hoddle could have done, and again questions Hoddle's man-management and media dealings. He does not find it easy, that's clear, but a simple telephone call would have prevented any confusion.

Hoddle is a master at controlling his emotions. He once rang me at my home, bitterly disappointed with a headline that my office had put on a story after Chelsea's 2-0 FA Cup semi-final victory over Luton at Wembley. Hoddle had revealed afterwards that a little voice had told him months before that Chelsea would get to the Cup Final. It was a vision, he said. Playing on his beliefs in God, the headline screamed: 'God Tells Hod Your Cup Runneth Over.' He did not like it, told me that he thought it poked fun at him and his beliefs and threatened to sue the paper. It was a no-nonsense phone call, but it certainly wasn't a shouting, really angry Hoddle.

I had a certain amount of sympathy with him but did feel he was overreacting. If you reveal your beliefs you open yourself up to smart headlines, particularly in the tabloids. Adams and Merson's booze problems will be used against them many times, probably for the rest of their careers.

Hoddle gave an insight into his emotions as he prepared for his first home game as coach. He admitted: 'There must be no emotion from me. You have to control it. The main thing for me and the staff to do is get the players relaxed and ready before they go out. If they see me uptight and nervous that's no good. If a player is too uptight he cannot perform.'

The crowd were certainly ready, waiting and emotional. After the passion and excitement of the European Championships, Wembley was on the edge of its seat again and the expectancy was high. Hoddle knew that it was important to use the backing of another capacity crowd, without letting the waves of patriotism affect his players. 'We have to use the crowd as a major advantage,' said Hoddle. 'They showed in Euro 96 how important they can be.

'I feel that the spectators have to be a part of what we are trying to create. Everyone must play a part in Team England. Having said that, players have to be able to cope with frustration from the fans. If things go wrong and the crowd are restless, you have to be able to cocoon yourself away – yes, even out there on the pitch. You must be able to do your own thing without being affected by supporters. You have to keep focused on things that will get us results. You must keep your nerve. That is when you need experienced players. Keep playing well and wait for the moment.'

Wait for the moment. It is a phrase continually used by Ruud Gullit at Chelsea and one that is popular on the continent. Hoddle added: 'At international level you have to wait because the moment does not come along so often as in club football. When it does, you must be mentally and physically ready for it.'

Winning was all-important to Hoddle and England. He knew that getting his team to France 1998 was more important than anything else: result first, performance second. It was not an argument close to his heart but one that was relevant.

'This will not be my England team until six or seven sides down the line,' said Hoddle. 'It will not feel like my team until probably after we have qualified for the finals. I can put up with a stop-start along the way just as long as we get there. Qualifying football is so different to that of a tournament. You have to pick a side to win an individual game. In tournaments a pattern develops and you keep it going; in qualifying you go for the win at all costs.

'I will put up with imperfections along the way just as long as we are getting results. I do not believe there is any such thing as perfection in football.'

It was funny to hear Hoddle talking like this, because here was someone you always associated with perfection. The perfect pass, the perfect temperament, the perfect player . . . the perfect manager? We were about to find out.

Hoddle, looking back to Moldova, didn't think England's passing had been good enough. 'We looked as if we had a cutting edge but there was not enough quality in the last third of the pitch.' Now Hoddle was confident. He expected to win the game, and expected to qualify. 'I would not have taken this job on if I did not expect to be in France.'

The team he sent out showed two changes from Moldova. Gary Pallister, who looked shaky and not completely fit in Moldova, was replaced by Steve McManaman. This meant a shuffle, with Gary Neville moving from wing back to one of the three markers and David Beckham taking over as the man to work the right flank. It was up front that was interesting. Hoddle left out Nick Barmby and paired Alan Shearer with his Newcastle partner Les Ferdinand. It was an explosive-looking attack and one that the country had called for, including Newcastle manager Kevin Keegan.

Like Hoddle, Wembley was significant for Alan Shearer because it was his first appearance as captain. How similar these two men are – cool, no nerves, solid temperament. Perhaps unfairly, some would say boring. Shearer, the established winner, the man who scores goals for fun. Hoddle, who so desperately wants to be a winner.

Nothing, it seems, ruffles Shearer. Not his price tag, not the media, not captaining England, nothing. He admits: 'I never suffer from nerves. Not inside or outside football. I can't think of anything that phases me.' Going for goal in the last minute of a World Cup Final? 'No, that would be enjoyable, not nervous.' Pressed, Shearer did say that emerging from the tunnel at Wembley for the first time as captain of his country would send the goosebumps on the back of his neck into overtime. So the ice can at least be cracked, if only on the surface. But thank goodness for Shearer. How we are going to need that ice-cool finishing along the way to France. His importance to the team was about to be proved.

It was an interesting team. Considering that Hoddle loves his sweeper system he had not yet seen an out-and-out man in that role in his first two internationals. This was probably due to the fact that in English football we do not possess a player who is marvellously comfortable on the ball in defence playing as the spare man. Frank LeBoeuf had arrived at Chelsea from France and was showing the rest how to do it. Hoddle himself played there at Swindon and Chelsea and we marvelled at the range of his passes, struck with time and space on his side.

In Moldova the three defenders were Gareth Southgate, Gary Pallister and Stuart Pearce, none of them graced with the touch of a paintbrush, and this time the three defenders were Pearce, Southgate and Gary Neville.

I have a lot of time for Southgate. At Palace he was an underrated player, a damn good leader and a sensible talker, and with England and Villa he has emerged as a professional footballer with real talent, on and off the pitch. He is a future England captain if he can continue his progress. However, Southgate's return to Wembley proved to be another nightmare for him. He looked uncomfortable from the first minute, and from his first ten touches, he gave the ball away eight times. His positioning was poor and his tackling sloppy, and his nerves soon spread to the rest of the side so that Poland took a shock lead through Marek Citko in the seventh minute. Football came home in June, but in seven minutes it was quickly going away again.

Southgate's performance – he later went off injured to be replaced by Gary Pallister – proved how hard Hoddle needs to search for his sweeper. He may have to convert someone, like he did himself towards the end of his career. Paul Ince is a possibility, but we would surely miss Ince's swashbuckling approach in midfield and his tackling, aggression and strength is needed on the road to the finals. Hoddle is known to like Liverpool's Jamie Redknapp, who, like Hoddle, certainly has the range of passing and the ability to strike a 40-yard pass from the depth of defence into enemy territory. And what about Paul Gascoigne? Does Gazza have it in him to play a more controlled game as sweeper? There is no denying his ability and it would suit his declining fitness. There are a lot of professionals who think Gascoigne would be the obvious sweeper.

Garth Crooks, who listened to Hoddle for years at Spurs, says: 'Has he got the players to do what he wants? It is the biggest question of all. Has he got defenders who are comfortable on the ball all over the pitch in the hot atmosphere of a World Cup? It is very difficult to teach an old dog new tricks. The young defenders coming through are players like Sol Campbell at Spurs. Is he good enough? Hoddle hasn't got that much time.

'Players can learn new things about themselves; have their minds opened. Terry Venables was very good at that. Terry asks questions about you. He makes you think. Glenn can do the same with Gazza. I am convinced that he can get a few more seasons out of Gascoigne. Sweeper could be his obvious position. It could open up a new chapter. I believe that Glenn is looking at

Gascoigne for the role. If Gazza can mentally focus on it I believe he can do it for Hoddle over the next few seasons.

'This question of players is interesting. Take Alan Shearer and Les Ferdinand. They are typical English centre forwards. Dangerous, quick, strong, good in the air, scorers of great goals, but are they international class as a pair? I'm not talking individually now. As a pair.'

There are times when you wonder if Shearer needs a partner at all. Wembley was one of them. He single-handedly won England the points and gave Hoddle the victory he so desired, with two superb first-half goals. The first, a header, was typical centre forward play. A cross from the right, the goalkeeper hesitant as he came out, almost certainly with one anxious eye on Shearer, who kept going, never flinching, to head England level.

The second was spectacular. A crashing shot from the edge of the area that gave him his thirteenth goal in 30 appearances and, most significantly of all, eight in his last seven games. It was finishing that had Hoddle drooling. 'He is already the best striker in Europe and wants to become the best in the world,' said the manager. 'You can see he has the credentials.'

Thank goodness for Shearer. No one else looked like scoring, especially Ferdinand. A draw would have been a fair result and for much of the game England were outplayed by a little Portuguese player called Piotr Nowark, who was everything Paul Gascoigne and Steve McManaman were not. Nowark, at 32, was the best player on the pitch by a distance. Hoddle would have admired his passing and his skill but not the beat he gave to his heart when in the second half he almost equalised himself and then set up chances that should have been taken.

It wasn't a good performance but it was a win, and Hoddle had told us that three points was all that mattered in these games, disregarding how you play. However, he could not have been satisfied with his team's performance – tactically, it was light years behind what Venables had shown the nation during Euro 96. Hoddle left to applause but the jury remained out. They would be back in February for the massive game against the Italians.

A lot had been made of Hoddle's nine days with the players. He had insisted on them staying together at the squad's Bisham training HQ near Maidenhead in Surrey, not even letting them go home for the weekend. He had been used to the pure professional approach of the continental player while living and playing in France, and he was determined to stamp that kind of ruling on England. 'I don't know what all the fuss is about,' said Hoddle at the time. 'This is what I want and this is what the players will do.

'They are representing their country and surely a few days of dedicated training and resting before an important international is not too much to ask? It's how they prepare abroad and if we're going to progress certain sacrifices have to be made. You can't achieve anything in life without dedication. A lot of people might feel we should do it differently. Well, my answer to that is that I'm the manager and we'll do it my way. The training needs to be right and the rest periods need to be right.'

Hoddle had his players for nine days altogether. Once training was over they were free to do anything around the hotel and a series of leisure activities were arranged by Hoddle and his staff, such as videos, snooker, pool and table tennis. The food was prepared especially and hand picked by Hoddle, and included plenty of pasta, soup and chicken with no skin. There was no red meat, no beer allowed before the game, and one glass of wine provided with the meal if they wanted it. If a player had a special request then the chef could prepare it, but only if Hoddle felt it was OK.

Pampered? Yes, but this is World Cup football. Getting to France means everything to so many people, and huge amounts of money to the country.

Sadly for Hoddle, you wouldn't have known the players had been together for nine days. There is a lot of work to be done. The only good thing to emerge from Wembley was that England won. Two games, six points, only one goal conceded. 'I would have settled for that,' said Hoddle. 'My job is to get England to the 1998 World Cup finals. If we do it we won't look back on this match and remember the disappointment.' Maybe not. It all depends on what happens in the future, of course. If England play like this again they won't qualify.

14 Game Three, Game Won

Saturday 9 November 1996
Georgia 0 England 2
Scorers: Sheringham, Ferdinand

This was unquestionably the greatest test of Glenn Hoddle's career and all eyes were on him. Would he, wouldn't he? And the subject was not even on-pitch. Hoddle, in his third match, found himself in the middle of a debate that split the country. Paul Gascoigne was a wife beater and there were admissions from Gazza and disturbing pictures of his wife to prove it.

Would God-loving Glenn forgive Gazza and pick him for England? Would the Football Association allow him to forgive? In the past they had frowned on certain selections and other controversies, so everybody was keen to find out whether the issue could be separated from the football.

You always had an opinion about Gascoigne. Wonderful player. Immature boy. Fool to himself. This, however, was different. He had beaten up wife Sheryl in a drunken rage and no one can condone such behaviour.

Hoddle had to decide. Gascoigne needs help, that is obvious, but could he have him pulling on the white shirt? And what would happen if Gascoigne scored the winning goal? Are we a country who can so easily turn a wife beater into a hero?

The mood swings of Gascoigne have been there for us all to witness, ever since he arrived into our lives during the 1990 World Cup, crying tears of heartbreak after being booked in the semi-final against Germany. The nation cried with him, and took this chubby boy, with the mischievous grin, to their hearts.

The headlines and the money rolled in. Gazzamania took over. Quite simply, he couldn't cope with it. This boy from Newcastle who happened to be born with genius in his feet became a millionaire almost overnight.

To cope he showed off. We loved him on the pitch when he acted the clown but then it went too far. We turned on him. It is a problem with the media today that we build them up and knock them down but some can cope with that pressure, some cannot. You just have to if you are in the public eye.

The pressure did eventually get to him, and he turned to drink. After the horrendous injury he suffered in the 1991 FA Cup Final, when he snapped knee ligaments following his ridiculous tackle on Nottingham Forest's Gary Charles, alcohol became a comfort and began to take over his life. He'd always enjoyed a pint but things quickly deteriorated into much more than that. I recall travelling with Gazza to Italy, on his way to meet his new club. When the stewardess asked Gazza, his brother Carl and infamous friend Jimmy Five Bellies what they wanted to drink, Gazza asked for a rum and port mix in a large glass. In the two hours it took to fly to Rome he had at least four of them. Later that afternoon he trained with Lazio.

Gascoigne's moods have dominated so many press conferences with England. One day he can be charming and chatty, the next he refuses to talk. He never attended a press conference during Euro 96, but he did talk before the 1996 match against Poland. I asked him a question and he snarled: 'You can fuck off, I'm not answering a question from you.' The next time I saw him he shook my hand and said, 'How are you, Brian?'

In there somewhere there is a different Gascoigne trying to get out. On odd occasions we have seen the caring, softer side of him. He does a lot of charity work and is exceptionally good when dealing with children. Hoddle saw that side of him. He looked deeper than most and decided that he wanted to help him – and that's why he picked him for the World Cup tie in Georgia.

What we will never know is whether it was the decision of a true Christian or an England coach determined not to lose one of his few world-class players, even if Gascoigne was half the player we had seen during and just after the 1990 World Cup. But Hoddle had to see enough good in Gazza to gamble on the fact that he wouldn't let him down. Hoddle the Christian, Hoddle the saviour – it would mean nothing if down the line Gazza went back to his old ways. There were a lot of people waiting to tell the England coach, 'We told you so.' Hoddle genuinely believed that Gascoigne could and would change his ways, something which many people, myself included, thought was wishful thinking. Indeed, there was the extraordinary situation after England's game in Georgia when Gazza, in his Glasgow Rangers gear, ran into the boardroom minutes before a Scottish League game and demanded a drink. He threw it down and went out to play.

Hoddle had always liked and appreciated Gascoigne the player. He had tried to sign him for Chelsea the previous season, at one stage asking to take him on loan. He also believed he could see beyond Gascoigne the footballer. From a distance Hoddle had become interested in the wayward character who could drink for England, let alone play for them. As Hoddle explained: 'I had always felt there was something there that I needed to talk to him about. This has brought it around.

'Had I signed him for Chelsea two years ago, when I first asked, then the problems might have been resolved by now.' This, perhaps, is the key comment by Hoddle in this amazing debate that dominated the build-up to a vital World Cup tie. Hoddle had wanted to help Gascoigne before he became a wife beater and long before he himself became England coach. The caring, forgiving side of the England coach's nature made Gascoigne a fascinating subject for him. It was like a doctor taking a great deal of interest in a patient and monitoring his rehabilitation. On that count, there was never a question in Hoddle's mind that he would discard Gascoigne. He told the FA that if Gascoigne was dropped it would push him back, perhaps beyond help and repair.

There is an argument, of course, that other wife beaters do not lose their jobs. But are they public figures, role models for kids, people who can influence so many?

Hoddle's explanation was deep, thorough and often touching. At his selection press conference he answered all questions honestly and didn't duck anything, apart from refusing to reveal details of Gascoigne's counselling, which was understandable. It was one of the best performances of Hoddle's management career in front of the media. It was a brilliant press conference and journalists afterwards couldn't believe how open the England coach had been. If only he could always be like that. It was a subject of course that allowed Hoddle to expand on something he had been interested in ever since he started to believe in God. Forgiveness.

In the two weeks prior to naming him in his squad, Hoddle met Gascoigne on a number of occasions. They met privately and Hoddle found that Gascoigne wanted to open up and discuss what he felt inside. The two men became close, and Hoddle established that Gazza did want help. Hoddle convinced Gascoigne that he would benefit from counselling and the sessions began immediately, Hoddle sitting in on some of them. Throughout this period he was constantly with Gazza. It was an extraordinary situation that developed behind the scenes, and only a few people knew what was happening – Hoddle and Gascoigne, of course, Gazza's Glasgow Rangers manager, Walter Smith, and one or two FA officials, including the new chairman Keith Wiseman.

'We all know that Paul needs help and guidance and that is what he is being given,' Hoddle explained. 'I have felt that Paul has needed this for some time [another significant Hoddle reaction] and his treatment will go on long after the Georgia match.

'I am prepared to give Paul this chance. To cast him outside now would be detrimental, long term for him and his family. I do not condone for one minute what Paul has done. But we all make mistakes; I made plenty when I was younger. I thought long and hard about this and this is my decision. He's in the squad.

'I think we should all realise that footballers have a lot more presure than other people. They are only human beings. Problems multiply because of the money, the fact that football is so big these days and the huge media attention.'

Hoddle is also determined to help Gascoigne the footballer by advising him on what to eat and drink, how to look after himself, when to take rest, and how to keep his body in better condition. Never before in the history of English football has a player received such treatment from his manager. Gascoigne is one lucky man. He is lucky that Hoddle was around to save him.

'For long-term recovery the best thing to do is keep him in the squad,' says Hoddle. 'I know that I'm not going to keep everyone happy over this, but I made the decision after talking to the boy and finding out all about him. There is a lot I cannot, and will not, discuss in public. This has taken a lot of energy and time. We have reached the first port of call with him. I have only just got my hands on him and significantly I have not had to persuade him to do anything.

'The ideal world would be for him to eventually become a role model, for kids and people with similar problems to those he has suffered. I know I keep going back to this thing of forgiveness but that is what this is. The very example of Christianity is forgiveness. If Joe Public had done the same and the police were not involved then he wouldn't have got the sack or lost his capacity to earn. We are helping Paul to change and that surely has to be a good thing.'

So Gazza was on the plane. So too were Paul Merson and Tony Adams, meaning that Hoddle had included a wife beater and two self-confessed alcoholics in his latest squad. Again, it was a first for England.

For Adams it was a significant return. Fit again and playing magnificently for his club, he was included while Alan Shearer was injured and not in the squad. No England team looks right without Adams. He is inspirational, a real leader and has grown even more in stature since revealing how he has been fighting the booze. There aren't many journalists on the England scene who don't have time for Tony Adams. Since his admission he has changed – he is easier to talk to, more approachable and someone who now offers a great deal of sense. The booze did terrible things to Tony Adams and now he is trying to find the real him.

The night of England's European Championship defeat by Germany was just a blur to Arsenal's captain. He had fought off the demand for a drink in China when the other England players went to the infamous session at the Jump Club because he knew what would have happened had he gone along too. Neither did he touch a drop at Bisham when the players locked themselves away for the Championships. Instead, he went to bed when the temptation was there.

But when Andreas Moller drove the decisive penalty past David Seaman, Adams's resolve broke. He had a drink in the dressing room after the match to drown his sorrow and bitterness, followed by a few more in the players' bar and then a lot more back at Bisham. He remembers talking to Terry Venables and Don Howe but not the conversation. When he woke up the next morning only Stuart Pearce and Gareth Southgate were left. The other England players had gone home, and Adams was amazed that no one was still drinking. But the skipper found some more mates and went on a three-day bender.

It was 16 August when the old life was left behind once and for all, a life that had seen Adams go to prison for a drink-driving offence. While he was in prison Glenn Hoddle wrote to him and advised him that he should try and sort himself out. Here again was an indication of the caring Hoddle, long before his religious beliefs were revealed.

Adams laughed out loud in his cell when he read the letter. Who was Hoddle to tell him what to do? He laughed even louder when Hoddle was named England coach.

But Adams and Hoddle were now together, in the coach's third match in control. The ice had been broken between them in a series of phone calls and Hoddle had spoken to Adams face to face after selecting him. Georgia was Adams's first long trip away since admitting his problem and it meant him missing regular AA meetings. He was helped with long telephone conversations with his sponsor, at £7 a minute, back to England, with the bill happily picked up by the Football Association. Adams was also assisted by talking to a journalist who is a reformed alcoholic. The pair, who are now good friends, spent a lot of time together in his hotel room, Adams knowing he could trust him implicitly.

'I'm trying to become a better footballer and, yes, a better person,' Adams confided. 'When I woke up in the morning before, the first thing I asked myself was, "how am I going to get home tonight?" Glenn must see a different me. We were together with England ten years ago. He can see the change.

'I'm doing this for me, not anyone else. This is for Tony Adams. I'm discovering things about myself every day. I need this. I really need this.'

Adams got the captaincy in Shearer's absence and it was the only choice. Adams loves being captain of England but he will always give everything for his country. 'It means a lot to me. But if Glenn Hoddle goes down a different road then so be it. I will get on with my job,' he said.

Adams captained a team that showed more changes. At the heart of the defence Hoddle gave a first cap to Spurs' talented but inexperienced Sol Campbell, who played alongside Gareth South-gate and Adams. It was the third different defensive trio we had seen under Hoddle in three matches. For the first time, however, there were three men playing in their club positions.

Hoddle asked David Beckham to do the right wing back role, another first, and gave David Batty a start in midfield, alongside Paul Ince and Gazza. Up front there was also a third different strike partnership under the England coach. In Moldova we saw Shearer and Nick Barmby, at home to Poland Shearer's partner was Les Ferdinand, and now, without Shearer, Teddy Sheringham returned to partner Ferdinand.

It was a good-looking team and one that proved Hoddle's flexibility, showing that he is prepared to change his thinking and his personnel along the way to the World Cup. The coach said of Adams as captain: 'It's the first that he has played and been captain since his problems. He is a super example of how people can turn their lives around.'

Hoddle clearly admires those who have done something for themselves. Adams is a fighter on the pitch and is showing those same qualities in beating the booze. He has made it clear how much he loves the job of captain. 'I want it long term,' he has said. Hoddle has stressed, however, that he has told Alan Shearer that he would have the job for three matches. 'If Alan Shearer is around in February then he will be captain,' said Hoddle. It was a comment that was to haunt him three months later.

Teddy Sheringham, a favourite of Terry Venables and so outstanding in the European Championships alongside Shearer, returned for the first time under Hoddle. The Spurs striker had been in all three squads although he dropped out of the trip to Moldova at the last minute with injury. Now he was in and quick to deny that he only played for Venables because they were good friends. 'No manager would pick a player just because he liked him as a person,' said Sheringham. 'You get into an England side on merit. I don't have to do anything different than I did for Terry. I am not the guy who gets the ball on the halfway line, beats three men and blazes the ball in. I have other strengths and believe that I should be in the team. That's my opinion.'

Hoddle never names his side until an hour before kick off. It is all part of the mind games coaches around the world play with each other. They refuse to show their hand and try and get an advantage over each other. Consequently, no one knew whether Paul Gascoigne would play or not. On the morning of the match, at around eleven o'clock, Hoddle took his players for a walk close to the hotel. Stretching the legs, footballers call it, and he broke the team to them then. Gazza was in. I suspect he always was in Hoddle's mind.

On this trip the media stayed in the same hotel as the team, which is not something that Hoddle likes or encourages. This time it was due to the fact that in Tbilisi there wasn't another suitable hotel. Hoddle prefers the team to be locked away from the glare of the media, and for the press just to visit when there is an arranged conference. Of course we weren't too disappointed, and were trying desperately to find out the team from contacts or bits of tell-tale gossip. But even on the morning of the game, when Hoddle and his players went for their walk, no one really knew. Adams, as captain, had been told, and he had consequently confided in his journalist friend who knew that it wasn't worth his while to breathe a word. So there were still plenty of guesses, although everyone expected Gascoigne to be in.

There was no getting near him, however, because the FA had given him his own personal bodyguard, which only added to the anxiety around him. In all the years I've been travelling with England, I have very rarely seen Gascoigne relaxed and happy, sitting with a group of journalists in a non-hostile environment. Some players, however, can handle the media – like David Platt. It's hard to keep Platt away from press conferences. He likes to chat and it has benefited his career greatly. Gareth Southgate is in the Platt mould. He is prepared to discuss issues with you, and knows that every word is not rushed off to the newspapers because, believe it or not, a lot of journalists like to talk to players just for conversation.

Then there is Ian Wright. 'Hey man, how's it going? What's happening? Sweet, cool, take it easy.' Off the pitch there isn't an ounce of malice in Wright. He likes to be liked and if you like your company to be a hundred miles an hour then he is your man. Wright was recalled for the trip to Georgia and couldn't believe his luck. At 33 years old he found himself on England duty, loving every minute of it. 'I never thought it would happen again and

I'm going to enjoy it,' he said. Hoddle picked him at 33 because he believes he is still one of the best strikers around in English football. 'When I was at Chelsea I tried to sign him last year; that is how highly I rate him. The money I was prepared to pay should indicate how highly I rate him,' Hoddle admitted.

That deal was close to going through. Wright had asked for a transfer because of his poor relationship with the then Arsenal manager Bruce Rioch. There were talks between the Wright camp and Chelsea, but Arsenal vice-chairman David Dein refused to let Wright go. It's said that he told Wright, 'You are going nowhere. The manager will go before you.' And Rioch did. He was sacked on the eve of the 1996–97 season. Wright blossomed, scored goals like before and forced Hoddle to pick him.

What about the other England players? I wouldn't say that any journalists are really close with them, although David Seaman is approachable and friendly and Stuart Pearce talks a great deal of sense and puts forward forthright, honest views. Pearce is the classic patriot. Like Adams, it will be Pearce in the dressing room who goes around pumping up the adrenalin. As former England manager Graham Taylor once said: 'Look into Pearce's eyes ten minutes before kick-off. He scared me, let alone the opposition.'

The Liverpool boys are not so forthcoming. Robbie Fowler and Steve McManaman didn't give one press conference during the European Championships because of the publicity surrounding the infamous Cathay Pacific Airline flight home from Hong Kong.

You don't get a family atmosphere at press days, unlike other countries. Italy, for instance, will invite the media to an open day where all the players will sit around, making themselves available for interview. With England the player is marched into a room, sat down at a table with an FA representative standing over him, and questions are often greeted with 'You cannot ask that.' You think to yourself, I just have, and if it wasn't for you we might get a good interview going here. Often the player is willing to talk but inhibited by the FA representative.

Still, the Georgia game saw a magnificent England perform-ance. Hoddle had told his players to be careful, especially in the opening 25 minutes – he didn't want Georgia, particularly the dangerous Georgi Kinkladze, to gain control of the midfield. Clearly Hoddle didn't want a repeat performance of England v.

Poland, with the Poles scoring first and almost putting the game beyond England. Hoddle need not have worried. This England were positive, controlled, strong, determined and eventually stylish. By half-time they had killed off the game with goals from Teddy Sheringham and Les Ferdinand.

David Batty produced his finest performance in an England shirt. The little Newcastle star plays his football nice and simple – he wins the ball and gives it – and there is a tigerish British bulldog attitude about him. Many people, myself included, had doubted his quality at this level, while Hoddle had said when first selecting him for the squad against Moldova, 'He is a much better player than people give him credit for.'

So he proved. Batty won every tackle. His anticipation was magnificent, his timing superb and his distribution better than I can remember. His attitude is as simple as his football. 'I play the game, do my job and go home to my family,' he says. Batty, in fact, would rather have been back home than on the other side of the world playing football. He loves representing his country and playing for England but doesn't enjoy the travel and being away from home. 'I've got 21-month-old twin boys and they are my satisfaction. Football is my job. My life is my family,' Batty said after his man of the match display.

Batty's inclusion was also a triumph for Hoddle, who had picked him ahead of Steve McManaman – a brave decision for a game that was a potential banana skin. He also gave Sol Campbell a debut against an attack that, on its day, can pull any defence apart.

The choice of Batty rather than McManaman threw up an interesting debate. Against Poland, England struggled in midfield, especially defensively, which questions whether Gazza and McManaman can play together all the time. They did in the European Championships for Terry Venables, but Hoddle's slight adjustment of the system opens up an old problem. Too many ball players in the side?

Gazza was . . . well, Gazza. He huffed and puffed a bit, but had a hand in both goals. At times he looked to have all the problems of his wife-beating debate on his shoulders, while at others he helped control the game with Batty, Paul Ince, Sheringham and the rest. I have to say that I still can't imagine an England side without Gascoigne. Correction, a winning side without Gascoigne. There are players emerging, however, and Gazza is going to have to get his off-pitch dedication perfect if he is to maintain his place under Hoddle. The coach's decision to play him despite the personal problems was justified. Had we lost and Gazza been poor, it would have been so different, of course.

The match also proved that Adams is the best leader of men in England, and the captain the players like and respect most. His tackling was magnificent and you could tell how pleased he was to be back in an England shirt, wearing the armband as he did through Euro 96.

It was a psychological victory – great for our morale and it would have worried the Italians. With three wins out of three, seven goals scored and only one conceded, England were in the box seat. 'It's a great way to end the year. I can have a good Christmas now,' Hoddle said. 'Everything went well and to plan. We passed the ball superbly and looked as if we could score every time we got into their box. I'm happy.'

Happy? I should think he was. No one could have asked more from Hoddle. England had maximum points and Hoddle had emerged as a coach who was very much in charge. Hoddle has an aura about him – because of his name, because of the way he played the game and because he is one of those people who doesn't give anything away. There remains a bit of mystery about him. He had put all that on the line as England coach and at the end of 1996 he had emerged flawless.

There was relief, of course, because this was one of the qualifying matches he had worried over. Georgia are capable of destroying sides. Hoddle had even showed his players a video nasty at their hotel – a video of Georgia at their best. But they were never allowed to reach such peaks and after three matches Hoddle's reputation was growing with every minute.

There was a sting in the tail from Hoddle before he said goodbye to his players for three months. The message was simple: Get on board, listen to me, do things my way or I will go elsewhere and get others who can carry out my instructions. 'Against Poland we veered away from the principles you need as a team at this level and the result was we did not play well,' he said. 'We gave Poland too much space and it made life hard. I told the players I didn't want to see the things I saw against Poland happening again. I didn't ask the team to play the way they did that night.

'Here [Georgia] the penny dropped. Maybe it has sunk in after three get-togethers. This was a great technical performance, coupled with some outstanding individual performances. We hunted in pairs and were tremendous.'

I have said before that Hoddle is tougher than you think. After three matches the players realised where he was coming from. Glenn Hoddle wants to win the World Cup and if certain players can't do the job his way, they'll be out.

The players took that message with them over Christmas, while Hoddle retreated into the background with three months to plot the downfall of the Italians. By the time he opened his presents on Christmas morning he had formed his plans in his mind – because Hoddle eats, drinks and sleeps football. Almost every minute of every day he is thinking about how to improve. He did it as a player, and certainly does as a coach.

As a player he was never completely satisfied in this country and at Swindon and Chelsea he left jobs unfinished. He set his heart on England because he always felt it was his job, and after three matches he was even more convinced.

He knew that nothing would be accomplished until he had led England to the 1998 World Cup, and that was only the start. The Italians now stood in his way. He couldn't wait for 12 February – it was his kind of match, his kind of occasion. 'I wish I could play in it,' he said as the countdown began.

15 Game Four, Game Lost

Wednesday 12 February 1997
England 0 Italy 1

I f England don't qualify for the World Cup then Glenn Hoddle will look back on this night, this game, this team and, most significantly, this player, as the moment he blew it. Who would have thought that Matthew Le Tissier would return to haunt an England manager?

Terry Venables was heavily criticised for not selecting the Southampton enigma, but he stood firm. Despite an onslaught of pressure from the media and within the game, he refused to pick Le Tissier. In fact, he discarded him without ceremony. When he made his decision, Le Tissier was playing superbly, scoring great goals and crying out to be selected. Venables said no and had a bust up with journalists, particularly me, about it. In the end he was proved right. Le Tissier shrunk backward, not showing the character to prove Venables wrong, and England went on to play magnificent football in the European Championships. Venables' judgement held up completely. He said Le Tissier wasn't a player for what he wanted and not a good enough team player, and so it was proved.

But then along came Hoddle to rescue Le Tissier's international career. He called him up for his first game in Moldova, and sent him on as a second half substitute. 'I feel better now,' Le Tissier said on the homeward journey. 'It's up to me now. I feel wanted at last.'

Le Tissier wasn't playing particularly well when Hoddle picked him, but Hoddle saw himself in the strolling Southampton minstrel who often burst into song with a superb goal or flash of genius. If Hoddle could nurse Paul Merson, Tony Adams and Paul Gascoigne through their off-field problems, he could certainly bring the best out of Le Tissier. Or so he thought.

The two men became close over the three internationals at the start of Hoddle's career. Hoddle liked Le Tissier. He liked him as a player and grew to like him as a person. They spoke the same language, and they spoke a lot. As players they both had the same attitude: 'No one likes us, we don't care.' Le Tissier was a challenge to Hoddle, and the thought of playing him against Italy was in his mind even before the crippling list of injuries forced him to re-think and re-plan.

It was the selection that was to surprise a nation and, sadly, backfire on Hoddle completely. It wasn't that Le Tissier played that badly, but he had to come off spectacularly in an England victory for Hoddle to get away with the biggest gamble of his managerial career.

Le Tissier isn't the type of player who can shrink into a team game, and he has to produce something special because he is that kind of footballer. So all eyes were on him. Stunned by Hoddle's selection in such a massive game, everyone agreed before the game that he would either be brilliant or be substituted after about 65 minutes. We were five minutes out. It was exactly an hour when Le Tissier was replaced by Les Ferdinand.

When the FIFA official stood by the touchline with the number ten card in his hand, Le Tissier was running across the halfway line. He looked up, glanced in the direction of the dugout and knew what to expect. He was well aware that it was him who had to come off because, with Italy winning, there was no other choice. It was one of the worst moments of his career. He was almost destroyed by Venables' snub, and now the nightmare had returned. In the players' tunnel half an hour after the game, Le Tissier emerged from the England dressing room alone, head down and unhappy. He wore his England track suit but didn't feel like an England player. He refused requests for interviews and just whispered, 'I want to be with my family.'

Hoddle put on a brave face. Was that the end of Le Tissier's international career? 'No way,' said Hoddle. 'In the first half he had our best two chances. At least he was in the right position.' Hoddle, however, cannot possibly play Le Tissier again in a qualifying match. Another gamble and another defeat would be the end of him.

Those two first-half chances will haunt Le Tissier for the rest of his life. If only, if only. The first came from a driven cross from Stuart Pearce which fell perfectly for Le Tissier. We've seen him accept such chances so many times in the Premiership, but this time, and for the first time in his career, he needed two touches. The Italians pounced and the opportunity was gone. Then came a headed chance from a David Batty lob into the Italian area. Goalkeeper Angelo Peruzzi committed himself to the punch but was too late, and Le Tissier was left with a free header. It went wide. If only it had been Alan Shearer there . . . if only, if only.

The gamble had failed and Hoddle must take the responsibility. He hadn't just gambled on Le Tissier, he had gambled on a nation's dream. Only one nation qualifies automatically from group two and England can't afford one more slip-up, not at home to Georgia, away in Poland, at home to Moldova or, most significantly, in Italy. The chances are that England will have to go to Rome in October to avoid defeat, or even win, to qualify without a play-off. We haven't won in Poland for 31 years, while in Italy it's 35 years since we were victorious. The defeat emphasised the size of the task now, and the size of the cock-up over Le Tissier. The chances are that England will need a play-off decider to go through.

In World Cup qualifying matches you have to win your home games. Graham Taylor was bitterly criticised for defeats in Norway and Holland when he tried to take us to America in 1994, but he argues that it was home matches against those two countries that robbed him. 'We were one-nil up against Norway and drew and two-nil up against Holland and drew again,' he says. 'Those are the two games I look back on and think what might have been. Those are the games that were responsible for my low moments. You have to win your home games. There is no getting away from it.'

This was England's first World Cup defeat at Wembley in our history of playing World Cup ties, spanning 48 years. Not even Taylor, the most criticised of all the England managers, managed that. However, Hoddle wasn't really criticised as a manager or person in the days that followed – he got quite an easy ride, in fact. There were question marks over his judgement, though. There was a touch of arrogance about the decision; a hint of 'I'll show you that players like this, players like me, can dominate and win matches that matter.' He threw Le Tissier to the wolves and then made it worse by taking him off.

This is a great example of the fact that Hoddle does things his way and isn't influenced by others. We all pick our England teams in pubs and homes throughout the country, and not once did Le Tissier's name come up in conversation during the build-up to this vital game. In six press conferences with Hoddle the name of Le Tissier wasn't mentioned once, simply because the media didn't see him as an important issue. No one expected him to play, and most didn't want him in the game because to most of us Le Tissier remains a luxury. You don't put your mortgage on him when it really matters. Hoddle did and the house fell down.

There was something throughout the build-up that wasn't right. OK, the injuries dominated, with a walking wounded roll call that included Tony Adams, Paul Gascoigne, David Seaman, Paul Ince, Alan Shearer and Robert Lee. But something else didn't feel right. All the mystery over the injuries and all the Will he? Won't he? conversations gave the impression that England, deep down, were worried. The Italians appeared relaxed and confident while England were cautious. 'We have nothing to fear,' said Hoddle. 'We should be on the front foot.' We never were on the front foot, however. Hoddle ducked bouncers all week before Italy took out his middle stump at Wembley.

Were the injuries just a smokescreen? Did Hoddle keep them going in an effort to try and fool and confuse Italy? On Monday he told us that Gascoigne, Shearer and Seaman were all fit. 'Good news,' he said. Gazza's ankle was so badly damaged he went for a scan on Thursday after the game. Seaman's knee was so bad that he was told that he would miss the next four Arsenal matches. Shearer, the England camp knew, was struggling, but it wasn't with the back injury that was made public. It was the groin once again that was worrying the England captain. He had undergone two operations already on the groin area and now there were more signs that the injury hadn't cleared up properly. Shearer had been playing in agony for weeks before the match and reported for England duty in discomfort.

Hoddle decided to keep the injury a secret. The last thing he wanted was for the Italians to know that the man they feared most was struggling, but we became so obsessed with keeping the injury a secret that we overlooked the fact that Shearer should not have played. It was another gamble by Hoddle. Shearer was only fifty per cent fit, and it was a classic case of the manager sending out a player not ready for such a huge match. He'd been getting away with it in the Premiership, but against the Italians it was different. It was a gamble that should never have been taken.

Paul Ince was the one player Hoddle said was a major doubt, but turned out to be England's best player.

After the game Hoddle's secret tactics were defended by the FA's head of public affairs, David Davies. 'There were no lies and no smokescreen. On the Monday we thought that Gascoigne and Seaman were fit. They trained and came through. It was only later that they suffered reactions. Tony Adams was always the most serious doubt.' Had it been a smokescreen, Davies said, then they would have admitted it after the game, although there wouldn't have been much point in that.

There was also a strange, rather childish reaction by the FA on the morning of the game to the breaking of the story that Le Tissier was in Hoddle's side. My colleague on the *Sun*, Martin Samuel, broke the news that Le Tissier was in and even printed Hoddle's complete side. It was a superb story and the third time, in four matches, that Samuel had named Hoddle's selection before he announced it.

The local south-coast radio station contacted Le Tissier's brother, Carl, and asked him to confirm the story. Carl did more than that. He sung like a bird about his brother and revealed the role Le Tissier would play, talked about Hoddle's tactics and told how the two of them had become close over the months of Hoddle's reign.

The FA didn't like it and there was even talk of leaving Le Tissier out of the team, which seems ridiculous. Who cares if Le Tissier's brother talks to a radio station? Did the FA think the Italians were going to pay any attention? England are far too wary in the approach to big games: smokescreens, kidology, cloak and dagger. Why not be bold, positive and show the opposition who's boss? I recall Bobby Robson before his first game as England coach in Denmark. 'There is my team and we're coming to get you,' he said at a press conference, before throwing his piece of paper on to the table.

The Italians did indeed expect Les Ferdinand and not Le Tissier to play, not thinking that Hoddle would use Le Tissier and Steve McManaman in the same side, but it didn't matter to them what team Hoddle sent out, or when he named it.

'There are no secrets in world football any more,' said coach Cesare Maldini, which made a complete nonsense of Hoddle's smokescreen.

Gianfranco Zola, Chelsea's little pocket dynamo who scored the match-winning nineteenth-minute goal, also stressed: 'I think you worried too much about me and Italy. You should have concentrated on what you are good at. We expected Ferdinand to play because his power, especially in the air, could have worried us.' The sting in the tail from Zola came like this: 'You cannot make one more mistake in the group now, otherwise the outcome will be exclusion.' Zola apologised for scoring the goal that might knock us out and said how much he loved England and Chelsea. 'England is my second home,' he said. 'I cannot imagine a World Cup without Italy, Germany, Brazil or England.'

There was yet another selection gamble by Hoddle. On the Saturday before the game he approached Spurs goalkeeper Ian Walker and told him to be prepared to play because David Seaman was struggling with his knee. Walker had to reveal that he too was unhappy with an injury, a shoulder strain that had been hampering him for some time. He had been beaten outside his area on a number of occasions, by Manchester United's David Beckham twice and Roberto Di Matteo of Chelsea, and there was a feeling inside White Hart Lane that he might need a rest. England sent Walker for a scan and on the Monday he had a pain-killing injection to help him through the week. Yet Hoddle still picked him, even though he had two other goalkeepers: David James of Liverpool and Blackburn's Tim Flowers. The most in-form goalkeeper at that time, Nigel Martyn of Leeds, had been overlooked completely.

Should Walker have stopped Zola's winning goal? He was beaten at the near post with the ball taking a slight deflection off Sol Campbell, Walker's Spurs team mate. Campbell afterwards held up his hands and said that he was to blame for the goal. 'The ball went over Stuart Pearce and I should have been across quicker,' admits Campbell. Would Seaman have saved it? Who knows? It was still a bad goal to concede. Yes, I think a top international goalkeeper, which Walker is not, would have saved it.

There were other question marks. With Tony Adams unfit, Hoddle went into the game with only one recognised central defender, Campbell, making only his second start. The others were Gary Neville and Stuart Pearce, both full backs with their clubs. Gareth Southgate was completely overlooked. Everyone agreed with David Beckham and Graeme Le Saux, the latter returning for the first time since his broken ankle. Ince, if fit, was automatic and David Batty deserved to retain his place following his magnificent game in Georgia. The Italians had a lot of respect for Steve McManaman but it was Shearer's partner that caused the greatest debate. Ferdinand or Paul Merson, who had been in outstanding form for Arsenal, but surely not Le Tissier.

England didn't create one clear-cut chance all night, which is a worry considering that goals could now be vital if we are to pip the Italians. There were those chances for Le Tissier and a shot by Pearce that crashed back off Angelo Peruzzi and Shearer almost got in. 'It didn't happen on the night for us,' moaned Shearer. 'We failed to create one good chance.' How many times have opponents said that about Italy? They came, they scored and they kept us at bay.

Hoddle's side showed seven changes from the one that performed so well in Georgia. It meant that in four matches he had used, including substitutes, twenty players. It was his fourth different partnership up front. It showed his flexibility and bravery and determination to do things his way, but it was also in contrast to the view of Italy's Maldini, who had been given charge of the side after Arrigo Saachi. Maldini complained that before he took over there were so many changes in the Italian side it became hard for the fans to recognise the players. He was going for stability in selection.

England thought they would beat Italy. The confidence had never been higher going into a game of this importance. Hoddle too was confident. He wouldn't admit it but he believed he would have one foot down the road to the finals after Wembley. Not in his wildest dreams did he expect to become the first manager to lose a World Cup tie at home.

The controversy over who was to be captain – Adams or Alan Shearer – wasn't a good start for Hoddle. At the squad announcement press conference, Hoddle had got into a mess, saying that he wanted to talk to both players before making a decision public, even though in Georgia he had said that Shearer, when he returned from injury, would be given three trial matches. He spoke to the players on the Thursday morning and the choice was Shearer, the man with no nerves, with Hoddle stressing that there would be no more trials and that Shearer was his choice all the way down the line. He felt that the days of the sleeves rolled up and swashbuckling skipper are over. 'That's old-fashioned and head in the sand,' he says.

Shearer, said Hoddle, would give England respect across the world, from players, fans and referees alike. 'Don't talk to me about captains having to be defenders. What about Platini with France, Maradona in Argentina and Johann Cruyff when he led Holland? We didn't question those decisions. Times have changed. Shearer will make us a great captain.' But his decision led to a dreadful piece of PR by the Football Association. The Thursday before the game was the first media gathering and, as usual, the FA press office nominated two players to talk to the media at an official press conference. They put forward Graeme Le Saux and David Batty.

What the FA failed to tell us – and journalists mixed with FA public relations staff for more than an hour before the press conferences – was that Hoddle was about to reveal that Shearer was his captain. It wouldn't have been difficult to tell us that Shearer was the captain and bring him to the press conference. Instead, Hoddle had almost finished his briefing, talking in detail about the injuries, when he announced who the captain was. It was too late to talk to Shearer, they said, and no, we couldn't speak to him the next day because on a Friday the Sunday newspapers get first choice of player interview.

It perhaps wouldn't have been worth it anyway. Shearer is getting a reputation for being unhelpful in press conferences. He straight bats all answers, giving nothing away. He knows as skipper he should talk to the media but he seems to take great delight in avoiding all questions. When we eventually spoke to him, on the Tuesday before the game, I'm sure there was a wry smile on his lips as he did his best not to answer with any kind of emotion. You know the kind of thing: 'This is such a big game, Alan.' 'Well, I wouldn't say that.'

All England managers have a honeymoon period. Because Hoddle stepped into a World Cup qualifying situation it was always going to last until he lost his first game. But had Bobby Robson or Graham Taylor picked Matthew Le Tissier and lost a World Cup tie at home, they would have been absolutely slaughtered by the media, because Robson and Taylor are more vulnerable characters. Hoddle has a tougher exterior. You don't crack it easily, and the confidence in him remains, even if it has been dented a little.

As for Gazza, you can't have an England international without something happening to him. If he isn't pulling down Paul Ince's shorts, he is allegedly beating up his wife. This time, apart from being injured, he was said to have slipped away from England's headquarters to go home to see his wife because there was a divorce pending. When Hoddle heard of these stories spreading when he returned to the team's hotel on the Thursday night, he was so angry that he issued a statement via the press office, describing the rumours as nonsense. 'Paul Gascoigne has not left the team's hotel,' said Hoddle. 'Nothing could be further from the truth. These things always seem to crop up around the time of an England international. Let's deal with them now and concentrate on the football after the weekend.'

Hoddle was particularly upset because he has worked hard with Gascoigne since the wife-beating business. Since the match in Georgia he has kept in touch with the Glasgow Rangers player and continually watched him on and off the pitch. All the reports delighted the England coach and, having got him into the squad again, he was furious with the rumours, and understandably so. 'Gascoigne has handled himself well since I left him last time,' said Hoddle. 'I did not exactly put my head on the chopping block as far as he was concerned but I made it clear where I was coming from. He has behaved well and significantly he hasn't been in trouble with referees at all.' Gascoigne should thank Hoddle from the bottom of his heart. There aren't many managers who would have taken such trouble with him. There are many critics who would like to see Gascoigne out of the side on performance alone, but he still remains the one Englishman who can win a match on his own, with one pass, or one stroke of genius. Had Gascoigne been fit there is no question that he would have started against Italy.

How we missed him. How we missed the one pass or that stroke of fantasy that means so much at international level. Hoddle said before the kick-off that it would be a game of one chance. He thought it would fall to us and that Shearer was the man to take it; never imagining that England wouldn't create one clear-cut chance on the night. Not one. It was tight, just as we knew it would be, but not once were the Italians opened up. In the last twenty minutes we huffed and puffed and the ball bobbed around their area yet we were never convincing. Paul Ince admitted afterwards: 'We missed Gazza. Even a half-fit Paul Gascoigne would have given us the chance to unlock the door.'

David Beckham's maturity at the highest level continues to grow. Apart from producing another impressive performance he gave his first real interview of the season. This time there was no Alex Ferguson or Glenn Hoddle sitting alongside him and Beckham responded well. He came over as a level-headed 21-year-old who knew he had the world at his feet. He spoke about his life, himself and how he sometimes pinches himself when he looks at all the material things that are suddenly his, like a home of his own, two cars, and a £7,000 a week contract. Plus, of course, the eye of every football-loving single girl in the country. It was interesting to hear Beckham reveal how closely Ferguson keeps an eye on him. The Manchester United manager decides if and when Beckham can do interviews, and every commercial offer goes through Old Trafford.

Yet despite some good individual performances, nothing can hide the fact that England lost. We lost the one match we knew we had to win. Were we, as a nation, over confident? Had we been carried along on a wave of optimism following the European Championships and the fact that Hoddle had won his first three matches? Did the excitement of Euro 96 hide the things that were wrong with the players and the team? Terry Venables was a vastly experienced coach who got the best out of a group of players over a two-year period. Hoddle has nothing like his experience and he was thrown into a game, against one of the best nations in the world, so early in his career.

It certainly wasn't a game to experiment in. Hoddle was without David Seaman, Tony Adams, Darren Anderton, Paul Gascoigne and Teddy Sheringham and still tried the impossible. It was an amazing show of either confidence, arrogance or just plain stupidity. What Hoddle did was make the mistake of believing he could beat Italy by being clever and, as we know in world football, it just does not work.

Amazingly, after watching a video re-run of the game, Hoddle even said that he wished he had kept Le Tissier on longer. 'He was someone who could have opened the door for us. I should have kept him on longer,' he said. Le Tissier should never have started and Hoddle shouldn't have tried to be so clever. The Italians were so delighted when they heard that Le Tissier was in that they ordered twelve bottles of champagne to be put on ice for after the match. It was a show of arrogance, for sure, but the Italians knew they would not lose after studying Hoddle's team. Nobody could understand what Hoddle was doing, or why. After the game, one of Venables' right-hand men said, 'I put £50 on England to win and then when I saw Hoddle's team I wished I hadn't bothered.' Another former England international, also a member of the Venables staff, had a bet on Italy to win when he saw the Hoddle team.

Hoddle will never admit he was wrong – he isn't that sort of person. He is stubborn and I suspect, having read every report and listened to every broadcast since the defeat, he will be sulking. Not on the outside, but certainly on the inside. He will be angry, a little with himself for getting it wrong but mainly with the media, for daring to suggest that he is not yet good or experienced enough. We are still behind him but England is public property – it's not Hoddle's team, it's the country's team, and he has to be big enough to except criticism.

The following weeks were lonely for him, but he had to look forward. He knows that Italy will probably qualify for the World Cup as group winners, and if you don't beat them at home, you can't expect to win in Rome. Hoddle's next game is at home to Mexico in a friendly, and that's the kind of game when he should be experimenting. It would have been the ideal start for Le Tissier. Then it's home to Georgia and away to Poland. Victory is absolutely vital. As Zola said, 'One more mistake and you are out.'

Venables was allowed two years of friendlies before he put his head in the noose. 'Judge me in 1996,' he said. 'Judge me after the European Championships.' He was right, and got it right. The man is a master tactician.

But after this defeat by Italy we don't know how good England are. Or how good Hoddle is.

16 With Hod On Their Side

'**M**um, this is Glenn. Glenn, meet my mother.'
A simple introduction. Boy meets girl who takes him home to meet her mother. It has happened millions and millions of times. But this was no ordinary meeting, no simple introduction. It was a coming together that was to change Glenn Hoddle's life. Glenn did not know it at the time but this meeting in 1975 was the making of the man, and, yes, the manager.

Mum was Eileen Drewery, mother of Michelle, a girl Glenn had met in a bar in his local Harlow town. Shy Glenn had plucked up the courage to introduce himself, which he was uncomfortable doing but he was attracted to the girl and something made him do it. Hoddle was eighteen years old at the time. He was never to forget Michelle Drewery, or her mother.

Eileen Drewery heals people with healing hands and spiritual belief. 'It is all down to love,' she says. 'It is about being aware and caring for my fellow man.'

In this chapter I speak to Paul Elliott, the former Chelsea and Celtic star whose career was ended by a knee ligament injury after a controversial challenge by Dean Saunders, then at Liverpool. Elliott was left bitter, frustrated and determined to take revenge on Saunders through the courts. Eileen Drewery healed his bitterness.

It was Hoddle who introduced Elliott to Eileen, and saw that there was an immediate bond between them. Although reluctant to talk in too much detail about how he feels now, Elliott believes he owes both Eileen and Glenn a lot. 'They are very special people,' he told me. 'My whole attitude to life has changed since meeting them.'

There is little doubt that Hoddle would not be the man he is today had he not met Eileen Drewery. He took time out to help Paul Gascoigne, and he stood by, talked to and understood the problems of Tony Adams and Paul Merson, yet without Eileen's influence I suspect that these three players would have been discarded by England in shame. There would not have been such forgiveness in Hoddle. He would, I am sure, gone with public opinion against Gascoigne.

Let us return to that first meeting between Hoddle and his girlfriend's mum. She noticed that he was limping – a football injury caused by a hamstring problem – and offered to heal it for him. Glenn, however, was reluctant and shy, and understandably wasn't keen on the idea of taking his trousers off. So he was surprised to be told that not only could he keep them on but that Eileen wouldn't need to touch him.

Later that evening, when Glenn said goodbye to Eileen, she said to him, 'Don't worry, Glenn, your leg will be OK in the morning.' Hoddle laughed.

When he woke the next morning there was no pain. He jumped out of bed, did a few stretches and kicks and ran to the phone to ring Michelle. 'What happened?' he asked. His girlfriend told him her mother had done some absent healing on him while they had been in the kitchen. Hoddle was gobsmacked – and hooked.

He was too embarrassed to tell the club, however, in case they thought he had been faking injury. He confided in physio Mike Varney, who was understanding but told him to keep things quiet. He did as he was advised, but he was determined to find out how such a thing had happened. Every time he went back to see Eileen he learnt more about her, the methods and, most significantly, himself. Hoddle admits that he was bemused and even scared at the changes taking place inside him and before his eyes. All the time, of course, he was developing as one of the best footballing prospects this country has produced. It was a critical stage of his life.

Eileen cured other injuries. She would lay her hands on the part of his body that was giving him trouble and Hoddle would sense a warm feeling spreading over the damaged area. He learned to relax and close his eyes. It was only later that he discovered she was praying while touching him.

There was another significant meeting between them when

Hoddle went to see Eileen with a knee injury. The longer they talked on this occasion the more Hoddle realised there was something missing in his life. This was the start of his strong religious beliefs.

He felt tremendous warmth for this person who seemed to have time for everyone. They talked for many hours and the more Glenn listened the more he realised that a change in his life was needed. He knew it meant an enormous sacrifice on his part because he liked going down the pub with his mates and didn't want to give that side of his life up, but he had to follow his instincts. 'I didn't consider myself a particularly horrible or bad person,' he explained. 'I just felt I would need to make an enormous jump from my middle ground to reach the sort of faith I was seeking. I thought I would have to change the whole of my life.'

This wasn't the first time he'd toyed with religion. After meeting Cliff Richard at a Christian in Sport dinner, Hoddle began reading much more, including the Bible. But the confusion stayed with him, and it wasn't until England played in Israel and the players were taken on a tour of Jerusalem that Hoddle finally realised what he wanted. After visiting the birthplace of Christ he was left with a feeling of fulfilment, although he returned to England needing many more answers. He and Eileen sat down and spoke for hours about faith, life and Christianity. 'Gradually my faith grew stronger,' says Hoddle.

Hoddle was surprised to find that his life didn't have to change dramatically for him to have a strong Christian belief. Hoddle believes in God, but he rarely talks about this in public – although he did touch upon it when answering questions about his handling of Paul Gascoigne. He certainly never pushes his beliefs on people, but he has often invited players to visit Eileen Drewery. He tells them: 'The opportunity is there if you want it. If you are comfortable then visit her and allow her to help you.'

One of those players was Mick Hazard, when he was playing at Swindon. Hazard says: 'The only thing that Glenn forced on us was his football beliefs. He is the manager and we would play his way. That was fair enough and we were comfortable with that. As far as his belief in God and faith healing was concerned, it never became an issue. It was there if we wanted to use it.

'I was once suffering with a stomach muscle strain. Glenn rang me one Sunday and mentioned the faith healer, but he said he wouldn't be offended if I didn't use it. Glenn said Eileen would come and visit me if I liked. We'd been given Monday off and although I was suspicious of anything like that, I decided to give it a try. I must admit, I thought it was going to cost me money because I always felt these people were in it for the cash. But Eileen wouldn't take a penny.

'The stomach injury was due to keep me out of action for a few weeks. She lay me down on the sofa and put her hands on my injured part. While she prayed she massaged the area. While I was lying there I did think to myself, what the hell are you doing here, Micky? I was sceptical and not convinced that it would make any difference. I did feel warmth under her hands, however. There was definitely a feeling of warmth.

'When she had finished she told me I would be fit to train on Thursday. I spoke to Glenn and he confirmed that I would be OK on Thursday and to report for training. I thought there would be no chance because I was still in discomfort. On Thursday morning when I woke up I didn't have any pain at all. I went into the club and told Glenn. He gave me that "I told you so" look. I trained and played on the Saturday.

'It was the first time I had experienced anything like that. I had always only believed in natural healing. I was fully prepared to sit out for weeks with that stomach injury. She cured me in three days and I have no real idea how it works. Glenn calls it faith and I'll have to go along with that.'

Eileen calls it a gift. 'That is what it is', she says. 'It began when I was a young women. A friend said her hand hurt and I laid my hands on her. The pain went and that was the start of it. I have never wanted to exploit my gift. Everyone I see is extremely pleasant. I do it because I love and want to help my fellow man. I have never said that I am something I'm not. I don't want publicity or material gains. Glenn has become part of the family. Listen, faith healing comes from God, not me. People find their faith in different ways and there are many ways of finding God.'

Paul Elliott's story is perhaps the most moving:

'I had gone through every medical angle possible in an effort to cure my knee injury. Every ligament had been torn and ruptured, my career was hanging by a thread and I was in despair at what to do. I was all gloom and doom. I was depressed because I realised that my days as a professional footballer were limited. They could be over. I had been told they were, although you still hope and pray that someone will find a cure.

'The lowest I felt was when Glenn Hoddle became Chelsea manager. I talked with him at great length about injury and he could relate to it because he too had suffered with injuries, when he was with Spurs and out in Monaco. He realised the mental dilemmas I was having with myself. I had suffered injuries before. At eighteen years old I suffered a double fracture of my leg. This was different. My ligaments were in a bad way and coupled with the mental strain, it was very difficult.

'The greatest thing that happened to me at that stage of my career and life was meeting Glenn Hoddle. I found him humble, understanding and warm and a great comfort.

'During our early talks he didn't mention a faith healer. He just said there was someone who might be able to help me. She had helped him, he explained, and there was no pressure to go and meet or see her. He left it to me. It was very relaxed.

'I went to see Eileen Drewery because I had nothing to lose; nothing. I had been told my career was over. When I went to see her I had exhausted everything possible. I was at my wits' end, as a footballer and a person. I found the realisation that my career could be over very hard to take.'

Paul Elliott stayed with Eileen Drewery for three days, talking and listening. He found out about himself, and genuinely believes he became a better person in those three days. The bitterness he felt about the injury, the end of his career and how it had ended left him. 'She gave me a great source of strength and optimism,' he adds. 'I stayed for three days because I felt it was right. I began to understand about her and how much good she had done for other people. It was important for me to have confidence in her. I couldn't just go along and say "Glenn sent me". It had to be more than that. She helped ease my mental problems.'

Elliott's injury was treated. Eileen put her hands on the damaged knee, just like Micky Hazard had experienced on his stomach injury. 'This is now a delicate subject for me,' says Paul. 'I feel it is private and I don't want to get into details of the treatment, or what she does. I want to protect the confidentiality of it. She is an immensely gifted woman. She is gifted in the way that Glenn is gifted in football.

'After spending so much time with her, and talking to Glenn, I find the whole thing fascinating. I had no idea that she was a faith healer. In fact, the faith healing is such a small part – there's a spiritual thing that is unique.

'It's difficult because so many people don't understand or want to know about it. I was probably the same but I've discovered that I *am* interested and want to know. One day the whole thing will come to the fore. It will be accepted and appreciated. There will be no dismissal. In years to come she will be the equivalent of a doctor. There is still a reluctance from the medical trade, but how can you ignore powers like this? I thought the same way as so many others before I saw her but not now.'

Elliott's career is over, but without meeting Glenn Hoddle or Eileen Drewery he believes that he would have been forced to retire feeling unfulfilled and discontented. 'She has been absolutely great for me. She doesn't look for glory; she just wants to help. I have no idea what was going through Glenn's mind when he recommended her to me. I'm sure he knew that she wasn't just going to treat me physically.

'I believe now that I was meant to meet her at that stage of my life. I was meant to see her for different reasons. One was a football thing but the more I spoke to her, other things came to the fore. Yes, I believe it was meant to happen.

'The more I spoke to her the more I found out about myself. I discussed things with her that I had no intention of talking about. I went with an open mind, because I'm that kind of person. I don't have an insular mind. Meeting her has broadened my horizons and changed my outlook on life. I can't stress more what a huge influence she has had on me.

'All this hasn't made me a deeply religious man. Everyone has their own faith and some people's faith is not to have faith, if that makes sense. I'm not anything when it comes to religion, but I believe there is something. I certainly believe that you should help other people and Eileen has brought that out of me.

'I find Glenn so easy to talk to. He's a wonderful man, you know. So often he is seen the wrong way. The great thing that comes across all the time is his humbleness. There is huge inner strength with Glenn; so much determination. He's got that strength of mind from different reasons and aspects of his life. I wish I had discovered all this before, but maybe it was meant to happen now, at the end of my career. Who knows?'

Elliott did try to play again, but his injury was too bad. David Dandy, the specialist who has treated so many footballers, told Elliott that his ruptured knee was the worst football injury he had seen. 'What I realise now,' says Elliott, 'is that I tried. I feel contented that I did my best to play again, and did the best for my injury.'

He is mentally repaired, however. 'I think she has done even more for me than making me play again,' he says. 'I feel that a new era has dawned in my life. I have seen so many other things, about myself and my life. I have different thoughts. A lot of things have happened to me since my first meetings with Glenn and Eileen. I hope I'm not being too vague but I must keep this as private as I can. I could have walked into her home and there could have been no chemistry between us. There had to be something – a wavelength – for me to have been influenced by, and I have. We speak a lot now and I don't have to be in her company for things to happen.

'I have discovered absent prayers. This opens up a whole different thing. Where does a person get those powers?

'Isn't it amazing how your life can change? If a few years ago you'd said all these things to me I would have laughed in your face. Yes, I would probably have laughed at the prospect of faith healing. I had no idea this was going to happen; it has just snowballed.

'Glenn and I speak occasionally. He has great loyalty and there are very few people like him. I didn't know him personally but the qualities he has makes him special. I played against him and admired his skill. He nutmegged me enough times. Now I feel I know him so well. He has helped me a great deal.

'I have learnt a great deal through adversity. Was this supposed to happen to me? I have no idea what will happen to me next. Take Matthew Harding. Is there a message there? Was his time up; had he served his purpose on this earth? I have no idea. What I do know is that it's best to treat every day as your last. To enjoy.'

It was on 5 September 1992 when Paul Elliott's life changed. 'Seven minutes past three at Anfield when Dean Saunders tackled me,' recalls Elliott. 'I will never forget it.' The pain from the impact was intense and Elliott knew something was seriously wrong. 'You get blows and breaks and injuries as a professional but when it's a serious one there's a realisation that runs through your body,' he says.

Today he has forgiven Saunders, with help from Glenn Hoddle and Eileen Drewery. 'Feelings of bitterness went out of my system long ago,' he says. 'It's not a problem now. It doesn't affect my life in any way. I realise that a lot of good things happened to me before the injury – and after it.'

In no way must we underestimate Hoddle's role in Elliott's mental rehabilitation. Hoddle was there when Paul needed him, taking phone calls and being available for chats when Elliott's morale was rock bottom. Significantly, Hoddle has never spoken himself about it, because loyalty is an important part of his make-up. 'When you talk to Glenn Hoddle about private matters you know that they stay that,' adds Elliott. 'I have one hundred per cent confidence in him as a bloke.'

Hoddle usually prays every day, but he hasn't forced religion on his wife Anne, or his children, daughters Zoe and Zara and son Jamie. He knows that religion has made him a better father, husband and family man. It has made him a better person. Religion has helped him as a person and he is doing the job he always wanted. God has helped him make decisions in his life and I am sure he believes God will help him make a success of England's bid for World Cup glory.

If he is not a success then he already has the inner strength to cope with that, too.

17 First Year As Coach – So Far, So Good . . . ish

Four matches, three wins, one defeat, seven goals scored, two against, nine points. In any other job it would be almost the perfect start. When you are England coach and trying to qualify for a World Cup, one defeat is a disaster. To lose to Italy at home was a nightmare for Hoddle, but it didn't put England out of the competition and he remained unflappable.

So how do we sum Hoddle up after a year in control? The game seemed to be in safe hands until that cock up against the Italians. Then it threw up all the old questions. Is he too young; too inexperienced? Will he be able to cope with real pressure?

He believes he can, and will. He called the defeat by Italy a set-back but not a disaster, pointing at injuries as the main reason. But was it just a set-back, or was there a total blind spot? There was an arrogance about the selection that we hadn't seen before. There was certainly a hint of 'Terry Venables couldn't find a place for this man (Le Tissier) and didn't think he could perform at the highest level. I will show you all. I will prove that I know best.' Well, he didn't – and it cost us dearly.

The secret is how you react. How many managers have you heard say that? After Italy Hoddle vanished into his other world. The life of an England manager can be a lonely one. You open the door for matches and then retreat behind it. When you've won you happily step out into the limelight, but when you've lost the curtains are drawn until the next match comes around.

In the first week after Italy, Hoddle and his assistance John Gorman locked themselves away in Hoddle's FA office and watched a re-run of the match on video six times. Every day they watched, analysed, re-ran the tape and looked for reasons why.

The result, sadly, stayed the same. They certainly didn't see anything wrong with Matt Le Tissier's performance and Hoddle has no regrets about playing him. Indeed, the manager contacted the Southampton enigma soon after Wembley and told him not to worry about the criticism and reaction. He told Le Tissier that he would definitely be in his squad for the next match – the friendly against Mexico at the end of March.

One defeat, of course, does not make you wrong. But it was a terrible game to lose – the biggest of Hoddle's career and the most important on the road to the World Cup in France 1998. What was slightly worrying was Hoddle's reluctance to blame himself or anyone else. We can only hope that in those lonely days after Italy he did admit to himself, 'Shit, I got that wrong.'

His bosses at Lancaster Gate were frustrated at the defeat, but certainly not in panic mode. They had given him the job and still believed that he was the right man to lead England a long way down the line. In fact, they felt for him.

Keith Wiseman, the new chairman of the FA, says: 'I didn't really know Glenn before he was interviewed for the job. I obviously watched him play and took interest in his career at Chelsea. I met him a few times while he was at Chelsea but not beyond that.

'The first thing I would like to say here is that Glenn was the first choice for the FA, despite what people have said. We didn't have to come down to a choice of choosing between candidates because Glenn emerged as the clearest possible name, and that was very early on.'

This is interesting, because it was generally thought that the FA wanted a number of men before Hoddle, including Kevin Keegan and Bryan Robson. Indeed, all the obvious successors to Terry Venables said no in public. Yet according to Wiseman, they weren't even asked. Hoddle, he says, was the only man offered the job.

'We developed a routine in our search for the right man,' he continued. 'We used Jimmy Armfield to go and get a feel about how the managers felt about the job, and what their opinions were. Listen, we had no reason to believe that Terry Venables would not be doing the job for quite some time. Goodness knows who would have been the top candidate down the line in five or six years' time had Venables stayed. Maybe had Terry stayed then an obvious person would have emerged from his backroom staff.

'It was far too premature to say that under Venables individuals were being groomed. He was just making best use of the people he knew had good international experience. What the Venables era proved was how short-term football can be, and how unexpected.

'Once we had appointed Glenn, I obviously had to get to know him better. In a club situation the relationship between the chairman and his manager is everything. It's the one that counts. With England there is so much back-up from other people involved in the professional game that it's different. The way I viewed the situation was that I was always available to him if he wanted any advice. We have said to each other that our doors are always open.

'During the build-up to an international I make sure I go along to our Burnham Beeches Hotel HQ and have a dinner with Glenn and all the training staff. We are also tripping over each other at Lancaster Gate. We operate from the same building and there are plenty of situations and opportunities for an off-the-cuff meeting. Howard Wilkinson, our director of coaching, is also there, and it's not as though meetings always have to be arranged. It's a consistent situation.

'One of the things that attracted me to Glenn almost immediately was the breadth of his own international playing experience. We certainly took into account his experience of playing with England abroad and playing club football for Monaco. I think it's recognised that international football is different to club football and he certainly seemed to have the right pedigree in that respect.

'It's also essential that the individual has the right diplomacy. We actually face some testing international situations and he has got to be able to handle those. In the new Eastern bloc countries things can be testing and you need to keep calm. We've also done a lot of groundwork in some countries which are less developed, and I am reluctant to call it missionary work although that gets near. We've done things with kids and we've tried to portray the right image of English football and a Western country in general. Glenn is ideally suited to do this as well as coach.

'Glenn doesn't only have to pick a winning side. He does work on other things with me, although not excessively – we don't want to burden him. He has to report to the International Committee six times a year but generally we leave the job up to him. A lot of people don't understand the committee system at the FA. The committees are there to run all sorts of things, like competitions, while Glenn is reporting to one committee on an infrequent basis, otherwise he's allowed to get on with the job in the way he thinks best.'

There is clearly respect from both men. Hoddle and Wiseman work together but only when it matters, such as the handling of the Paul Gascoigne situation. If Italy at home was Hoddle's biggest match, Gazza's wife-beating scandal and whether to pick him or not was Hoddle's biggest off-pitch test. Wiseman adds: 'The only time Glenn came to me for advice was over the Gascoigne affair.

'I think Glenn showed us that he's very much his own man. He wanted to deal with it in his own way and I was happy to give him full backing on it. It was a storm for a while and he remained calm in the middle of it. Glenn wanted to give Gascoigne the chance to get things right for him and I don't think he wanted to be left with other people's decisions. That turned out to be a perfectly justified way of handling it.

'What Glenn now has to consider is the actual playing standards involved. Is Gascoigne still good enough to play for England? Once the storm had blown away I think most people were happy with the outcome. Glenn has done a lot for Gascoigne, I have no doubts about that, and I sincerely hope that Gascoigne doesn't let Glenn down in any way. I have no doubts either, however, that Glenn would deal in a proper fashion with anything that arose now. I don't think Glenn was being soft with Gascoigne, I believe that he gave him a final chance of getting it right for himself.'

There is no question about Gazza only having one chance left now, and it is clear that Hoddle has told Wiseman and his bosses that Gascoigne would be ditched and disciplined if he let him down now. But as Wiseman asks, is Gazza still good enough for England? Would Gascoigne have played against Italy had he been fit? Hoddle indicated afterwards that he would have used him as a sub, yet his staff are convinced he would have started. Whatever, it is clear that the most controversial player in our history is on trial, as a player and a person, as Hoddle continues his career as England coach.

Wiseman adds: 'Soft is not a word you would use for Glenn. In a way, because he is calm as a personality, it takes a little while to realise that he is pretty tough under the surface.

'I'm getting to know him better as the months and the matches pass. I've had a good club training as far as a chairman and manager is concerned. I'm not a dressing-room man, win or lose. I believe that the dressing room is a private place. In my own experience of playing tennis I know the hour or two after a match is important. If you've lost, for instance, you want to be on your own. I'm much happier talking to my manager the next day rather than getting involved with him while he's doing his job.'

Wiseman certainly didn't enter the dressing room after the match with Italy, but he and Hoddle have spoken at length since. Being vice-chairman of Southampton, Wiseman is particularly interested in the debate about Le Tissier. 'To be honest I felt slightly sorry for Matt. I felt that he should have played more often for England over the last few years, then he would have been better equipped to handle a match like that. To suddenly come in and be expected to do a Roy of the Rovers job when you've hardly had a game or friendly is unrealistic.

'The whole spotlight was on Matt. Glenn tells me he has analysed the first half of that match at length and there would be no reason to pick out Le Tissier for criticism at all. It's just one of those things that he subbed him – it didn't reflect on Matt. I think there were perhaps one or two other players who could have felt quite pleased to have stayed on. Because it was Le Tissier he has had to live through the "I told you so" headlines. A little unfair on him, I think.'

Wiseman calls his role as chairman 'an incredible professional challenge', but it's one that he's enjoying immensely. 'There are a large number of legal or semi-legal situations that come up and it's a testing job as well as an enjoyable one. I'm a football nut – you have to be – and I've had some wonderful opportunities to see matches and deal with situations. I just hope that everyone feels that over a period of time I've done a reasonable job.

'The goal for Glenn is to win the World Cup; the goal for me is wider. I am certainly desperately interested in winning the World Cup, but it's only twenty per cent of the challenge for me. That's important because it reflects on the whole buoyancy of the country and the way the game is perceived, and the ability to obtain sponsorship and all sorts of things. It's absolutely vital for all-round success.

'There is, however, so much development work going on, starting under Howard Wilkinson. There is a lot going on that the people on the outside aren't aware of. Trying to build the inner structure of the game. I have been amazed myself at what takes place inside Lancaster Gate. The coaching, the referees' structure, courses, thousands of things that keep the game going. I'm conscious that I have to take a much wider picture, but that doesn't mean to say that I don't get pretty worked up about the national team.

'This job is pulling me in many directions. I have a business to run too and I suppose I'm trying to find nine days a week in which to work. Somewhere further down the line something will be sorted out on that too. The chairmanship is an annual election and in my first year I've got to make sure that people want me for a period of time, before I get too worried about some of these other things.

'If it becomes clear that it's going to be a long-term situation it's obvious that a number of things, like my business, have to be resolved. With so much going on it's not easy to fit everything in, but the next few months will see it being sorted, I'm sure. In the meantime we must carry on trying to qualify for the World Cup because that's of vital importance. It'll be interesting to see if Italy can drop something along the way. Let's hope so.'

Wiseman seems to be the ideal chairman for an England coach to have. While the manager learns his own ropes, Wiseman provides an open door, an educated head and an outlook that allows Glenn to do his own thing. 'Basically, we allow Glenn to get on with the job the way he sees best,' says Wiseman. 'There are no pressures put on him by the International Committee, certainly not me.'

What about the players? He has picked the best there are – 32 so far – and used 22 of them in a match situation. There have been two new caps under Hoddle, Andy Hinchcliffe and David Beckham, and the only player who has been unexpectedly overlooked is Dennis Wise, his skipper at Chelsea and a member of the Venables squad until he named his final Euro 96 party. There hasn't been a place for Stan Collymore yet, and Phil Neville has been unlucky with injury. It will be interesting to see if Hoddle picks Dominic Matteo again, after being included twice but dropping out with injury.

So how have his players reacted to him after four matches? Players are an interesting lot. At club level they will sniff out any new manager, testing him to see what he knows and how he reacts to situations like turning up late for training and not dressing how he wants. These games are played early and as long as the manager wins then he will have the players respect.

Managing England is different because when you are chosen by your country to be the coach then, hopefully, you are the best. You do not have to prove anything to the players. That is how it was for Hoddle when he was waiting at the Burnham Beeches Hotel for his squad to report for duty before his opening game against Moldova. Hoddle was slightly nervous – after all, this was *his* day and he hadn't met all of the players before.

The story of Hoddle's first year in charge from a player's point of view is told here by Gareth Southgate. The Aston Villa defender is friendly, articulate and ambitious, and enjoyed the European Championships like nothing he had experienced before. He also played the best football of his career. He expected to be included by new manager Hoddle, although it is still a relief when you know for sure, especially at the start of a new era.

'On that first day back after Euro 96 it was like going back to school after a summer holiday. There was a great atmosphere in the air. Glenn was at the door of the hotel to meet us and shake hands and do a general welcome.

'We had a meeting later and he was quick to praise us for the summer, but he also pointed out that we had a major task ahead of us to qualify for the World Cup. He made it clear that it was back to work. I hadn't met him before; only played against him at one or two testimonial games.

'We had a couple of days training together before he held his first real team meeting. It was at that meeting when he told us how he wanted his team to play, and the way to progress under him. There was respect for him because of who he is. The name Glenn Hoddle speaks for itself and that's definitely an advantage.

'At a club level it doesn't take players long to work out a new manager. It probably seems quicker because we are working with him every day. With England we've only had four games to date and that means in a year we've only had four weeks with Glenn. That's just hours, which seems incredible, and so it's diffiult to work out exactly what type of manager he is, or person for that matter, or what his strength and weaknesses are. And don't forget that he's still working out the best and worst bits of the players he's chosen.

'Glenn has stated already about the frustration he has of not being able to work with the players directly after a game. He has to say goodbye virtually at the final whistle and we don't meet up again for weeks. He would like a period after a match to go through it with us. It's an old complaint and one you can have sympathy with.

'If training is interesting it helps because the players are immediately enjoying themselves. With Glenn you're learning while you're watching because his ability and skill is still there.

'The training under Glenn is similar, with minor changes, to the Terry Venables way. There has been nothing wide scale which has made us say, "Oh, hang on a minute." The biggest changes have been with the diet. There are no fizzy drinks up to three days before the game; even sparkling water is stopped. The staff of the hotel are instructed not to serve it three days before each match. Things like chips and any food high in fat also disappear off the menu as the week progresses.

'He's very keen on a lengthy warm up with a lot of stretching. He obviously felt that this benefited him as a player and he is passing on that knowledge. I'm sure his interest in diets and stretching came from his days playing for Monaco.

'At home I don't have much fatty food or fizzy drinks although all sportsmen and women break out and you slip into bad habits. When you're away with England it's not an option. The choice isn't there. Glenn Hoddle makes the rules and that is that.

'My life as a professional footballer has not altered a great deal. When I was at Crystal Palace we weren't at the stage when players had steak before a game. Things like bananas are pushed more these days; food containing carbohydrates is continually encouraged. For instance, they put jelly babies on the bus after training with England. They believe it's a way of putting the carbohydrates back into the body quickly.

'The training is becoming more scientific, and that's the same at club level. People are putting a lot of research into ways of training and how to get the best of your body. Hoddle has introduced a full-time masseur, which we don't have at Villa. I think it's an important part of training. Our top athletes use them and feel the benefit. I talk to runners and they are staggered that football clubs don't have a full-time masseur.

'If Glenn gives us the weekend off to do our own thing and some of us have played golf, then he insists we have a massage before we start training again. It's what he believes in. Quite honestly, professional footballers in this country have been so amateurish in their outlook for so long. For years the rugby players and athletes were better prepared, and when you think of the sums of money involved in football and what's at stake for the clubs, it's incredible that the best has not been organised for the players before now.

'Our preparation has been pathetic for too long. It's only now that we're thinking on the right wavelength. I spoke to Jimmy Greaves recently. When he went to Inter they had three coaches, a manager, two physios, a full-time masseur. Most Premier League clubs don't have that now and we're talking twenty-five years ago in Italy.

'There aren't many players who bring training home. Some do extra weight training but all the top clubs now have all the facilities you need. For the first couple of games under Glenn we did extra training in the afternoons. We didn't do it in the build-up for Italy although that probably reflected the fact that there were a lot of injuries and it was much further into the season, and players are as fit as they are going to get. Most clubs have cut down their physical training by the time you get into the spring months.

'The evenings with England are relaxed and you can do what you want. There are good facilities laid on at the hotel; a cinema with a different film each night, snooker room, video games. The manager will also go through a video of the opposition, or a previous England performance, more than once.

'I've found Glenn easy to talk and listen to and I appreciated him telling me before Italy that he was leaving me out rather than finding out in the media. It is simple man-management. Whether it made me feel any better is debatable but at least I went home afterwards thinking that it was good of him to tell me. I haven't had as much to do with him on a one-to-one as some other players, for obvious reasons, but I have been influenced by him, as I was by Terry Venables.'

Southgate's reference to man-management is interesting, because it has never been Hoddle's strong point. He admitted later to Venables' physio Dave Butler that he should have told him he was no longer needed himself, rather than Butler finding out from a journalist. Hoddle never told goalkeeping coach Mike Kelly that he wasn't wanted and Ted Buxton was hardly spoken to, even though he spent months after Euro 96 working out his contract at Lancaster Gate in an office next to the new coach. 'I think I became an embarrassment to him,' admits Buxton now.

Southgate adds: 'I always try to take the best things from everybody. It probably happens without you even realising. The things they encourage you to do are taken back to your club. I was first called into the squad a year and a half ago and I'm sure I've improved in that time as a player. This season has been up and down and, if anything, I have taken a slight step back since the summer. But I've learnt a lot and it stands me in good stead for the future.

'In the summer of '96 I was playing better than I had ever experienced. There's bound to be a levelling-off period when you don't play as well. The important thing is to keep learning.

'It is often said that players don't care or get paid too much. Just to be part of the England squad gives me immense pride. I love meeting up with the other players and getting together. When I was first picked I read about it on Teletext. I was staggered because I thought the letter inviting a player to join England came from the FA in the post. The letter didn't arrive until the next morning.

'I treasure my caps. I keep some of them in a cabinet and others in a drawer. I hope I can keep playing well enough under Glenn Hoddle for there to be many more before I finish.'

That is down to one man. Glenn Hoddle. Who will be in Hoddle's World Cup side in France? If, in fact, we get there. Will there be new faces? Will Gazza still be there, or will he have let Hoddle down? Or will his form have deserted him?

Hoddle himself dedicated his first year simply and solely to the England job. He didn't allow himself to be sidetracked in any way. There were no outside interests and no huge commercial deals like Venables struck. Hoddle and his agent Dennis Roach made a decision before the first game that he would get his feet under the table and be successful before accepting the many offers that were thrown at him from the first day he walked into Lancaster Gate.

A £300,000 book deal was put on ice and Clive Anderson's BBC chat show was rejected, as was *Hello* magazine for an 'at home' feature. *The Big Breakfast* was desperate for him to appear and companies wanting to put the name of Glenn Hoddle to their product bombarded Roach with requests. At one stage he was receiving twenty faxes a day with lucrative commercial deals. Hoddle politely turned them all down.

They were rejected because first he wants to be a winner. When he can hold his head up as a World Cup winner, or at least qualify for a major competition or two, he will open the door to the extra millions he can make, but only then.

The jury is still out on Glenn Hoddle. The man and the manager is being tested like never before. He wanted the job and is determined to be successful. He is loving every minute of it but whether the nation end up loving him remains to be seen.

Ramsey is still respected and idolised, Revie was a traitor, Greenwood failed to deliver, Robson ended up a loveable success, Taylor was sacked and Venables is a hero. Who can tell what Hoddle will be eventually remembered as? As a player English football didn't completely understand him. If he fails to take us to the World Cup, English football will never forgive him.